ADVANCE PRAISE FOR *FILTHY SUGAR*

Filthy Sugar brings the Depression-era life of a young, single, desirable woman alive with Wanda Wiggles, a sensuous, curvaceous model and burlesque dancer who is driven by sexual appetite and a desire to stay alive in a world of dire penury. Never downtrodden, despite the many men in her life who use her financially, she maintains a sass, is naughty, and breaks social rules. Underneath this camp and well-researched historical novel is a strong feminist story of the multiplicities of female sexuality, of an unstripped agency and, in the final scene, an empowerment that will leave you clapping and laughing. Masterfully written with the sensibility of a poet, Heather Babcock is a writer to watch.
—BRENDA CLEWS, author of *Tidal Fury* and *Fugue in Green*

Filthy Sugar is so delicious, it's positively sinful! Wanda Wiggles will take you to another time and place, but a place where love, lust, greed sex and power are just as heartbreaking and complex as they are today. Wanda Wiggles is a stellar female character — she is a dame not to be messed with! Her heart is as soft as a kitten's fur but the claws come out when they need to! She's sensual, sassy and stunning and she isn't afraid to be her true self, even when that self lands her in some hot water. I hope this exquisitely written debut novel will enjoy the love and attention it deserves. Superb, poetic and cinematic, *Filthy Sugar* will transport you into another world and you won't want to leave!
—LISA DE NIKOLITS, author of *No Fury Like That* and *Rotten Peaches*

Filthy Sugar takes us to the mid-1930s, from the struggles of a working class slum, to the hustle and excitement on and off the burlesque stage. Here, we follow redheaded heroine Wanda Wiggle's rise and fall from fame in a journey of self-discovery that reveals desires and reserves of strength she never knew she possessed. Erotic, compelling and full of richly textured characters, Heather Babcock's storytelling is equal parts moxie and poetry—tinted with the heartbroken nostalgia of memory and lost dreams; and sparkling with striking, evocative imagery. More than a backstage pass into this world, *Filthy Sugar* shines a light on the challenges faced by working-class women. Dancing as fast as they can in order to survive, they must navigate the unapologetic misogyny and hypocritical social codes that govern their bodies and behaviour as they pursue their hopes, dreams, and desires. Sounds kind of familiar, doesn't it?

—CATE MCKIM, Life with more cowbell arts & culture website

With the grit and desperation of the Depression, the forgotten man, the sassy dames, and dirty little secrets sprouting out of dandelions, *Filthy Sugar* is a dream wrapped up in a sassy pre-Code cinematic adventure and its heroine Wanda Wiggles is all the parts of a swell dame made up of a fine mix of Barbara Stanwyck, Thelma Todd, Jean Harlow, Joan Blondell and Clara Bow. Heather Babcock has captured the pure essence of the 1930s with eloquent, colourful words that flourish across the pages. You literally feel as if you are part of the audience in the burlesque house, hooting and hollering as Wanda wiggles across the stage. You don't need to be a fan of pre-Code movies to enjoy this wonderful debut novel.

—LIZZIE VIOLET, writer, poet & spoken word artist

Heather Babcock's *Filthy Sugar* is both a sweet and saucy journey behind the curtain. Vicariously through Wanda's trials, tribulations, and triumphs, we're taken through the tapestry of a difficult and opportunistic time. The characters are alive, and full of antique and vintage sentiments. The narrative is stark, romantic, and eloquent, while the dialogue all but inspires the crackling of a Victrola sound for every scene. A time-travelled, tantalizing, and tumultuous tale, to be sure.

—Valentino Assenza, Co-Host/Co-Producer HOWL, CIUT 89.5FM

Heather Babcock's novel, *Filthy Sugar,* artfully takes the reader into the Jazz Age of flirty flappers and boozy philosophers, an era which has always captivated me. Her vivid descriptions and strong use of language take you right into the action, and her knowledge and passion for the period are clearly vast. However, there is also a sensitivity to her characters, and insights into human nature, which are timeless.
—PAT CONNORS, Toronto poet

Filthy Sugar is a real time-travelling excursion. Heather Babcock brings alive the era of Trilbys, hoofers, and two-bit scriveners with vividness, imagination and striking description. A good read—and how!
—JEFF COTTRILL, writer, actor, journalist and spoken-word artist

FILTHY
SUGAR

We gratefully acknowledge the support of the Canada Council for the Arts and the Ontario Arts Council for our publishing program. We also acknowledge the financial support of the Government of Canada.

Filthy Sugar is a work of fiction. All the characters and situations portrayed in this book are fictitious and any resemblance to persons living or dead is purely coincidental.

Cover design: Val Fullard

Library and Archives Canada Cataloguing in Publication

Title: Filthy sugar : a novel / Heather Babcock.
Names: Babcock, Heather, 1977– author.
Series: Inanna poetry & fiction series.
Description: Series statement: Inanna poetry & fiction series
Identifiers: Canadiana (print) 20200204149 | Canadiana (ebook) 20200204157 | ISBN 9781771337175 (softcover) | ISBN 9781771337182 (epub) | ISBN 9781771337199 (Kindle) | ISBN 9781771337205 (pdf)
Classification: LCC PS8603.A253 F55 2020 | DDC C813/.6—dc23

Printed and bound in Canada

Inanna Publications and Education Inc.
210 Founders College, York University
4700 Keele Street, Toronto, Ontario, Canada M3J 1P3
Telephone: (416) 736-5356 Fax: (416) 736-5765
Email: inanna.publications@inanna.ca   Website: www.inanna.ca

FILTHY
SUGAR

HEATHER
BABCOCK

Inanna poetry & fiction series

INANNA PUBLICATIONS AND EDUCATION INC.
TORONTO, CANADA

CONTENTS

For all of the forgotten dames...

I call her the Queen of the World Behind the Market: the majestic creature, with her crown of Harlow curls and weather beaten face, plastered across the backside of an abandoned five and dime store. Her dark esoteric eyes keep silent watch over the Market's grass widows and forgotten men. As they shuffle past her, knees bent and arms laden with parcels and barrels, the Queen smiles. Her painted lips slightly parted as though the people have given her a secret too illicit to keep. Beneath her slim, bejeweled throat, the cigarette advertisement's original slogan has been ripped away and in its place are the following words, carved into the wall with a pocket-knife:

A pretty girl
Without a fighting spirit
Is like a stray cat
Without claws

1. MILK AND DIAMONDS

IN THE WORLD BEHIND THE MARKET, death is always close, but life is stubborn.

Birds, mistaking gold stars for the sky, fly into closed windows; their bodies sustenance for maggots and clandestine cats in the garden of faded flappers where young men trample through tobacco Tulips and lipstick Lilies. Where babies are born. And where more babies are born.

Daddy didn't trust the automobile. So when the other milkmen traded in their horses for trucks, Daddy doggedly held on to his beast—a gentle white and grey mare named Sadie.

"Ya can't trust anything that doesn't need ya," Daddy explained to me one day, as he filled Sadie's feedbag with oats. "This girl needs me as much as I need her. Now what mess of steel and rubber is goin' ta beat that?"

That was as most as he ever said to me. Daddy wasn't much of a talker, but he was friendly enough and well-liked in the world behind the Market. His only enemies were the 'milk snatchers': a group of young boys with hard, hungry faces and eyes like broken beer bottles: sharp and empty. *"Ol' one-eyed Joe!"* they'd taunt my Daddy; one or two of them jumping in front of Sadie and distracting both driver and horse while the others would steal as many jugs of milk as their scrawny pink arms could carry. My Daddy's name was Albert, not Joe. It was true though that he only had one eye.

On a colourless November day—the kind of cool, muffled day where the world feels as placid and dreamy as a silent film without organ music—Daddy spotted one of the milk snatchers, uncharacteristically alone, pulling a wagon full of milk jugs in the direction of Mr. Tootsie's grocery store.

"Hey you!" Daddy shortened his reins, calmly bringing Sadie into a trot alongside the boy. "How much Mr. Tootsie payin' ya for my milk?"

The boy, startled, broke into a run as my Daddy tapped Sadie lightly on her haunches and charged after him.

"Come back here, ya mug!" He cried, his buggy whip raised in his tightly clenched fist. "Ya little dime store hoodlum!"

The kid turned around and threw one of the milk jugs in Daddy's direction, striking the alabaster forehead of the Market Queen who hit back in an explosion of milk and diamonds.

Daddy was livid. It was one thing to snatch milk for food or profit, but quite another to so deliberately and maliciously waste it. Red-faced and furious, he dismounted Sadie and ran out into the road, in pursuit of the quickly vanishing boy. The buggy whip jumped from his hand, cracking the cruelly reticent air, as a Cadillac V-16 roadster swerved out from behind Tootsie's Grocery and flew through my Daddy's body like a mad bird on a blind night.

2. THE DAME IN THE FOX FUR COAT

LESS THAN A MONTH AFTER Daddy's death, Mama got Evelyn a job working beside her as a seamstress at the glove factory. I wanted to work at the factory, too, but Mama said it would give me a hunchback and jaundice my skin. I said what about Evelyn and Mama said that my sister was lucky, because she didn't have to worry about being pretty. Mama and Evelyn's jobs at the glove factory are seasonal though, so I still needed to look for something steadier than my casual taxi-dancing gig. I found a job modelling fur coats at Blondell's department store, three trolley rides away from the Market.

Under an opaline sun, I strut up and down the aisles of Ladies Wear, my peep-toe high-heeled shoes keeping in time with the sinfonietta of the wishing well fountain, the cash register bell, and the mechanical cry of *"Forty-eight weeks to pay, oh-kay!"* from the ceramic ringmaster planted in the centre of Blondell's marble atrium. I am encouraged by management to approach the male customers, but only if they are wearing a wedding ring or a three-piece tailored suit.

"Fox fur, like to touch?" I ask as I smooth my hands over the coat, its folds as soft as a rich woman's flesh. I give the customers my smile, but I keep my eyes to myself.

"Oh, Henry! Look at the darling thing!"

Greedy, bony hands claw at my sides. I keep my lips stretched into a smile even though the tiny woman's rain blue eyes are focused solely on the coat. She pulls at my shoulder, her helmet of lemon-yellow finger waves wobbling as she tries to tear the coat off of my back. I look helplessly at her companion, an older gentleman dressed in a dark blue three-piece suit with a matching silk tie and pocket square. A cashmere overcoat with a mink collar is draped over his forearm.

"Norma, please," he says in a stern tone of exasperation. "You're terrifying the poor girl."

"It's all right," I say, still smiling. I turn to the blonde woman. "You're much more slender than I am. You'll swim in this. Come with me and I'll help you find your size."

As I lead the couple to the fur department, I can hear the blonde chattering behind me.

"She *is* right, Henry. I'm much slimmer than she is. Personally, I've always found the hourglass figure rather gauche, wouldn't you agree, Henry? Especially," she adds, "when combined with red hair."

I feel my face burning as I comb the racks for her size.

"Here you go," I say, holding out a smaller coat. The blonde snatches the fur from my hands, her eyes avoiding my face.

"Oh, Henry!" she exclaims, slipping into the coat. "Henry, it's *adorable!*"

She preens in front of the oval mirror and gleefully claps her hands together like a six-year-old child. "Don't I look grand, Henry?"

"Exquisite," her companion answers, his eyes on me.

I start to feel hot again, but pleasantly this time, as though I am sinking into a warm bubble bath. The man is tall and broad-shouldered with thick, neatly combed grey hair and a jawline that could cut glass, but there is something off about his face. After sneaking in a few glances of my own, I realize that his eyes are two different colours: his right eye is blue while his left is a dark shade of warm honey. I also notice that, unlike the blonde girl, he is wearing a wedding ring.

"Oh, Henry," the blonde sticks out her baby-pink bottom

lip. "This coat was *made* for me." She wraps her arms around his neck. "*Please,* Henry."

"That is an excellent choice?" Ann, my supervisor, suddenly appears at the gentleman's shoulder.

Ann's voice always turns up at the end of her sentences when she speaks to the customers, so that everything she says sounds like a question. The habit used to disgust me until I realized that I do the same thing—when I am afraid.

"The coat really suits the lady? Let me ring it up for you?"

The man nods and reaches for his wallet as Ann whispers to me, "Nice work, Wanda. It's past five now. You can blow."

It is almost seven o'clock by the time I reach the World Behind the Market. Under the light of the retiring sun, the falling leaves look like fire. Cigarette butts, broken bottles, and decapitated flowers artfully litter the concrete, as though part of a crude museum piece—remnants of an already forgotten good time.

An elderly woman, barefoot on the wet pavement, plays a ukulele. I dig inside the pockets of my cloth coat and give her the last of my coins. I walk on, looking up at the tiger velvet sky.

"Please, God," I whisper. I think of the man with the different coloured eyes. "Oh, please, God."

Two men, their hands and faces devastated by years of labour, sit on the steps behind a fruit and vegetable store, slicing giant pumpkins in half. Nearing my rooming house, I spot the skinny rump and docked tail of my neighbour's Doberman Pinscher and I freeze.

"You're not afraid of that dog, are you sister?"

I turn to face the men behind the store, who are both grinning at me in amusement.

"Yes, I am."

They chuckle at my honesty.

"Aw, you don't need to be scared," one of the men says. His smile is forsaken of teeth, but his eyes are full of merriment. "He's a nice dog."

"No, he isn't," I say. "He always barks at me. Look at him." The Doberman is now in a standing position, a low growl rippling through his body as his eyes fix on me. "He'd rip my throat out if he wasn't on a leash."

"They'd never let him off his leash."

The other man stands up and removes his hairnet. "My wife is afraid of dogs, too," he says kindly, falling in step beside me. "Dogs can sense fear, but that's nothing; cats can sense danger and that's much more useful. There you go, sister," he winks at me as we reach my door. "You're not in danger anymore."

"Wanda, take your dress off." My mother greets me this way every other evening. I only have one dress suitable enough to wear to work under the fur coat, meaning that it is bland enough not to divert any attention away from the fur and sturdy enough so as not to look cheap. On alternate nights Mama soaks it in the galvanized tub by the stove, which we use for both laundry and bathing. .

"Mama, you don't have to do this," I say. "I can wash it myself."

She waves my protestations away. "You've been on your feet all day, Wanda." She turns her back to me as I change into my pink terrycloth robe. "I'll have to go ask Myrtle if we can borrow some of her soap. There's stew on the stove for you. Go sit down with your sister and eat some supper."

"Are you going to eat too, Mama?" I ask as I hand her my dress.

"I'm not hungry."

I scoop the last of the cabbage stew onto a plate and join Evelyn at the kitchen table. She waits until Mama goes out into the hall before speaking. "Our hours got cut," she says impassively, staring at her plate.

"But it's almost winter!" I gasp incredulously. "People need gloves."

"Yeah," Evelyn agrees, sighing. "I guess we worked too fast this summer."

Mama returns from our neighbour's carrying a box of Lux soap bubbles in one hand as she balances a washboard on her hip. Evelyn shoots me a look that signals the conversation is over.

"How was work today, Wanda?" Mama asks as she pours a kettle of warm water into the tub.

Evelyn snorts and continues picking at her stew. I know she doesn't approve of my modelling job. *Those capitalists are using you like a puppet,* she told me when I'd first gotten the job.

"I sold a coat today," I answer and hesitate before continuing. "To this really interesting man. He was with this very rude, very skinny blonde girl but I don't think that he liked her too much..."

"Did he buy the coat for her?" Evelyn asks.

"Well, yes but... "

Evelyn snorts again.

"I've never met anyone like him before," I continue. "He looked like he walked right off of a movie screen. He was so handsome and confident. He was perfect—well, except for his eyes."

"What was wrong with his eyes?" Mama asks, joining us at the table.

"Nothing was wrong with them—they were beautiful—but they were two different colours."

"Like Shadow," Mama smiles, referring to our beloved late cat.

"Yes, just like Shadow."

"He sounds married to me," Evelyn says.

"He is, but he was really nice," I counter, digging lamely into my bag of impotent adjectives.

"Was the blonde dame his wife?"

"No, I don't think so," I answer, wishing now that I hadn't mentioned Henry. *He's only a fantasy to me anyway,* I think bitterly. Fantasies are like bubbles: once they hit the outside world, they pop.

Mama parts the kitchen curtain and looks out.

"November," she says softly. "Everything is grey in November, like a charcoal picture." She pulls at her shawl. "It's getting rather cool in here. Evelyn, why don't you put some fresh coal on the stove?"

My sister crouches by the stove, the coal tongs in her right hand. "It's been three years," Evelyn says.

Mama nods and continues to gaze out the window at the bony, naked trees.

"I miss Daddy."

Evelyn's words hover over us, heavy like a dust cloud.

I want more than anything to wear the blonde girl's coat; I want to live inside of her flesh.

This is why my work dress, still slightly damp from Mama's late night washing, is folded up in my cubbyhole, along with my camiknickers. This is why I am walking up and down the aisle of Ladies Wear with nothing between me and the fox fur but a light sprinkling of Evening in Paris, borrowed from my friends at the perfume counter.

I run my hands over the coat as I pose for the customers. Today I meet their eyes.

If you like what you see, it is me. It is all me.

Toe, heel, toe. I strut my stuff to the big band orchestra playing inside of my head. I'm Toby Wing in *42ⁿᵈ Street* or maybe Ruby Keeler in *Dames*—the only girl Dick Powell has eyes for.

"A beautiful coat." The woman's words, spoken in a strong British accent, reach out to me over the swell of the band. She is speaking directly to me, not to her plump, besuited male companion, who is standing slightly behind her.

"Fox fur," I say, stretching out my arm. "Like to touch?"

She peers at me over her elegantly framed spectacles. I notice that her swirl of grey and white hair match the coat perfectly.

"It is absolutely splendid," she says, ignoring my invitation. "May I try it on?"

I contort my face into a mask of cheer as my soul pushes up against my rib cage in fright.

"I don't think this will fit you," I say quickly. "Here, let me help you find..."

"Oh, I think it will fit me just fine," she interrupts. "You're much bustier and wider along the hips than I am, yes, but I like for my coats to be a little roomy."

"Please," I can feel my mask beginning to falter. "Please, let me find you another."

The woman's own mask of cool elegance disintegrates and her next words tear out at me through gritted teeth.

"Let me try on the coat, little girl. *Now.*"

Her male companion inches forward. "Give my wife the coat!" he barks.

I step backwards and shake my head. The woman's eyes and mouth open wide as her claws descend upon me.

"You stupid little fool!" she cries, ripping open the coat.

Her screams slash at my bare skin, exposing my nudity as I fall into a rack of bathing costumes.

I jump up, wrapping the coat around me quickly and run out, past the woman's violently gaping mouth and Ann's puzzled pink face. Through the haze of indignation, I spot a pair of eyes smiling at me in amusement:

One blue and the other a dark shade of warm honey.

I return to Blondell's the following morning. Ann doesn't need to tell me that I've been sacked but she does anyway.

"This is only for Monday," she says, handing me my pay-cheque, along with my dress and camiknickers. "Mr. Adams says that we aren't going to pay you for yesterday."

Mr. Adams is our manager. Although he's skinny and doesn't smoke, he always has the look of a fat man chomping on a cigar. I blush at the thought of what Ann has told him.

"I figured," I say. "I only wanted to give back the coat."

I attempt to hand over the fur, which I've wrapped in a paper bag, but Ann stops me with a yielding gesture. "It's yours."

I gape at her in confusion as she rifles through the drawer behind the counter. "That man—the handsome one with the funny eyes—he bought it for you. He said his name was Mr. Manchester and," she produces a tiny cream-coloured envelope, "He told me to give you this."

Ann's manner has changed from one of business solemnity to school-girl giddiness. I take the envelope from her and gently remove the small gold embossed card. The address of the Apple Bottom burlesque theatre is printed in tiny cursive below a bold font:

A TREMENDOUS OPPORTUNITY
AWAITS THE FEW WOMEN
WHO ARE SELECTED AS APPLE BOTTOM GIRLS

I turn the card over and silently read the message, handwritten with a fountain pen, on the back:

4:00 Thursday afternoon. Ask for Raul.

"What does it say?" Ann asks, craning her neck over the counter.

I smile at her and drop the card into my faux crocodile handbag, enjoying the accompaniment of Ann's disappointed sigh as my purse snaps shut.

"Goodbye, Ann."

I turn on my snub-nosed heels and make my final strut through Ladies Wear. Before I reach the exit though, I stop and unbutton my cheap cloth coat, letting it fall to the freshly waxed floor. Aware that Ann and the customers are watching me, I toss my hair back like a silver screen queen and slip into the fox fur coat. Their sea of gawking faces resemble a drawer full of rolled up pink socks as I blow them all a big farewell kiss and push my way through the exit doors.

3. A SWELL WIGGLE

"I LOOK LIKE AN OVERSIZED TAP DANCER who's seen better days." Standing on top of the toilet seat in the washroom we share with the other tenants, I gaze morosely at my reflection in the cracked looking glass above the sink.

I am wearing Evelyn's knitted black bathing suit over a pair of cheap stockings. My chubby toes crawl out of the silver high-heeled sandals—one size too small—that Myrtle, our old maid neighbour, lent me.

Evelyn leans against the windowpane. She takes a drag of her cigarette and appraises me under heavily lidded eyes.

"You don't look bad, little sis," she says as she exhales. "Just take those pins out of your hair and put on some red lipstick and you'll be fine."

I step off of the toilet. "You promise me that you won't tell Mama?"

Evelyn nods. "Yeah, I promise."

Mama is out looking for more work. Evelyn faked a cold so she could stay home and read Theodore Dreiser. She picks up her book and hops on the window ledge. "We'll tell Mama that you've taken up a night job as a typist or a telephone operator."

"Even if we get into a spat? You still won't tell her the truth?"

"I still won't tell her the truth."

I move towards her. "Thanks, Evelyn."

She waves her hand in the air dismissively and opens up her

book. "Besides," she says, "dancing at the Apple Bottom is a hell of a lot more honest than what you were doing at the department store."

"I don't even know if I'll get in," I say, ignoring the jab. "It's just an audition."

Evelyn doesn't look up from her book. "You'll get in," she says.

"You're really okay with me doing this?"

Evelyn takes another puff on her cigarette. "Sure, it's not like the Apple Bottom's a flash house. It's a classy place—the girls all wear pasties."

"How do you know?"

She shrugs, still not looking at me. "A date once took me there."

"You'd better go," she says quickly, before I can inquire further. "Break a leg, little sis."

When I step off of the streetcar, it is still day and the lights of the marquee above the Apple Bottom theatre are unlit. Its sign, however, still feels imposing:

The Apple Bottom Presents:
Burlesque Royalty *QUEENIE ROSE*
With *BROCK BAXTER & LILI BELLE*
Plus over a dozen *GORGEOUS GIRLS!!!*

An old man dressed in rags and pushing a cart full of his treasures, stops and stares at me. "Hey Big Red," he says, "Where'd ya get that fur?"

I flash him a smile, the kind that I used to give to the customers. "I stole it."

The lobby of the Apple Bottom theatre is stifling hot. Even so, I keep my fur coat on as I study the colour-tinted photographs of the featured dancers that decorate the lobby's velvet walls. Several photos are of a petite woman with short spit curls and plump thighs. *Lili Belle*, the text under one photo reads, *The Doll Next Door*. With her Cupid's bow mouth, large round eyes, and playful curves, Lili Belle resembles a naughty cartoon flapper brought to life.

The largest photograph is of an unsmiling, statuesque brunette with sleepy eyes and lips like two red rose petals resting upon a bed of pearls. Sitting naked on a backwards facing chair, she holds her head up in a dignified, regal manner; seemingly oblivious to her bountiful breasts, which spill out over the top of the chair like mounds of whipped cream. *All Hail Queenie Rose*, the caption reads, *And God bless her land of plenty, of which she rules.*

A thin elderly man whistles to himself as he pushes a manual vacuum over the lobby's red carpet.

"Hello," I approach him shyly. "I'm here to audition." I hold out the card from Mr. Manchester. "Do you know where I should go?"

The man doesn't look up at me as he continues with his work. "Go see Joe," he says.

"Joe?" I ask. "But Mr. Manchester told me to see Raul."

"Go see Joe," he says again. He bends down to pick up a stray cigarette butt.

"Well, where is this Joe?"

The man drops the butt into his breast pocket and points to a door marked "East Stairwell. Staff Only."

I nod my thanks and push it open. The air inside is thick with the effluvia of bodily waste. After making my way up four flights of stairs, I am met with a dead end: a knobless yellow door, tinctured with smudged lipstick and shoe prints. Pressing my ear against it, I hear a cacophony of running water, female laughter, and Cab Calloway's "Minnie the Moocher." I knock and the laughter becomes louder. Feeling despondent, I turn to leave just as the door creaks open. A petite girl, a cap of shiny yellow hair framing her boneless face, sticks her head out and blinks at me.

"Hello," I say, apprehensively. "My name is Wanda Whittle. I'm here to audition."

The girl blinks again.

"I think I'm supposed to see Raul," I laugh nervously. "Or Joe, I'm not sure."

Blinking twice, the girl opens the door and waves me inside. The damp mist of perfume and sweat make me feel as though I am stepping barefoot through a lush meadow, albeit one with Lux soap bubbles in place of clouds and wet stockings in lieu of trees. Naked skinny chorines congregate around a large vanity table, jostling for a sliver of mirror in which to rouge their lips or curl their lashes. In my fur coat, I feel like a mammoth bison surrounded by prancing, lissome deer.

I sequester myself between a rack of sequined brassieres and a large sign that reads:

NO MEN!!!
(Small dogs OK)

I peel off my coat and dress and stash them both behind the rack. I feel no less extraneous in my dancing costume as I make my way toward the stage door, fully aware, in this land of sinewy, blonde abundance, of my ponderous breasts and the loud persistent whisper of my thighs rubbing together. I pause at the door, wondering if I should wait for the other girls, but spotting not one friendly face in the bunch, I decide to step out on my own.

"Is she wearing a *bathing suit?*" a shrill voice cackles as the door slams shut behind me.

Two men, one old and one young, are seated at a small round table in the middle of the empty theatre. The older man is writing in a notepad as the younger one looks over his shoulder and smiles amenably. They both look up at the sound of my silver shoes clacking across the stage. "Holy Mary Mother of God!" the older man exclaims. "Come here, girl."

The two men watch me as I hop off the stage and make my way over to them. The younger one has shiny, slicked back hair and leech-like pouches under his dark eyes. I can tell by his bone structure that he's usually good looking—he's just having a bad day. He smiles at me kindly. The older man is ugly in an interesting way, with a large hooked nose and long lines, like cat scratches, on his saggy face.

"Hot damn!" the old man says. He stares at my breasts as though he's watching an oncoming tornado or a plane crashing. "You've gotta be Wanda!"

"Mr. Manchester told us about you," the younger man explains, his eyes sparkling with joviality.

I keep my face stretched into a stupid smile. "I'm here to audition…"

"Henry sent you—you ain't auditioning," the older man interrupts. He tears his eyes away from my chest and breaks into a smile. "A redhead!" he claps his hands together gleefully. "Finally! We've got too many fucking blondes in this joint."

The younger man winks at me. "What he means to say is welcome to the Apple Bottom." He puts his hand out and I shake it. "I'm Raul. I choreograph the show. This here is Joe, he does everything else."

"How do you do?" I nod.

"*How do you do!*" Joe laughs. "Jesus, you're a cute kid. Listen girlie, how old are you, anyway?"

"Nineteen. I'll be twenty in the spring."

"Education?"

"Does it matter?"

Joe laughs. "Of course not. I was just curious."

"I've finished the ninth grade. My family couldn't afford to send me to high school."

Both of the men nod.

"Have you ever danced before?" Raul asks.

"Well, I've never done burlesque before, but I used to work a little as a taxi dancer."

"Same thing," Joe says. Raul purses his lips in quiet dissent.

"Look, doll," Joe is suddenly all business. "We'll pay you fifteen dollars a week. How does that sound?"

"Gee, that sounds swell!"

"Good," Joe claps Raul on the back. "Raul will show you the ropes here. I'll go get the other girls. What's taking you dames so long?" he shouts as he climbs onto the stage. "Powdering your pretty little asses? It's only a fucking rehearsal!"

I turn to Raul. "I thought this was an audition. I didn't know it was an actual rehearsal."

Raul smiles at me warmly. "You'll be fine, Wanda. Here," he puts his hands on my shoulders. "I'll show you some basic moves. Do you bake?"

"Do I *bake?*" I laugh in confusion. "No."

"That's okay. I like to use baking chocolate biscuits as an analogy for burlesque. I think you'll catch on anyway. Now, watch me."

"Flour!" Raul shouts, jerking out his left hip.

"Butter!" He bumps his right hip.

"Beat it!" Raul grinds his hips in a sexy, circular motion.

"Roll the dough!" He turns around and wiggles his bottom.

"Stir the cocoa!" He faces me again and thrusts out his chest, shaking imaginary breasts.

The other girls arrive and Raul takes me by the hand as we join them on stage.

"Girls!" he shouts. "This is Wanda."

A dozen painted eyes graze my body with a mixture of curiosity and contempt. I notice that the other girls are all wearing white shirts tied at the waist and black tap pants with bare legs. I feel silly in my sister's bathing costume.

Raul arranges us into a straight line.

"Follow along with me," he says. "And remember, you'll each get a turn to stir your cocoa. One at a time."

"Flour!" he shouts. I shake my hips to the left, along with the other girls.

"Butter!" I bump out my right hip and almost trip over the skinny dame beside me.

"Don't you even know how to butter?" she whispers derisively.

When he gets to "Cocoa," Raul points to a tall girl with Harlow-blonde hair. She struts to centre stage and shakes her tiny breasts.

"Ooh, you're giving me a toothache!"

We all stop and look up as a curvy woman wearing a black silk turban, matching gloves, and a fitted red coat enters the theatre. I recognize her from the lobby posters.

"Lili Belle!" Raul purrs. He kisses her outstretched hand. "How wonderful of you to join us!"

"Hello Lili Belle!" the other girls sing out in unison.

The surly dame beside me has stretched her mouth into a slavish smile.

"So lovely to see you, Lili Belle!"

Lili Belle ignores her. "Mr. Manchester told me that we've gotten some fresh meat," she winks at me. "Mind if I steal her away for a bit, Raul?"

"Not at all," Raul says as Lili Belle takes me by the hand and leads me out the side door.

Backstage, Lili Belle takes off her coat and positions me in front of a full-length oval mirror. "So what are your issues?" she asks.

I laugh self-consciously. "Everything."

Lili Belle shakes her head and looks at me kindly. "Mr. Manchester wouldn't have sent you here if he didn't think that you have what it takes. Besides," she adds, "I was watching your walk; you already know how to strut. You've got a swell wiggle."

"Thanks," I say. "But I feel clunky." I frown at my reflection. "Especially next to those other girls. They're so slender and elegant and I'm…" I sigh and gesture toward my hips.

Standing behind me, Lili Belle takes my hands and places them on my ribcage, just below my breasts. "There!" she says, her eyes bright. "You already look pounds lighter and inches taller!"

I look at my image in amazement. She's right—with my hands in this position, I appear much slimmer.

"Unless you're carrying a prop, always walk with your hands on your ribcage, never on your hips," Lili Belle continues. "Remember to be very aware of your hands, wrists, feet, and ankles. Burlesque isn't just about curves, it's also about lines." With her own hand under one breast, Lili Belle stretches her other arm up and over her head in a perfectly straight line. She dips her wrist gracefully.

"See?" she asks, wiggling her fingers.

I nod and mimic her pose.

"Good," Lili Belle turns away from the mirror. "We need some music in this joint!" She begins fiddling with a small teardrop radio on the dressing table. The room suddenly blossoms with the galvanizing sounds of jazz. Then she turns toward the looking glass and starts to wiggle her hips. Unlike Raul's, Lili Belle's movements are smaller and more contained. I can't take my eyes off of her.

"How long have you been dancing at the Apple Bottom?" I ask her.

Lili Belle continues to dance in front of the mirror. "Oh a little over five years or so," she says, smiling in satisfaction at her reflection. "This joint is much classier now that the customers don't need a password to get in," Lili Belle winks at me. "I remember the night that Mr. Manchester made me a feature. He took me out to see *The Broadway Melody* and afterwards he told me that I reminded him of Bessie Love. Or," she laughs. "Bessie reminded him of me."

"I remember her," I say. "She's a swell actress."

Lili Belle slides her eyes at me. "Do you think she's pretty?"

"Sure!" I say. "She's very pretty."

"She always plays the plain girl, though," Lili Belle says.

"Yes, but pretty girls always play plain girls in the pictures."

"True." Lili Belle dances over to me and places her hands on my hips. I attempt to follow her movements.

"I see Lili Belle is *working* you very hard, Wanda!"

We both look up as Joe enters the room. A dour-faced older woman follows behind him.

"I was just showing her some moves, Joe," Lili Belle says, putting her arm around my waist protectively.

"*Showing* or *making?*" Joe smirks at her.

Lili Belle licks her right palm and walks over to him. Joe visibly flinches as she raises her hand. "Oh, Joey," she purrs as she brings her hand down to smooth his wayward cowlick. "You always miss a spot."

Lili Belle turns to me. "See you tonight, honey," she says, kissing me on the cheek. "You're going to be swell."

With a pronounced shake of her behind, Lili Belle exits the dressing room, a waft of peaches and talcum powder lingering in her wake.

"Wanda," Joe says gruffly. "This is Geraldine." He gestures to the woman standing beside him. "She's our costume lady."

Geraldine gapes at me behind thick Coke-bottle spectacles. "She's too fat, Joe," she says bluntly. "She won't fit into any of my costumes."

"So make 'em fit," Joe snaps. "But keep 'em tight." He waggles his eyebrows. "We want to showcase Wanda's *assets.*"

Geraldine purses her thin lips. "You men are all the same." She cups my face between her coarse red hands. "Pretty girl, though," she says. "That hair'll stand out on stage."

Joe leaves as Geraldine begins to take my measurements. She clucks her tongue in disapproval as she pulls the measuring tape tightly around my waist. "What do you eat?" she asks, but doesn't wait for me to answer. "To reduce, you should only eat grapefruit and oranges," she continues. "Grapefruit, oranges, and black coffee. Oh, and have a steam bath every Friday."

I look at Geraldine's own lumpy, potato-like body and say nothing.

"Stay here," she instructs me as though I am a dog. Geraldine crosses the room and begins rummaging through a rack of clothing.

"A-ha!" She pulls out a black, whale-bone corset bustier. It is hand-beaded with red sequins and silk ribbons.

"It's beautiful," I say, reaching out to touch it.

"Let's see if it actually fits you." Geraldine yanks down my bathing suit.

"You're going to need some silk stockings," she says. "Those I can lend you. You have nice legs, at least." Her rough, sausage-like fingers scrape at my flesh as she ties up the corset.

"Joe wants it tight, does he?" she mumbles to herself. "Well he doesn't need to worry about *that.*" I fight back tears as she yanks at the ribbons. I think of the British woman in the department store. My body warms with shame.

Geraldine turns me around. "Good," she nods her approval. She digs into her dress pocket and hands me a pair of black French knickers.

"Put these on," she instructs me. "Oh, and this is important: always, always wear pasties. Otherwise, Mr. Manchester will get arrested." She looks down at my feet. "Are those your own shoes?"

"They're my neighbour's."

"Well, I like 'em." Geraldine nods again. "You can wear them tonight." We are interrupted by a clamouring of female laughter as the other chorines begin to file in. "If you ever become a headliner, I can custom make your gowns," Geraldine says as she turns to leave. "On a deposit," she adds just before the door shuts behind her.

I smooth my hands over the silky corset. It occurs to me that I should have gone to the powder room *before* Geraldine dressed me, but it's too late now.

"Excuse me," I approach the lanky chorine who had been the first to "stir her cocoa." "Can you please tell me where the powder room is?"

"The *powder room?*" Her thin red lips curl up in amusement. "Why, *this* is the powder room, doll!"

"No," I stutter nervously. "I-I-mean…"

"You mean the *toilet?*" she chortles. "Why it's just out the left door, down the hall and to your right, *doll.*"

"Look for the *green* door," another girl calls out among hushed giggles.

"Thank you." I follow their directions, sighing with relief as I locate the green door. Hurriedly, I push it open.

"Say, what's the big idea!"

A young man, wearing nothing but an unbuttoned dress shirt and BVDs, glares at me in angry indignation.

"Oh! I'm so sorry!" I shield my eyes with my right hand. "They—the other girls told me that this was the powder room." My tight corset, Geraldine's rough fingers, and the chorine's mocking smile all suddenly coalesce and I burst into tears.

"Wait," the young man's body visibly sags in contrition. "I should have known it was those dizzy dames!" He buttons up his shirt. "Here," he says, pulling a handkerchief from his front pocket. "I shouldn't have snapped at you like that. I'm sorry."

I accept both his apology and his handkerchief gratefully. "I'm Wanda," I say, extending my hand. "I was just hired on today."

He takes my hand and kisses it in showy gallantry. "Pleased to meet you, Miss Wanda. My name is Brock."

"Oh!" I look up at him. With his heavily lashed blue eyes, pronounced cheekbones, and small angular body, Brock resembles a wooden toy soldier. I want to put him in my pocket. "I saw your name on the sign outside!"

"Yes," Brock rolls his eyes towards the ceiling and laughs bitterly. "'*The Master of Ceremonies,*' better known as the comic. Not that it matters—the audience in this joint never looks at me anyway. And," he continues, bringing my hand again to his lips, "if you'll beg my pardon, Miss Wanda, with *you* on the stage tonight, I might as well not go on at all!" His smile lets me know that he's only flirting.

I squirm, both from embarrassment at his compliment and from the fact that I still have to go pee. "Brock, would you mind please pointing me in the direction of the powder room?"

"I'd be glad to!" He winks at me. "Just give me a moment to put on my trousers." In the hallway, Brock puts his arm around me amicably as we pass the showgirl's dressing room.

"Hey girls!" a shrill voice calls out. "Looks like Wanda found the *toilet!*"

"Go pour yourself a saucer of milk!" Brock shouts back. He turns to me kindly. "Don't let those dames buffalo you, Miss Wanda. Here," he points to a door at the end of the hallway. "That there's the ladies room. And if you'll beg my pardon again, Miss Wanda, *you* are one of the few 'ladies' in this joint!"

"*Of course* a burlesque dancer has virtue!" Brock merrily bellows from the stage. "She has a brassiere too, but does she wear it?"

Even from backstage, I can sense the impatience behind the audience's polite laughter.

"Think you're ready, girlie?"

I turn to face Joe. "I guess I better be."

He smiles. "That's the spirit! Remember doll," he lowers his voice. "The audience here *wants* to like you. So it's easy—you just give 'em what they want."

"I better bring out the tomatoes," Brock continues, addressing the crowd in his smooth, jovial tone, "before you all start *throwing* tomatoes!"

The orchestra strikes up a jazzy number as Joe pushes me and the other girls forward. "That's your cue! Move it, girls! Go!"

Following behind the other chorines, I stumble on stage and straight into a hot ball of stupefying yellow light.

Daddy and I are sitting on the beach, eating hotdogs. A swarm of seagulls hover above us in the cotton blue sky. "Rats with

wings," Daddy calls them. Every time one of them gets near
me, I flinch. "Don't be scared of them flying rats, baby-girl,"
Daddy says, laughing. "Even if one of 'em did once mistake
my eye for a gobstopper!" That was Daddy's story of how he
lost his eye. It was a lie, but I didn't know that at the time. I
look up at the light disappearing behind the clouds. "Don't
do that, baby-girl," Daddy puts a hand over my eyes. "Don't
you never look directly at the light—it'll blind ya more than
any bird ever could."

But the light has already conquered all of my senses, along with
most of my will. Licked by the merciless heat of its flames, my
body bends and quivers, submitting to its ravenous commands.

Even though I am unable to see him, I know that it is Mr.
Manchester who is directing and controlling the blaze. And
when it is my turn to take centre stage, I can feel his approval
as the audience embraces my body with its fervent applause—
curbing the flames, but unable to extinguish my fire.

As the curtain closes, Lili Belle meets me backstage, engulfing
me in a giant bear hug. "I said you'd be swell," she cries out
happily. "I knew you'd be swell and you *were* swell!"

"You really think so, Lili Belle?"

"Do I really think so?"

Lili Belle steps back and takes both of my hands in hers.
"Sweetie, didn't you hear that audience?"

I laugh. "I couldn't *see* that audience."

"Those footlights are pretty blinding," Lili Belle agrees. She
lets go of my hands and does a little twirl. "Say doll, what do
you think of my new glad rags?"

I let out a low wolf whistle as Lili Belle preens before me in
a figure-hugging shiny black dress with peacock feather trim
and a matching headband with an extra-large feather fastened
to the back.

"Hey, Lili Belle," Joe sneers from his position by the curtains.
"Did Geraldine pluck a bird to make you that frock?"

"Sure, Joe," Lili Belle haughtily replies. She tilts her chin in his direction. "But *you* needn't worry—she's got no use for chicken feathers."

Lili Belle winks at me. "I better get my pretty little bee-hind on stage before Joe has it!"

Most of the girls are already in various stages of disrobement as I enter the dressing room. The surly chorine from rehearsal is sitting at one of the cluttered vanity tables. "All of this war paint for one lousy picture number," she grumbles to no one in particular, smearing globs of cold cream on her face.

"Girls!" Geraldine bends down to pick up a discarded bustier. "*Please* be more careful with my costumes!"

A freckled, gum-chewing chorine hops up and down as she tries to remove her skin-tight dress. "Say Geraldine!" she snaps. "You ever heard of buttons?"

"Say Dottie," Geraldine replies, "You ever heard of the Depression?" She gives the showgirl's behind a swat. "Zippers are a helluva lot cheaper than buttons and besides, the dames who feature here prefer 'em."

She unzips Dottie's dress before turning to me. "You better let me help you with that corset, Wanda."

The chorine who had played the mean trick on me earlier, whose name I have learned is Penny, watches with a smirk as Geraldine unties the back of my bustier. "*Ba-ba-BOOM!*" Penny cries as the final ribbon is undone, my breasts bouncing free.

The other girls, to my relief, don't laugh.

"Here," Geraldine hands me a fluffy white robe. "Put this on and go watch the rest of the show from backstage. You've probably missed Lili Belle but you should be able to catch Queenie."

I look at her in confusion.

"Listen," she lowers her voice. "I've been here for over eighteen years and I know a headliner when I see one. Go out there and learn from the best and trust me, honey," she continues as I slip into the robe, "Queenie is the best."

4. DIAMONDS AND CRACKER JACK

QUEENIE JIGGLE-STRUTS ACROSS THE STAGE in a shiny, floor-length evening gown with a sequined fishtail hem, playfully swinging a lacy parasol back and forth in her right hand. Stopping centre stage, she extends her left leg, exposing her silk stocking and garter belt. She looks out at the crowd, her smile as sweet and warm as a deep dish apple pie, and slowly runs her hand from her ankle up to her thigh, clearly delighted by her own magnificent form.

"She has beautiful skin, doesn't she?" Lili Belle whispers. "I know why, too."

Turning her back to the audience, Queenie begins to unzip her dress while shaking her ample bottom in time to the house band.

I want to swat Lili Belle away and submerse myself in Queenie's honey, but she's been so nice to me and I can tell that she really wants me to ask her why, so I do. "Well, I probably shouldn't tell you, because she told me in secret. All the other girls think it's because she bathes in coconut oil, which she does, but that's not the *real* reason why her skin is so smooth."

"What's the real reason?" I ask, indulging her.

"Well," Lili Belle leans in closer, her sticky pink lips brushing against my ear. "She told me it's because she shaves. Not just her legs but her entire body and even her face. *Everything.*"

"She shaves?" I ask incredulously.

An attendant makes a dive for Queenie's dress as she tosses it backstage. She has opened up the parasol and is now twirling it in front of her chest demurely, teasing the audience.

"She doesn't *look* like she has a beard," I say and Lili Belle laughs.

"Of course she doesn't have a beard, sweetie! She shaves to get rid of dead skin cells." Lili Belle touches her own face. "I was thinking of trying it myself but I don't think I have the dedication."

Joe comes by and tells Lili Belle to shut up. I'm thankful because it is at this precise moment that Queenie drops her parasol. Her breasts remind me of the frosted pink cupcakes in the window of the department store's bakery except that, instead of cherries, Queenie's nipples are topped with sparkly tasseled pasties. She stretches her arms over and above her head and gives the audience a wink as her breasts bounce, swing and twirl in a hypnotic dance all their own.

"How..." I realize that my mouth has gone dry and I attempt to clear my throat. "How does she *do* that?"

"I don't know," Lili Belle's voice takes on an air of deference. "No one does. And don't ask her either—she'll think that you're trying to crab her act and then she won't tell you anyway."

The curtain drops to rapacious applause. Backstage, Queenie glides by me, a dampened pink cloud of sugar and sweat. "Queenie," I call out. Stopping, she turns to look at me, her eyes like those of a bored house cat.

"You were wonderful," I say. "You were so wonderful."

Without a word, Queenie flips her dark hair over one shoulder and disappears out the side door, leaving me feeling like an empty-handed fool. I had given her my praise as though my words were precious diamonds, when in Queenie's eyes my opinion is worth less than a plastic Cracker Jack ring.

Lili Belle touches my arm in sympathy. Before she can speak, a pretty brunette resembling a busty canary in a low-cut bright yellow dress approaches us. "New girl," she points at me. "Mr.

Manchester is waiting for you outside. Look for the green and blue Rolls."

"Waiting for me?" I ask in confusion, but she's already gone. Lili Belle squeals and hugs me. "He probably wants to talk to you about featuring. Oh, Wanda, you're so lucky! I was a chorine for months before Mr. Manchester let me feature." She takes a step back and scrutinizes me. "What are you going to wear?" she asks.

"The dress that I came in wearing, I guess."

"Oh, no," Lili Belle shakes her head dramatically. "You can't wear that old rag. Come, I'll lend you one of my dresses." She grabs me by the hand and we skip together to the dressing room like school girls.

It isn't until I've poured myself into Lili Belle's sparkly skin-tight dress though that I really begin to feel giddy. "I'm spilling out of this," I say, appraising myself in the dressing room's finger smudged oval mirror. I try to pull the dress up higher over my bosom, but Lili Belle smacks my hand away.

"Don't do that!" she admonishes. "What do you think these guys are paying to look at anyway? Your face?" She kneels before me and reaches her hands up, under the dress.

"Hey! What are you doing?"

Her pretty brown eyes wink at me as she pulls down my French knickers.

"You don't want any lines," she says. She stuffs my underwear into the pocket of her robe and stands up. "You look swell, Wanda. Mr. Manchester is going to make you a feature for sure!"

"You really think so?" I ask. I turn back to the mirror and look at myself sceptically.

Lili Belle comes up behind me. She smiles at my reflection and takes one of my curls between her fingers, giving it a light tug. "Why, it's cream in the can, baby!"

5. BETTER THAN A KISS

WHEN I WOULD STRUT UP AND DOWN the aisle of Ladies Wear, I always felt that, although my physical body was moving inside of brick and mortar, my soul was floating somewhere outside of it all, in a different dimension. I felt light. I do not feel that way tonight. Exiting the back door, ignoring the "Hello, dolly!" come-ons from the stage door Johnnies, wearing another girl's dress and another woman's shoes, both my soul and my body are very much a part of this world. I feel heavy.

Mr. Manchester is leaning against his Rolls Royce, the doors of which have his initials, *H.M.*, printed in gold. When he sees me, he drops the cigarette that he'd been smoking, and gallantly opens the passenger door for me. "Your chariot, Madam," he says, bowing.

His attempt at humour is stiff, underscored by my forced laughter.

"I can't do this every night," he says, as he helps me into the car. "But you are much too beautiful to ride the streetcar."

"Thank you," I say. "But where's..." I hesitate. What do I call the blonde woman—his girlfriend, or his mistress?

"Norma?" Mr. Manchester smiles, settling into the driver's seat. "I had my driver take her home in my other car." He puts his key into the ignition. "There's something that I would like to talk to you about, Miss Whittle."

"You can call me Wanda."

"Wanda," he draws my name out slowly. "This is strictly business, mind you."

"Of course," I smile, although inside I feel almost as foolish as I did earlier with Queenie. *All I did was offer you my name,* I want to say.

"Where do you live, Wanda?" Mr. Manchester interrupts my thoughts.

"Behind the Market."

"Behind the Market," he repeats and nods as though he had known all along. "Listen, Wanda, it would be much more practical for us to have this," he pauses, "*business* discussion at my apartment. I'll drive you home afterwards, of course."

He mistakes my silence for hesitation and continues. "Or should I just take you home right now?"

"No," I say. I look out at the Apple Bottom as Mr. Manchester slides the car straight into the glittering wet mouth of the city. The theatre looks like a small yellow box. A child's toy. A doll's house.

I sit up tall, push my shoulder blades down my back, and turn to him. "I want to go to your apartment."

"Please, Wanda, remove your shoes." I obey, turning away from Mr. Manchester as I slip off my silver peep-toe stilettos, fearful of my bosom falling out of my low-cut dress. Mr. Manchester opens the door to his apartment and gently leads me inside.

I gasp in delight as my bare feet sink into the white velvet carpet, stretching before me like a four-a.m. snowfall. Wall-to-wall gilt mirrors, framing the elegant yet sparsely furnished room, make any kind of corporeal escape impossible. In their reflection are three images: in two, Mr. Manchester is standing slightly behind me. In the third reflection, his hand is hovering above my bottom.

"Please sit, Wanda, and I'll get us something to drink. I have some champagne in the icebox." Mr. Manchester removes his

Trilby hat and motions to a tufted red-velvet couch, situated rather oddly in the middle of the apartment like a large blooming tulip. I feel self-conscious under his steady gaze and so I perch rigidly on the edge of the sofa's creamy cushion, unsure of whether to cross my legs at the knee or at the ankle. There is a potted peach tree to my right; I gently touch the fruit's silky skin.

"They're real!" I exclaim in amazement.

Coming out of the kitchen, Mr. Manchester smiles in naked amusement. "Yes, you can grow a peach tree indoors," he says. "The trick is in the progenitor fruit: the riper the peach, the stronger its seed."

He hands me a glass of champagne. "A toast," he says, raising his drink. "To the most beautiful showgirl at the Apple Bottom."

I smile and take a sip. The liquid gold gives me a soft, deliquesce feeling. I have the sudden urge to curl up in Mr. Manchester's lap like a kitten.

He puts his glass down on the floor. "I think you'd make a wonderful tassel dancer, Wanda. I'd like to make you our headliner. Tell me dear, what did Joe say we were paying you?"

"Fifteen dollars a week."

I catch the hint of a smirk on Mr. Manchester's lips before he clears his throat. "We'll pay you forty dollars a week then. But first," he continues gravely. "First I must see your breasts."

I swallow the last of my champagne. "I'm a little self-conscious..."

Mr. Manchester interrupts me with a laugh that sounds more like a cough. "Why would a girl as gorgeous as you are feel self-conscious? Besides, you needn't worry; I've seen many, many breasts in my time. They're as common to me as tires are to a mechanic."

"You'll really pay me forty dollars a week?"

"Of course," he answers. "And it will only go up from there."

I look down at my dress. "Can I have some more champagne please?"

Mr. Manchester shakes his head sternly. "No, Wanda. Too much alcohol will dry up your beauty."

He takes my glass away from me and I notice his hands for the first time: they are large, calloused, and, in sharp contrast with his otherwise pristine appearance, slightly dirty looking. *He wasn't born into money*, I think, *he has worked very hard for all of this.*

I look up and Mr. Manchester is staring at me. As though I am a marionette and his eyes are pulling the strings, I unzip my dress down to my waist, exposing my naked breasts.

Mr. Manchester continues to watch my face. "What are you thinking about, Wanda?"

"I'm thinking that you're always looking at me," I say. I place my hands under my breasts and hold them out to him like gifts of ripened fruit. "And I think that I like it. I like that you're always looking at me."

Mr. Manchester smiles. He looks down at my chest. "You're a very naughty girl, Wanda."

He moves in closer as though he is about to kiss me but instead he grabs me by the waist, taking me over his knee. Lifting the skirt of my dress, he begins to squeeze and massage my buttocks. "I don't mix business with pleasure, Wanda," he says before bringing his hand down on my bottom with a resounding smack.

I watch myself in the gilt mirrors as he continues to spank me. My derriere quivers and my breasts jiggle in time with his every slap. I can feel Mr. Manchester growing hard against his will and I wiggle my hips, grinding myself into his inadvertent erection.

"Please, Mr. Manchester," I beg. "Please."

Don't stop. Take me. Throw me down on your snow-white carpet and take me. Now. Please.

The more I squirm though, the harder he spanks me.

"Oh, please, Mr. Manchester..."

I squeeze my thighs together. A river roils inside of me; it

bursts the dam open and floods my body like a hurricane.
This is better than a kiss.

THE DAILY NIGHT BEAT

A Dream Named Wanda Wiggles
Norman Fingerhead, Night Beat Reporter

The Main Avenue streetcar stop, just steps from the front door of the Apple Bottom, seems a suitable analogy for the burlesque theatre.

There a man stands waiting. In his left hand, he holds a broken cardboard suitcase. With his right, he absentmindedly scratches his sagging unshaven jaw. Peering out from under his crushed derby, the city lights make the man think of plastic flowers planted in mud. And yet, as his streetcar approaches, the man catches a glimpse of a smile. A fat curl tucked behind a delicate ear, a shoe dangling from a recherché foot, and a forgotten or long buried dream begins to blossom inside of him.

Last night, such a dream descended from the rickety, splintered roof top of the Apple Bottom. A voluptuous dream sweeter than a whipped cream strawberry sundae.

A dream named Wanda Wiggles.

Entering atop a red velvet swing and joyfully kicking her shapely bare legs beneath a white cloak (a garment loose enough to reveal her gams but fitted enough to more than hint at the rich bounty underneath), Wanda tosses her long red curls and smiles at the audience with her plump, cherry lips as though to assure us that if she truly is a dream, then so are we. She twists her swing around so that her back is to the audience as she dismounts. Throwing her cloak off stage, she falls into a small pool made up to resemble a lake. With her back still to us, Wanda emerges from the water, clad only in her string knickers, and offers up the sweetest apple bottom of all. She looks over her shoulder, giving the audience both a coquettish smile and a tantalizing side glimpse of that aforementioned bounty (and oh, how bountiful!). Then, with all of the disillusionment of a blaring alarm clock, Wanda mounts her swing again and disappears, ascending once again to the roof top.

The audience doesn't cheer: they howl with hunger, crying out for just one more lick of this curvaceous candy cane.

Mercifully, the house band sounds the drums to announce that sustenance is coming and Wanda reappears on the swing: wet, naked, and now full frontal. Her body is a garden of plenitude, the fruit of which could fulfill even the most hopeless glutton. Still with that hypnotic smile, our dream girl continues to swing, her long wet hair whipping to and fro as she wiggles and bumps to the drum beat.

Rocking the audience to a dream that they never want to wake up from.

6. BLESSINGS AND DOUGH

THE WIND RATTLES THE FLAG atop the Mission but the men standing in the breadline keep their hats. As I pass them, I feel callous in my new astrakhan-trimmed cap and I try, unsuccessfully, to contort my lips into a smile. Only a handful of the men look at me, a vestige of momentary interest illuminating their hungry faces. The rest look down at their shoes or up at the cruel blue sky.

This hat isn't paid off yet, I want to assure them. I pull the brim of the cap down over my eyes. No, I will *not* feel guilty for taking twenty dollars out of my weekly pay for the installments on it. I know that I should hand over all of my earnings to Mama, but if I'm going to be an Apple Bottom feature, I need to look glamorous. Besides, it wouldn't be believable anyway for an evening stenographer to be making forty dollars a week. Why, Mama was flabbergasted when I brought home twenty.

"This man, this Mr. Manchester, he pays you twenty dollars a week just to take dictation for his memoirs?" she had asked me, her mouth agape. "Who has twenty dollars to give away these days?"

"Wake up, Mama," Evelyn had coolly replied, looking up from her copy of *The New Masses* magazine. "In order for a Depression to exist at all, *somebody's* got to be flush."

Mama had turned on Evelyn then, lashing out at my sister for her blossoming "Red sympathies." Thankfully, Mama had seemed to have forgotten that I don't know shorthand.

I look back at the men standing in the breadline. Every once in a while, when I'm riding the streetcar or sipping a chocolate soda at the drugstore, I see my Daddy's face in a crowd, but only until I blink. Sometimes it feels like his death was just a dream. Other times it feels like he was just a dream.

In the dressing room that Lili Belle and I now share, I sit before the looking glass and wonder where my own face has gone. Perhaps I left pieces of it behind the Market: rats nibbling on my lips; my mouth full of ashes; the neighbourhood kids playing "kick the can" with my nose. At least I still have my eyes, though. And, like the pointy-eared little carnivores hiding out behind the trash bins, I know how to see in the dark.

"Why so down, baby?" Lili Belle's melodious giggle cuts my melancholy in half. "You're the talk of the town!" She slaps the newspaper down on the vanity table with Mr. Fingerhead's review facing up.

"You look sweet, Lili Belle," I say, by way of changing the subject. She does look charming though, dressed in a black net-gown with red velvet trim. "I wish I could wear fancy dresses like that, but Raul only has me doing skinny dipping and bathing beauty routines."

Lili Belle takes a seat beside me and begins rummaging through her handbag. "Count your blessings and your dough, dearie! These frocks don't come cheap." She pulls out a small rectangular box. "You want an Olive tablet, honey?"

"No thank you, Lili Belle."

She shrugs and pops the laxative in her mouth.

"Say, Lili Belle," I turn to her. "Do you think Mr. Manchester will be in the audience tonight?"

Lili Belle gives me a sidelong look. "I have no idea," she answers. She takes out a jar of Vaseline and begins to smooth the jelly over and along the curve of her eyebrows. "Why do you ask, hon?"

"No reason. It's just that I haven't seen him since he made me a feature and I…"

"You ain't sweet on him, are you?"

"No, no, it's just that…"

"Wake up and smell the other dame's perfume, dearie," Lili Belle continues, as she feathers a soft brown pencil across her lashes. "Mr. Manchester is a happily married man and he has a very nice girlfriend."

"Well, I don't know about that," I reply, unable to keep my disdain for Norma out of my voice. "I wouldn't exactly call that stuck up dame 'nice.'"

Lili Belle signs and puts her makeup pencil down on the vanity table. "It doesn't matter what you'd call her, Wanda. Mr. Manchester is a professional man. He's strictly business. Now if you're looking for a sugar daddy, and I'm not judging you if you are, one of 'em stage door Johnnies should be good for a bit of jack."

"I'm *not* looking for a sugar daddy!" I exclaim angrily. "I just dance better when Mr. Manchester is around, that's all."

Lili Belle gets up and stands behind me. "Don't be sore," she says, wrapping her arms around me. "I'm just looking out for you, doll." She leans forward as though to kiss the top of my head. Suddenly, she jumps back.

"Pee-yew!" she cries. She pinches her nose between her finger and thumb. "I better lend you some of my lavender water, honey. Your hair reeks of the Market!"

I turn back towards the mirror and, for the first time all day, I smile.

7. HIGHBALLIN' HARD TIMES

"**H**IGHBALLS AND HARD TIMES! Diamonds and bread-lines!" Clad in his trademark checked suit and comedy derby, Brock belts out "Highballin' Hard Times," a song he wrote to commemorate the one-year anniversary of the repeal of Prohibition. A row of chorines dressed up as nineteenth-century saloon girls dance the can-can as I bathe centre stage in an elephantine cocktail glass filled with real champagne.

Humming along with Brock's booze tune, I joyfully kick my legs out towards the Apple Bottom's newly installed mirrored ceiling.

"My pockets are empty but my honey's got money!"

I dunk my head under the golden liquid, not caring if my hair gets sticky.

"As long as I'm with her all my days will be sunny!"

I take a generous gulp of fizz water before coming up again for air. Happy and dizzy, I shake my golden tassels at the mirthful audience, who roar their approval. I wonder if Mr. Manchester is in the theatre tonight. Just the thought of him watching me like this, with my wet, near naked body glistening under the hot lights, excites me. I have only ever known one man "in the biblical sense": Guy Bacon, a rather plump banker, eleven years my senior, whom I had met while taxi dancing when I was sixteen. I had not found Guy particularly handsome or interesting, but he was very persistent; I was kind of bored. So, one evening, after he had spent all of his tickets on me,

I agreed to go for a ride down to the lake in his cherry-red Chevrolet Sports Cabriolet.

It was late spring and the nights were still very chilly. I knew that the beach would be deserted; a fact that, undoubtedly, Guy was also aware of when he stopped his car by the boardwalk and suggested an evening stroll. Walking hand in hand with Guy, my wine-coloured dancing shoes slung over my shoulder, my world seemed as blind and as certain as the moon. Guy took me in his arms and pointed up at the ink-black sky.

"See those stars?" he whispered. "I'll buy you one. I'll buy you the whole sky full just to see you shine." He said the words mechanically, as though he was reading them out loud from a script. Playing along, I put my arms around his neck as he gently pushed me down onto the sand. I was so worried about getting my dress dirty though that I must have forgotten my lines, because moments later, after he had emitted what was either a groan or a whimper, Guy squinted down at my face and asked me why I wasn't crying.

"I'm sorry," I answered.

"I thought you were a virgin."

"I am ... I mean, I was."

"Well, most girls cry."

The truth was that I hadn't felt anything that night. Neither pleasure nor pain. Warmth, excitement, desire: these feelings were not to be found on the beach with Guy, but rather over Mr. Manchester's knee: my body at the mercy of his hands.

"Cause we've got highballs and hard times! Diamonds and Breadlines!"

Brock crosses the stage and hands me a martini glass filled with a thick pink liquid. "Ladies and gentlemen," he turns back to the audience and raises his own glass. "Let's have a toast! To the tastiest dish at the Apple Bottom, our very own Golden Delicious Girl, Miss Wanda Wiggles!"

"We should bottle this champagne," Joe says. He props a

small ladder up beside the giant cocktail glass and holds his hand out to me. "We could sell it to the stage-door Johnnies. Betcha we'd make a mint."

As I gingerly step out of the glass, my foot slips on the ladder and I fall into Joe's arms.

"Easy there, doll," he says, helping me down onto the stage floor. "Good thing she's got a lot of padding here, eh Benny?" He pats my bottom and waggles his eyebrows at the janitor whom I had met in the lobby on my first day.

Benny grunts non-committedly, a limp cigarette anchored between his teeth, and sweeps his mop forward to soak up the pool of alcohol at my feet.

Embarrassed, I wriggle out of Joe's arms. I wish that I could smack him across the face with a smart remark, like Lili Belle would, but the most that I can do is muster up what I hope is a dirty look before whirling around and gracefully stumbling backstage.

"Miss Wanda!" Brock rushes towards me, his arms full of towels. "I thought you could use these."

"Oh, Brock, how thoughtful!" I take one of the smaller towels from him and wrap my hair up in a turban. "You sure are regular!"

Brock's pretty soldier-boy face turns pink as he glances down at my bare chest.

"Miss Wanda," he looks down at the floor. "I was wondering—if you don't need to go home right away that is—if you'd care to join me for some supper?"

"Oh, Brock, that's very sweet of you, but I don't know—my belly's so full of bubbles that eating supper now would feel a bit like putting the cart before the horse!"

"Aw, please Miss Wanda? I know a really swell chop-suey place." He looks at me pleadingly; his face as nakedly honest as a puppy dog's. How can I resist?

"Oh-kay, Brock. Just give me a few minutes to pretty myself up."

I close the door to the dressing room and feel a little silly for doing so; after all, Brock has already seen almost all of my "goodies."

Why buy the cow when you can get the milk for free?

I smile at both the popular expression and Lili Belle's follow up: *How are you going to get anyone to buy it if you don't give them a little taste?*

Giggling, I remove the towel and turn to face the dressing room mirror.

Oh dear, God.

I stop laughing. I may be a little zozzled but at least I'm still sober enough to see that I look a fright. My hair, clumped and matted from the champagne, resembles a ginger squirrel with mange, while the black lash tint streaking my stark white face makes me look like a ghoul to rival *The Phantom of the Opera.*

I sit down at the vanity table and get to work. After wiping my face clean with cold cream, I tie my hair up with one of Lili Belle's silk scarves and apply a bit of Flame-Glo lipstick. Leaning back, I appraise myself: simple, yet glamorous. A vast improvement.

Standing up, I remove the sparkly dress that Lili Belle gave me off of its hanger. The frock is a little fancy for a chop-suey date, but I don't want Brock to see me in an old Market rag. As I run my hands over the sinuous flimsy fabric of the gown, a warm sensation stirs within me and I remember Mr. Manchester's hands on this dress. His hands on me. How he had grabbed me as though it was the most natural thing to do—as though I belonged to him.

Slipping the dress over my naked body, I decide not to put on my cami-knickers.

"Gee, Miss Wanda, you sure look swell," Brock says to me over supper. "I usually don't like seeing a girl in a turban, but on you it looks elegant."

Blushing, I look down at my dish and try, unsuccessfully,

to secure the precariously wet noodles between my wooden chopsticks.

"It's just..." I look up. Brock's pretty face is pinched with concern. "What's the matter Brock?"

"Well, Miss Wanda, I hope that you don't think that I'm rude for saying this..."

"Saying what?"

"It's just that I've noticed that you don't wear a, uh—well, a brassiere," he rubs the back of his neck nervously.

"That's because I'm a burlesque dancer," I put down my chopsticks, not bothering to hide my annoyance. "Or haven't you noticed?"

"I know that, but you're not dancing right now."

"Jean Harlow doesn't wear a brassiere," I say defensively.

"No, but Jean Harlow is a little, uh, well she's a little bit smaller than you are."

I push my chair back and stand up.

"I don't want to embarrass you, Brock. Maybe I should leave."

"Wait, Miss Wanda," Brock reaches for my arm. "Please don't be sore. I didn't mean to offend you, honestly I didn't. I'm sorry. Please stay."

Slightly mollified, I sit back down. I poke at my food, refusing to look up at him. Across the street, a woman exits a bar wearing nothing but a long thin coat over a pair of step-ins. Her mouth hangs open, revealing a row of teeth like bashed in window panes.

"Miss Wanda, please believe me when I say that I love the way you look. I just don't love the way that *other fellas* look at you."

"Mr. Manchester pays me so that 'other fellas' can look at me." I say, my eyes still turned to the window. I can't tell if the woman is laughing or screaming.

"Mr. Manchester," Brock spits out his name in disgust. "Please don't mention that masher, unless you want me to lose my appetite."

"He's not a masher!" I exclaim, turning angrily to Brock and he laughs.

"Of course he's a masher, honey! Everyone at the Apple Bottom knows that. Say," his voice grows serious, "he's never laid a hand on you, has he?"

"No," I look down at my lap, my face burning.

"Good. You don't know how glad I am to hear that."

"Mr. Manchester doesn't fraternize with his dancers," I mumble, not meeting Brock's eyes. "He's a professional."

Brock laughs again. "Oh, he's a professional, all right! A professional cad!" He reaches across the table and takes my hand in his. "You're so innocent, Miss Wanda. I think that's what I love most about you. You're soft—not like the other dames at work who are all so hard-boiled."

"You don't seem to like showgirls very much." I snatch my hand away.

"Oh, but you're wrong, Miss Wanda!" Brock's large painted-doll eyes look up at me imploringly. "Why, my own mother was a showgirl!"

"On the level?" I ask incredulously.

"You know it! My mother was a hoofer and my father was a comic. Honey, I was born in a trunk!" He smiles at me charmingly, bringing to mind the sweet boy that I had met on my first day. I feel my anger starting to melt away and I'm happy for it, because I really do like Brock.

"That's how you became a comic?" I ask. "Because of your parents?"

"I didn't have a choice," Brock pushes his now empty plate aside. "Show business is my family's business. At least the Apple Bottom is a regular gig." He puts his elbows on the table and rests his face between his fists thoughtfully. "I love my parents, but I don't want my own kids to grow up like I did—eating candied fruits for supper, going to bed at four a.m., finding out about the facts of life behind stage door left—that's no life for a child. Or a wife," he looks up at me bashfully.

"If you don't want to be a comic," I begin to ask, ignoring the meaning behind his last sentence, "then what do you want to do?"

Brock takes my hand again. "I'd like to be one of those newspaper men. A reporter," he says and then smiles. "I've never admitted that to anyone else before."

"I'm flattered that you told me, Brock."

"I think I'd be really good at it," he continues. "I write my own material at the Apple Bottom. I could do a helluva lot better than that snotty Mr. Fingerhead."

"I think you'd be a swell reporter, Brock, but I don't really like newspapers. My sister Evelyn says that if you're searching for the truth, you should look for it in literature, not newsprint."

Brock wrinkles his nose in disgust. "That doesn't make any sense. No offense, Miss Wanda, but your sister doesn't sound too smart."

"Oh, she's very smart! Evelyn is the smartest person I know. She's read every book at the public library. *Every* book. Some of them she's even read two or three times."

Brock takes a sip of his tea. "Well, I guess some of them books have strange ideas then."

"I don't know," I say. "But Mama's worried that Evelyn might be becoming a Red."

At this, Brock's pink face turns scarlet.

"Reds!" He exclaims hatefully. "Your mama *should* be worried. Those commies are plotting to destroy the country! And they're sly, too! Why, I found one of them union fellows chatting up Dottie and Penny the other day. Trying to organize hoofers—can you imagine!"

"Evelyn says that it is important for working people to organize. That the only hope for prosperity and a quality of life for the working class is through unionization."

"That's a flock of salami!" Brock's face is now purple.

"Evelyn says that unions protect workers," I continue. "She

says that they make sure that people are paid fairly and treated with dignity and respect."

"Well if your sister won't read the papers, Miss Wanda, *you* should at least." Brock shakes his finger at me across the table. "Then you'd know what monsters these..."

"Hi ya, kids! How's tricks?"

Lili Belle appears before our table, dressed to slay in a leopard-print bolero jacket and a matching beret cheekily worn on the side of her head. A nervous looking middle-aged man, his egg-shaped body threatening to burst the buttons on the vest of his three-piece suit, stands behind her. "I hope I'm not interrupting anything," Lili Belle winks at me. "Say, either of you got a snipe I can bum?"

"Wanda and I are just finishing supper." Looking like a huffy rooster, Brock pulls a package of cigarettes out of his suit pocket and tosses it to Lili Belle without glancing up at her.

"That's swell!" Lili Belle rips open the box and sticks one of the cigarettes between her plump pink lips. She leans across the table, motioning for Brock to light it. Her dress is cut very low and I can see that she also isn't wearing a brassiere. Reluctantly, Brock lights Lili Belle's cigarette and tosses the match into his teacup with disgust.

"When you're done," Lili Belle says, standing up. "The two of you should join me and Daddy Whipplebum at the Stone's Throw."

"What's the Stone's Throw?" I ask.

"It's a tea pad," Brock answers, his tone dark. He squeezes my hand and turns to face Lili Belle. "I don't think that Miss Wanda would feel comfortable in a sleazy joint like that."

"Why, the Stone's Throw ain't sleazy!" Lili Belle puts her hands on her ample hips in mock indignation. "Come on, you two, we'll have a swell time! It'll be a romp!"

"I've never been to a tea pad," I say excitedly. "Isn't that where you smoke reefer?"

Lili Belle winks at me again. "Whatever gets you hot, dearie."

"Please Brock?" I squeeze his hand back. "I've always wanted to try it."

"Then it's settled!" Lili Belle exclaims. "Two blocks down and then you turn to the left. We'll meet you there." She threads arms with her male companion. "Ring-a-ding-ding!" she cries as they turn to go.

"I don't think that I like Lili Belle," Brock says as he watches her leave. "There's something about her—I can't put my finger on it."

"And you ain't never going to neither!" Lili Belle shouts over her shoulder. Her laughter tinkles like a wind chime as the door shuts behind her.

8. THE STONE'S THROW

"WHY, IT'S NOTHING BUT A PILE OF BRICKS!" I stare up in disappointment at the shabby four-storey tenement building.

"What did you expect?" Brock asks, his feathers still visibly ruffled by Lili Belle's unexpected appearance at the chop-suey restaurant. "Buckingham Palace?"

"Well, not exactly, but…"

Brock opens the front door. "It's in the basement. Don't worry, Miss Wanda, you're safe with me."

I follow Brock slowly down the darkened staircase. On the bottom step I almost slip on a dead mouse. *Aren't there any cats in this joint?* I wonder. A feast like that wouldn't last long behind the Market.

"This is just a coal cellar," I say, looking around at the bleak grey walls and dirty, tileless floor.

"Like I said, Miss Wanda," Brock smiles at me and knocks on the brick. "I love how innocent you are."

A human eye suddenly appears in the wall. Stifling a scream, I clutch at Brock's arm.

"We're here for the Stone's Throw," Brock calmly says to the eye.

"Sorry, Mac," the eye responds. "Don't know what you're talkin' about." The eye disappears back into the brick.

"Jeez!" Brock pounds his fist against the wall. "Lili Belle sent us!"

"Lili Belle!" The eye appears again. "Well, why didn't you say so!"

Like sunshine breaking through clouds, the wall slides open to reveal a yellow and gold drawing room with a screen made of narrow panels of mirror set in chromium-plated frames, against which stands a group of the most beautiful people that I have ever seen. They aren't all standing of course; some are dancing, but most are lounging contentedly on the large, soft pillows strewn across the room's lush yellow carpet of three-dimensional roses. The people themselves are like flowers in a garden: different shades, different shapes, uniform only in their beauty.

Stepping inside, I am greeted with a strong, sweet, and almost skunk-like scent; a smell not uncommon to the world behind the Market. At the end of the room, a handsome man plays a Baby Grand while an even handsomer woman, dressed like Dietrich in a wide-shouldered trouser suit and a man's hat, stretches her lithe body across the piano, her pencil-thin eyebrows dramatically arched towards the mirrored ceiling as she sings a sad tune, the kind of song filled with so much sorrow that it makes you feel glad to be alive. "Why, Brock, this place isn't sleazy at all! It's perfectly wonderful!"

Brock shrugs at my enthusiasm. "Just don't go in the bedroom," he says. "It's full of lice."

"Isn't she swell, Brock?" I gesture towards the woman on the piano. "She looks like she should be starring in a talkie!"

"That crusty ol' canary?" Brock scoffs. "I've heard she has the clap."

The man with the eye holds his hand out to Brock. "Half a dollar each, Mac."

While Brock settles up the entry fee, I search the room for Lili Belle and find her cozied up with Queenie on a buttercup yellow loveseat. Mr. Whipplebum and Eddie, the drummer at the Apple Bottom, are standing like mismatched bookends on either side of the sofa.

"Hi there, cutie!" Lili Belle waves me over. "Come sit with us."

"Gosh, Lili Belle," I say as I bend down to accept her kiss. "This place is really swell!"

I smile shyly at Queenie, silently admiring her orchid-white silk shantung beach pajamas. I feel a little stuffy in my sparkly glad rags and when Queenie pulls a smirking Eddie down next to her and begins whispering in his ear, I am sure that they are making fun of me.

"You can have my seat, Winnifred," Queenie says, standing up. She waves a hand in front of her face. "I need to step out for a bit. The air in here is getting rather *thick.*"

"It's *Wanda,*" I say quietly as she brushes past me.

"Glad to see ya, baby." Eddie, wearing a loose pinstriped drape suit and a fedora placed haphazardly over his carrot curls, perches on the arm of the loveseat and gives me the once-over. "I see ya brought a spare tire," he motions towards Brock, who is still standing by the doorway, now in conversation with a skinny blonde. "Too bad it's a flat."

"Brock is oh-kay," I say defensively.

The dimples around Eddie's mouth deepen as he smiles. So much so that they almost look like scars. "Aw, Brock's a pill!" he laughs. "Say, speaking of medicine," he pulls a slim hand-rolled cigarette out of his jacket pocket. "Try some of dis."

He lights the reefer with a match. I take it from him, holding the cigarette up between my fingers nervously. "I-I've never smoked reefer before."

Lili Belle puts an arm around me. "It's easy, honey," she whispers in my ear, her signature peach scent tingling my nostrils. "You just pucker up and suck."

I do as she directs, inhaling so deeply that my eyes water. A violent cough overtakes my body and I cover my face in embarrassment.

Eddie gently thumps me on the back. "Easy there, doll!"

"You'll be okay, sweetie," Lili Belle says soothingly. "Give her some water Eddie."

I keep my eyes squeezed shut as I drink from the glass that Eddie offers me, which I discover is filled with the same type of "water" that I had been bathing in earlier at the Apple Bottom.

Lili Belle's beau whispers something in her ear and she pushes him away, rolling her eyes comically. "Not yet, Daddy! Wanda just got here!" She turns back to me. "That's the trouble with married men, honey. They're always in a hurry!"

Dejected, Mr. Whipplebum moves to a lone chair in the far right corner of the room; his waxy white body resembling a soft-boiled egg as he sinks into its golden marshmallow cushion. His pig-like eyes watch Lili Belle as though she's a pet puppy that he's let loose to play in the park.

"Is he the same Mr. Whipplebum whose family owns the soap company?" I ask Lili Belle. I place my now empty glass down on the telephone table in front of us.

"The one and only!" Lili Belle exclaims. She blows a kiss across the room to Mr. Whipplebum who squints in return.

"Do you like him?"

"Oh, I don't know," Lili Belle answers. "He's good for the occasional supper and the not-so-occasional bauble." She stretches out her right arm, displaying the dazzling diamond bracelet hanging from her wrist. The light from the chandelier snatches Lili Belle's jewels and tosses them up into the space between my pretty friend and Mr. Whipplebum like pieces of cheap confetti.

"I think Mr. Whipplebum got the better end of the deal," I say, catching on.

"Ain't you a doll!" Lili Belle kisses me loudly on the cheek.

"My daddy used to work at the Whipplebum soap factory," I continue. "One year, during Christmas time, your boyfriend's father made the employees work ten sixteen hour days, with the promise of a bonus at the end. Well, the bonus never came, so the fellas held a strike. Mr. Whipplebum Sr. called the flatfoots and they roughed up the workers something fierce, but then he fired them all anyway." I don't tell Lili Belle, but this is the true story of how my Daddy lost his eye—not to a hungry seagull but to a copper's nightstick.

"Oh, honey, I'm sorry. The cad!" Lili Belle turns around to glare at a puzzled Mr. Whipplebum. "I'm glad to be giving his son the merry-go-round! Where does your daddy work now?"

"He worked as a milkman for years afterward but he doesn't work anywhere now. He's dead." I feel defiant saying it like that.

Lili Belle brings a hand to her throat in sympathy. "I'm so sorry, Wanda. My own father passed away some years ago, too. How did he...?"

"I don't really want to talk about it, Lili Belle."

"I understand, honey," she nods and pats my knee. "Say, Eddie, how about sharing some of that mootie."

Eddie slips down onto the loveseat and in doing so, unintentionally (or perhaps intentionally) shoves me onto Lili Belle's lap. "Eddie!" Lili Belle exclaims in mock anger. "Ooh, you nasty man!"

I take another drag off the muggle. Snuggled between Lili Belle and Eddie, I feel as soft and vertiginous as a feather in a pillow. I reach out to simultaneously touch their faces, checking to see if they feel as silky as I do.

"You sure are a beautiful dame," Eddie whispers to me.

"Everybody's beautiful," I say.

The canary is now singing a song about a lover who's disappeared like a wet snowflake. I stretch my legs out over Lili Belle's lap and hold onto Eddie's neck. I feel like I'm a figurine in a snow globe.

"Let's go now, Miss Wanda!" Brock's angry face flies at me like a snowball full of ice.

"Noooo," I moan. I push him away. "You're so cold..."

Brock's face begins to melt, dripping icicles onto the yellow roses. "He's melting!" I cry as his face disappears. "Brock's melting!" I try to stand up. "*Brock!*" Tripping, I fall into the flowers.

"Aw, let dat wet blanket go," Eddie says as he pulls me back onto the sofa. I curl up in his lap and press my ear against his chest.

"Boom, boom, boom," I sing, listening to his heart. "Just like your drums."

Eddie presses a hand against my hip and squeezes me tight. My scarf has fallen off and I know that my hair must look horrifying, but I also know that Eddie doesn't mind. He tucks a sticky curl behind my left ear.

"Come to da bedroom wid me," he whispers.

"'We can't," I say, remembering Brock's warning. "We'll get the louse."

"Aw, dat's just a rumour," Eddie stands up and cradles me in his arms. "I've been wantin' to get you alone since yer first night at da Apple."

Eddie carries me into the warm, candlelit bedroom and lays me down onto a queen-sized bed with a buttoned satin headboard and creamy silk sheets. The room's walls and ceiling are painted a pale blue, making me feel as though Eddie and I are floating in the middle of the sky. I clutch at Eddie's upper arms, which are surprisingly muscular under his baggy suit.

"You won't let me fall, will you Eddie? It's such a long way down..."

His mouth crushes mine; his tongue twisting and squirming like a vulnerable animal searching for its shell. I push him back gently and wriggle out of my sparkly dress. Eddie gasps in delighted surprise.

"No knick-ahs?" he whispers, bringing his large hands down upon my naked flesh. "Ya bad girl."

I lay back, staring into the endless blue as Eddie's fingers pinch my nipples and his tongue explores my body. I imagine that we are in the snow globe again except that this time the globe is so small that Mr. Manchester can hold it between his hands. Rolling the sphere over and between his palms, he studies Eddie's love making and my writhing body with detached interest before tossing the globe up into the air and catching it like a ball.

Miles away, a door creaks open and the shy sonance of approaching feminine feet, high heels tapping against the naked wooden floor, adds an aural stimulus to my fantasy. Eddie stops, sitting back on his haunches, and we both watch in gaping silence as a phantasmic being, glowing white against the room's fading candle light, appears above our bed.

"Don't let me interrupt," the ethereal voice coolly says and I see that the apparition is in fact Queenie, in all of her tangible, voluptuous flesh.

"Please," she continues, the pull of her desire cracking her icy tone. "Pretend I'm not here."

Eddie turns to me questioningly and I nod my approval. He looks at Queenie and then back to me again, smiling naughtily as he unbuttons his trousers. Apparently done with the preliminaries, Eddie parts my thighs and, after a bit of anxious fumbling, enters me.

I keep my eyes locked with Queenie's as Eddie thrusts away. Although her face remains an impenetrable mask of ice, her luminous green eyes betray her excitement and curiosity. For her benefit, I begin to stroke and squeeze my breasts and as Eddie's movements accelerate, I throw my head back and close my eyes in feigned ecstasy. When I open them, Queenie is gone.

"Queenie!"

I roll out from under a now very sweaty Eddie and pull my dress on.

"Hey!" Eddie cries. "Where ya goin'? I ain't done yet!"

"I'll buy you the book so you can read how it ends!" I shout over my shoulder as I rush out of the bedroom.

Pushing my way through the languid mass of beautiful people, I search for Queenie, but she is gone. On the floor by the yellow loveseat, I spot the skinny blonde, whom Brock had been chatting up earlier, lying face up and glassy-eyed on top of my fox fur coat. Angrily, I pull it out from under her. The blonde sits up and blinks at me in confusion. "Dingy hussy!" she sneers.

Ignoring her, I wrap the fur around me protectively and cross the floor toward the exit.

"So long, Red! So long!" The handsome gent at the Baby Grand smiles at me, his hands dangling over the piano keys like handkerchiefs in farewell.

9. GOT TO ACT PRETTY

THE BLISTERS ON MY FEET TELL ME what my mind has already forgotten: how far I have walked from the Stone's Throw back to the World Behind the Market. I am not wearing a watch, but judging from the retiring moon, it must be close to morning. I've never seen the world so quiet. The only sound comes from the eerie whistle of men's undershirts and long johns limply swinging from rooftop clotheslines. Tired ghosts.

A skinny black cat glances at me with a strange mixture of curiosity and indifference, before disappearing through the slats of the picket fence, which surrounds the rooming house like a row of broken teeth. A small lonely light glows in the second floor window: Mama is waiting for me.

"Where'd you get that fur coat?" Mama stands in our doorway, her weary yet shrewd eyes flashing at me in interrogation.

Nerts!

I've been trying to hide my fox fur from Mama, but in my rush to get ready for Brock earlier this evening, I'd forgotten to bring Evelyn's old cloth winter coat, which she lent me to wear around the Market.

"I ... I borrowed it from a friend," I stammer.

Mama crosses her arms over her ample chest. "Who's your friend? Howard Hughes?"

"No, Mama. A girl friend."

She slaps my face. Hard. "Don't you lie to me, Wanda! You used to be a good girl—a girl to be proud of—but now," Mama sighs, her fleshy body visibly deflating. "Now, you make me feel ashamed. Staying out until odd hours, walking around these parts with a painted face and draped in fur. People are saying bad things about you and the people who aren't saying them are thinking worse."

"What are people saying, Mama?" I can't keep the cry out of my voice. My face still stings, but the anger behind her slap hurts much more.

"They just have their own ideas about how you got that fur coat. Your mama, though, I don't *want* to know how you got it and neither will any halfway decent man." She drops down onto a chair and motions for me to join her at the kitchen table. "Sit down, Wanda," she says, her voice softening. "It's long past time that we had a talk."

"I'm not a bad girl, Mama," I say, tears strangling my words. "I'm not."

Mama takes my hand and pulls me down beside her. "I know the people around here like to grease their gums, but Wanda you've *got* to be more careful. Now, be honest with me baby, you've been running with a different crowd lately, haven't you?"

"Yes, Mama," I nod, unable to meet her eyes.

"And these new friends—they aren't from around here are they?"

"No, Mama."

Mama gently squeezes my hand.

"Wanda, there are things that some girls, girls from well-to-do families, can do that you can't. Things that might slide like water off another girl's back will stain you for the rest of your life. It isn't fair, but it's the way that the world works. Do you understand what I'm saying, honey?"

I shake my head. "No, I mean, I'm not sure…"

"What I'm saying is that when you live in ugliness, you've got to act pretty. You want a nice man, don't you, Wanda?"

"Yes, Mama."

"Well, a girl as beautiful as you are can marry up and out

of these parts, but only if she's very careful."

"I … I think I understand now, Mama. I'm sorry." I cry even harder then, my snot and tears soaking the fur coat.

Mama takes me in her arms. "Shhh, baby," she coos. "Just be a good girl and everything will turn out all right." She sits back and smiles at me. Reaching out a hand, she strokes my hair lovingly. "I'm glad that we had this talk, Wanda. You need to get to bed, though," she stands up. "And I need to get these old bones off to work."

Mama takes her coat and hat off of the nail by the door.

"But the factory isn't open yet, Mama," I say.

"I know," Mama pins her black hat into place. "But I've taken up some cleaning jobs across the city. I can get two houses finished before I have to catch the streetcar to the factory and two more done before I come home to fix supper." She looks at me proudly. "I'll never let you or your sister starve, Wanda. Whatever it is that you've been doing these nights with that Mr. Manchester, you don't have to do it anymore."

"I'm just a stenographer, Mama," I stand up in protest. "Honest I am! It's true that I've been running with a wild crowd—and I won't anymore, I promise—but please don't make me quit my job!"

Mama sighs in surrender. "Okay, Wanda." She buttons up her thin grey coat. "Now, go get some sleep."

I watch Mama from the window as she leaves the World Behind the Market. With her saggy body, more ill-fitting than her old coat, and her slow, jerky movements, she resembles another tired ghost.

No! No! No! Not a ghost! Not Mama!

My heart pounding, I rush to the bedroom that I share with Evelyn. My sister is asleep, the light from the slow rising sun hesitantly touching her face. As I undress, I marvel at how beautiful my sister is. Mama always says that I'm the pretty one, but with her strong, prominent features, Evelyn looks so regal. Even in sleep, even in a lumpy old bed in a creaky rooming house, she appears as powerful and majestic as a queen.

I slip under the covers beside her. Stirring, Evelyn rolls over and sleepily wraps an arm around my waist. I fall asleep with my sister's heart beating against my back.

10. CHRISTMAS PRESENT

MY AUNT FLO' ARRIVES THE MORNING of Christmas Eve. I walk down to the Market's pharmacy to call Joe. "Joe?" I say into the mouthpiece of the brass-plated telephone. "I can't come in tonight. I have, uh, female trouble."

"Say no more, girlie!" Joe interrupts.

"I'm sorry."

"Don't worry about it, kid. It won't be busy tonight, anyway. Nobody wants to go to a titty show on Christmas Eve. See you next week, doll. Raul has a new routine for you to try on."

After we hang up, I fish a nickel out of my change purse and hand it to the pharmacist, an older man with taped up spectacles. "Thanks for the phone call, mister."

His eyes take in my new slim black dress with its shiny buttons and white ruffled collar. "You must work at that big bank downtown," he says admiringly.

"That's right," I say.

"You like it?"

"Oh yes, sir. It's a swell job."

As I turn toward the door, I spot Evelyn stepping off of the streetcar. "Evelyn!" I call out. I crack the door open and wave her over. She looks up at me, the wind whipping at her hatless head so severely that her hair resembles a small but furious bonfire. Her limp winter coat blows open to reveal a plain gingham dress. "Get in here!" I cry. "You'll catch your death!"

"Why aren't you at work?" I ask her as she joins me inside

the warm pharmacy with its recently installed radiators.

"The foreman laid a bunch of us off just before lunchtime," she answers. She runs a hand through her wayward curls and shrugs. "Merry Christmas to me."

After her hours had gotten cut at the glove factory, Evelyn had found a job wrapping lollipops at a bon-bon factory. They had promised her steady work throughout the Christmas season and had strongly hinted that the job would last long past the holidays.

"I'm sorry, Evelyn. Gee, of all the lousy, rotten things!"

Evelyn sighs. "You said it, little sis."

"Sit down, honey," I say, taking her coat. "I'll buy you a soda." I turn to the pimply kid behind the counter. "Two cherry sodas, please."

"I think I may need something a little stronger than that," Evelyn laughs bitterly. She rests her elbows on the shiny marble counter. "What am I going to do, Wanda?"

"Wait, I've got it!" I exclaim as the soda jerk plunks the tall glasses down in front of us. "I heard Joe say the other day that one of our hatcheck girls quit. I could talk to Mr. Manchester…"

"Ugh!" Evelyn interrupts. "Mr. Manchester!" she spits his name out in disgust. "That capitalist pig!"

"You don't even know him, Evelyn!"

"I know that he pays you a measly twenty bucks a week. *You're* the one bringing in the customers—what does *he* do?"

"How much do you think he should be paying me?" I ask cautiously.

"Well, I dunno," Evelyn takes a sip of her soda. "I heard this burlesque dancer talking on the radio the other day —Dee Dee Diamond I think her name was—she was saying how she pulls in over two hundred and fifty a week and I bet she's not half as pretty as you are. You know, little sis," Evelyn waves her spoon at me. "If I were you, I'd organize with those other dames and open up your own joint. Cut out the middle man.

You do all the work—you keep all the profits. That's how it should be."

"I don't think it would be that easy, Evelyn."

"It would be if you all were in it together," Evelyn drains her soda and pushes her glass across the counter. "If workers everywhere united! Could you imagine? The capitalist pigs would be shaking in their BVDs! There's more of *us* than there are of *them*."

"Are you a Red, Evelyn?"

Evelyn laughs and shakes her head. "I'm a member of the proletariat, little sis. The same as you and Mama—and Daddy." Evelyn looks down at her hands sadly.

"Well, Mama thinks that you're a Red," I say by way of moving the subject away from Daddy. "And Brock, the comic at the Apple Bottom, he seems to think you are, too. I was telling him how you don't read newspapers..."

"I read them sometimes," Evelyn says defensively. "But I never trust them. Every time that the capitalists haul out a new gadget or machine, the newspapers hail it as some kind of victory for the workers; it'll make our lives easier, they say. We'll get to spend more time with our families, they promise. Horse feathers!" Evelyn slams her fist down onto the counter, startling the soda jerk. "We'll have more time, yes, but only because the machines have stolen our jobs. The machines don't even really make the capitalist's life any easier, since they do exactly the same work that we proletarians were already doing. All they do is save the capitalists a few nickels and dimes and if us workers have to starve so their bank accounts can grow, so be it, but goddamn it! Aren't those cats fat enough already?"

"So," I venture, after she's gone quiet. "You want me to ask about that hatcheck girl job?"

Evelyn looks at me and we both burst out laughing. "Sure, little sis!" she says, playfully punching me on the arm.

I slide two dimes across the counter to the soda jerk. "Keep the change," I say.

Evelyn and I button up our coats. "I guess you better be heading over to the Apple Bottom soon," Evelyn says, glancing at her wristwatch.

"No, I got the curse this morning. Nerts! I almost forgot," I quickly head back to the pharmacist's counter to buy some pads and a new Kotex sanitary belt.

When I return to the front of the pharmacy, Evelyn is standing at the window with her nose pressed against the glass. "Evelyn!" I admonish. "Your stockings are all full of cobwebs!" I look down at my own legs. "Although mine aren't exactly ring-less either. How does Mama expect us to find husbands with stockings like these?"

Evelyn turns and glares at me. "Shush, Wanda! Nobody's getting married these days. Look," she points out the window and I follow her gaze.

Across the street, our neighbour, Myrtle, is being helped out of a green Hudson-Sedan by a bearded fellow wearing a bowler hat and a catalogue suit. He gallantly kisses her hand before stepping back into his car and driving away.

"Old maid Myrtle, so what!" I huff dismissively.

"Shhh!" Evelyn shoots me another dirty look before returning to the window. "Don't you think it's strange that he's dropping her off here? Why doesn't he drive her home?"

I shrug in disinterest.

"Well," Evelyn continues. "I think he must be one of her johns."

"One of her johns!" I laugh. "Old maid Myrtle? That's a hot one!"

"She's not that old, Wanda. She's only got about fifteen years or so on us. I heard Mrs. Merriweather tell Mama that Myrtle is a 'lady of the evening.' Mrs. Merriweather says she doesn't care just so long as she pays the rent on time and doesn't bring any of her johns over."

"A lady of the evening!" I watch Myrtle's stout form as she crosses the street towards home. Plain in both face and body, she makes a pretty disappointing prostitute.

Evelyn and I step out onto the street. The afternoon's cold air has stripped the Market down to its bare flesh, the sharp scent of fish, fire, and horse shit making my sister and I breathe through our mouths.

As night begins to fall, I step out onto the front porch of the rooming house so that Evelyn can speak to Mama alone. Snowflakes scatter in the wind; little bits of beauty that melt quicker than you can see 'em. I wrap my fur coat around me tightly. The neighbour's Doberman is outside again. Fixing his cold dark eyes on me, he bears his teeth and growls. I run down the stairs to the end of the front yard and raise my arms in the air, curling my fingers into claws.

"*Grrr!*" I shout. The Doberman yelps and spins around in confusion. "*Meow!*" I cry, my claws at the ready. Slowly, he backs away from me, his usually taut body sagging with defeat.

Victoriously, I return to the porch. Throwing my head backwards, I begin to bay at the rising moon, the light of which catches the Market Queen; her Harlow-halo glowing in the soft grey night like the most impetuous of stars. "*Awoo-ooo-ooo!*"

I stop to listen to my echo in the near empty streets.

"*Awoo-ooo-ooo!*"

The echo that greets me is not my voice at all but that of a rich male baritone.

Startled and embarrassed, I watch as the slight form of a man cuts out of the darkness, like a silhouette portrait. "Hiya, doll."

Eddie, the drummer from the Apple Bottom, hooks his thumb under the rim of his newsboy cap and grins up at me. "Merry Christmas, baby. Ya got any mistletoe?"

"How'd you get here?" I ask. "I didn't hear the trolley pull up."

Eddie casually cleans his nails with a pocketknife. "I walked."

"*Walked?*"

"Sure. Say, I only live about two blocks from here. What?

D'ya think I live uptown with Mr. Manchester and the rest of them high-hats with low IQs?"

"Well, what are you doing here? What do you want?" I try to sound more contemptuous than I feel. Eddie and I haven't spoken since the night at the Stone's Throw. I'd like to think that I've been avoiding him, but he hasn't exactly sought me out.

"I wanted to give ya a Christmas present," Eddie fishes a crumpled paper bag out of his overcoat and tosses it up to me.

"Gee, thanks Eddie," I say sarcastically. "You wrapped it real fine." I open the bag. Inside is a pair of beautiful black silk stockings with red seams. I take one of the stockings out and drape it over my hand, admiring its delicacy. "Eddie, these are really swell."

"S'nothing," Eddie puts his pocketknife away. He leans on the stair railing, not looking at me. "I just thought that a dame with gams as gorgeous as yours shouldn't have to borrow from Geraldine. You should have yer own things."

"Eddie!" I rush down the steps and attempt to take his hand. "I had no idea you were so sweet!"

He shrugs my hand away. "I said it was nothing, didn't I? Say, ain't ya gonna invite me in?"

I look up at the rooming house. "My mama's inside."

"Aw," Eddie groans in disappointment. "I don't wanna meet yer mama."

"No," I smile. "I didn't think you were the kind of fellow who would."

"Ya wanna meet my mama, baby?" Eddie's eyes watch me searchingly. I can't tell if he's joking or not.

"No," I answer honestly.

Eddie laughs and takes a seat on the bottom step. "Dat's why I like you, Wanda," he says, patting the space beside him.

"Why haven't you come by my dressing room then, if you like me so much?" I ask as I sit down beside him. Eddie doesn't answer me.

"Well," I attempt again. "Why haven't you...?"

"Shhh," Eddie says. He points to an elderly man standing alone under the Market Queen. "Listen Wanda," he whispers. "Just listen."

The man removes his crushed-in derby and places a gloveless hand over his heart. With his bald head and toothless face, he resembles a baby bird as he opens his mouth to the sky and begins to sing: "*Siiigh-lent night. Hole-eee night...*"

He's far from being Bing Crosby, but in the darkness of night, with the snow and the flawless moon, his voice is beautiful.

Across the way, a greasy looking middle-aged woman opens her window. Resting her heavy breasts on the sill, she looks up at the sky and smiles dreamily.

"Ain't this place something, baby?" Eddie puts his arm around me. "Everybody else calls it a slum, but that's only cuz it ain't their home. It's not a slum, is it Wanda?"

"No Eddie," I say, snuggling into him.

Eddie tilts my chin up between his thumb and forefinger. "Listen, I can't be your fella and I don't think ya want me to be anyway. But I like ya. I like ya a lot. Yer different than most dames."

"I don't know what that means," I say. "Brock said the same thing to me. I guess it's a compliment or an insult, depending on how you feel about 'most dames.'"

"Well, I like most dames," Eddie brings his lips to my cheekbone. "But I like you better."

We kiss as the elderly man finishes his song.

11. TAP DANCING ON A TIGHTROPE

BACKSTAGE, GERALDINE HELPS ME into a custom-made long satin dress with beaded straps. "There," she says, her mouth full of bobby pins as she piles my hair up. "You look pretty elegant for a fat girl."

"Button up, Gerri!" Lili Belle approaches her from behind. "Wanda's the juiciest tomato in this joint and you know it!"

Geraldine turns Lili Belle around and inspects her maid costume. The frock is certainly shorter and tighter than anything that the maids I know would wear to work.

"If you ask me," Geraldine says, securing Lili Belle's garter belt into place. "This here is the tawdriest routine that Raul has come up with yet."

"Aw, don't be a crepehanger! Men love to see two pretty girls on stage together, especially when one is undressing the other." Lili Belle winks at me.

"That's exactly what I mean!" Geraldine huffs. "I think it's scandalous!"

"Well *I* think it's brilliant," Lili Belle counters.

"And *I* think," I say turning towards the mirror to admire my reflection, "That I'm just happy that it's 1935 and I finally get to wear a fancy frock and keep my hair dry."

The stage is made up to look like a lady's bedroom, with a thick pink throw rug, a plush dusty-rose ottoman, and an ornate pink and gold vanity table. The only thing missing is an actual bed—both for economic reasons ("*Beds are damned expensive!*" Joe had protested) and in deference to the censors.

Raul meets us backstage. "Listen girls, we've only got time for one rehearsal before tonight, but it's a fairly simple routine and it'll be duck soup for two pros like you." He turns to me and nods in approval. "You look gorgeous, Wanda. Just perfect. Now, I want you to play it up really hoity-toity like. *Don't* be your sweet self. Pretend that you're one of those high society dames. Lili Belle," he smiles at her with obvious affection. "I want *you* to be exactly as you always are: flirty, fun, and adorable."

Lili Belle grins and pinches his cheek. "No problem, sweetie!"

Raul pinches her back playfully. "Okay girls, let's do this. Oh, and not to make you nervous or anything, but Mr. Manchester will be watching the show tonight from the balcony seats."

"Mr. Manchester?" The mention of his name jolts me like an electrical current.

"Sure, honey," Lili Belle answers. "Mr. Manchester always checks out the new routines."

"Don't worry, Wanda," Raul says soothingly, mistaking my excitement for nervousness. "You'll be fine."

Before I step on stage for the rehearsal, Geraldine hands me a large white fur stole, so ostentatious that it would put Mae West to shame.

"Come up and see me some time," Eddie mouths from the orchestra pit.

I turn my nose up at him in what I hope is a "hoity-toity" gesture.

As the curtains open, I cross the stage towards Lili Belle, who bows and curtsies in greeting. Tossing the stole carelessly in her direction, I throw my head back in mock laughter as she rushes to retrieve it. I pull the hem of my long dress up to my knees and place a high-heeled foot onto the ottoman. I pantomime for Lili Belle to remove my shoe. She gets down on her knees, her body twisted sideways so that the audience will view her in profile, and takes off my shoe, quietly setting it down on the soft rug. I place my other foot on the ottoman and Lili Belle, following Raul's instructions, runs her hands seductively up my leg, toward my garter belt. Pantomiming still, I lean forward and wag my finger at her in reprimand.

Lili Belle brings her hands to her cheeks in mock contrition. She jumps up and jiggle-walks to the vanity table. Bowing again, she pulls out a small pink stool with a buttoned satin cushion and gestures for me to sit. Turning the chair so that I face the audience, Lili Belle begins to remove the pins from my up-do, letting my hair fall in heavy waves around my bare shoulders. I smile at her in showy approval as she takes a hair-brush from the vanity table. Lili Belle smiles back naughtily and, under Raul's direction, slips the strap of my dress down my shoulder, revealing most of my right breast, with its heart shaped pasty, to the audience.

I stand up and bring my hands to my hips in mock anger. Taking the hairbrush from her, I pretend to spank Lili Belle with it. After I'm done, I turn my back to the audience and order for Lili Belle to undress me.

"Nice and slow, Lili Belle," Raul calls out. "Pretend that you're a sculptress and Wanda is your clay."

I feel Lili Belle's fingers fumbling with my zipper. Actually "fumbling" may not be the right word—shaking is more like it. When she finally gets it undone, she stands up to slip my dress off but her hands are so clammy that her fingers leave visible prints on the dress and her body is trembling so violently that I'm afraid she is going to faint.

"Are you okay, Lili Belle?" I whisper.

She bites her lip and nods.

"What the hell's a matter, Lili Belle baby?" Joe's coarse voice travels across the theatre like a hungry hawk. "We all know how you've been dreaming of this moment!"

Lili Belle's face turns pinker than the throw rug. Pressing her hand against her mouth, she turns and runs backstage.

I gape at Raul in shock. "I don't know what happened," he says, his beautiful dark eyes full of concern. "I better go check on her." Joe's smug laughter fills the theatre as Raul heads backstage.

"Joe, you dirty louse!" Eddie jumps up from the orchestra pit, drumsticks raised in his clenched fists. The saxophone player pulls Eddie back down before he has a chance to gouge Joe's eyes out.

Moments later, Raul returns. "Is Lili Belle okay?" I ask him.

Raul nods. "She'll be alright, Wanda. She just needs to rest for a bit." He steers me towards stage right, behind the curtain. "Listen, Wanda," he whispers. "Would you mind changing places with Lili Belle for this routine? It's just that Mr. Manchester will be watching tonight and I can't take any chances. I know Lili Belle is a little smaller than you are," he adds. "But Geraldine should be able to let out the maid costume for you."

"Swell," I mumble, not bothering to hide my disappointment. Nerts! I think, I finally get to wear a nice frock and Lili Belle goes and crabs it. Never mind that—I really wanted to shine for Mr. Manchester tonight; now I have to play second fiddle to Lili Belle!

Suddenly, I have an idea. "Raul," I say, "don't bother getting Geraldine to let that costume out. I want it tight."

Lili Belle is getting fitted for her gown so I have our dressing room to myself. I shut the door but I don't lock it. Standing before the full-length mirror in my frilly black tap pants and the silk stockings that Eddie gave me, I step into the maid costume. Even with my stomach sucked in, I can't get the zipper all the way up. The tight bodice barely contains my breasts and already I can see red indentations forming just above my nipples. I hunch my shoulders together and lean forward. *Perfect,* I think, smiling.

"Oh, hello, Mr. Manchester," I say to the mirror. "Oh dear,

do you *really* think this dress is too tight for me? Perhaps you should help me take it off then."

I slip my hand into my tap pants. Leaning against the wall, I close my eyes and imagine Mr. Manchester tearing at my costume with his bare hands: ripping open my bodice, he yanks down my tap pants and bends me over the vanity table.

I rub myself furiously. If only he'd walk in now ... if only ... or Eddie ... oh, God, even Brock would do now!

But no one comes. And, as I remove my hand in frustration, neither do I.

"And now," Brock bellows from downstage. "If the drinks aren't enough to lubricate you, our next act certainly will!"

Hidden behind the curtain at stage left, I take a deep breath and clutch my hand to my heart; it's beating faster than Eddie's drums. *Why am I so nervous? This is going to go over big!*

"Wanda!"

I turn around at the sound of my sister's voice. "Evelyn?" I whisper. "What are you doing here?"

"I'm sorry," she says. "I know I shouldn't be backstage, but I wanted to give you the news. I just spoke to Mr. Manchester and guess what, lil' sis? He gave me the job!"

"But I was going to talk to him for you," I say in disappointment. The hatcheck girl job had been the perfect excuse for me to approach Mr. Manchester.

"I know, but I had nothing to do today, anyways. I stopped by in the afternoon and got talking to Benny—he sure is regular! A really swell guy! He took me to Mr. Manchester himself."

"That's grand, Evelyn," I say.

"*Grand?*" Evelyn laughs.

"Okay, swell. It's really swell."

I spot Joe approaching. "You better blow, Evelyn," I whisper. "I'll see you later tonight."

I turn back to the stage as Brock continues with his introductions: "The Apple Bottom proudly presents the loquacious and lusty, the lovely and luminous: our very own luscious lollipop *Lili Belle*! Oh yeah," he adds as the curtain begins to rise and Joe pushes me forward, "And her little rusty-haired assistant, Wanda."

I stumble onto the stage and curtsey for the audience. Stretching my face into a smile, I try to push down the hurt that Brock's obvious snub has caused me.

Lili Belle enters from stage right, resplendent in a white silk Empire line gown. She slips off the Mae West stole and vigorously tosses the fur in my direction, narrowly hitting me in the face with it. The audience howls with laughter.

"Sorry," Lili Belle mouths, assuming her position on the ottoman.

I throw the ridiculous stole backstage and jiggle-strut towards Lili Belle. Falling to my knees, I take her left calf in my hand and slowly remove her shoe. Seductively, I run my hands up along her leg, towards her thigh, but as Lili Belle bends forward to scold me, I surreptitiously pull the front of my dress down, allowing my naked breasts to spring free from the corset.

I turn to the clearly delighted audience and bring my hands to my cheeks in mock embarrassment. They hoot, whistle, and roar their approval as I pretend to struggle to get my breasts back into the corset. Lili Belle remains in place as though a statue: her mouth a tiny "O."

"Wanda! Wanda! We want more Wanda!" The crowd cheers as the curtain closes.

"What the fuck was that, kid?" Joe grabs me roughly by the arm. "This isn't a flash house. Didn't Gerri tell you? No nipples!"

"Get your hands off me!" I snap. "The audience loved it, didn't they?"

"Oh, Wanda," Lili Belle says, her eyes blinking back tears. "How could you do that to me?"

"It was an accident!" I say. I yank my arm out of Joe's grasp.

"Leave me alone, both of you! I've gotta get out of this stupid costume!"

On my way to the dressing room, I pull the maid uniform off over my head. Standing in the doorway, I twirl the dress in the air like a lasso and toss it across the room, where it lands in a crumpled heap behind the vanity table. "You can stay there!" I shout and then laugh. I feel high, but dangerously so, as though I am tap dancing on a tightrope.

I sit down at the dressing table, still in my tap pants and stockings, but naked from the waist up. Dipping my fingers into an unscrewed jar of cold cream, I sweep the white goo over the bridge of my nose, onto my cheeks in a wide, circular motion. Someone knocks at the door.

"Just a minute!" I sing. Quickly, I reach for some tissue to wipe the cream off my face.

The door swings open anyway and Mr. Manchester steps inside. He regards me gravely, his mouth set in a thin horizontal line.

"Oh hello!" My heart is beating so hard that I can barely hear myself speak. "Mr. Manchester, what a pleasant surprise!"

"Put your robe on, Miss Whittle."

"But why?" Imagining myself as Jean Harlow, I lean against the vanity table; hand on hip, breasts thrust forward. "Am I making you," I raise an eyebrow in the direction of his crotch, "uncomfortable?"

Mr. Manchester grabs Lili Belle's silk robe from behind the door and throws it to me.

Still playing my role, I slip the robe on, but I don't bother to tie it.

Mr. Manchester looks down and clears his throat.

"I want to talk to you about that dirty little stunt you pulled, Miss Whittle. Now, you're just lucky—we're *all* just lucky— that there weren't any coppers in the audience tonight, but if there had been…"

"Mr. Manchester, you're trembling!" I pull him to me,

the way that I had seen Jean do with her prey in *Redheaded Woman*. "I'm trembling, too," I press my chest against his. "Can you feel it?"

Above Mr. Manchester's shoulder, Brock's head pops up in the doorway, like a "Whack-a-Mole" at the summer fair. At the sight of our embrace, his soldier-boy pink face turns tomato red.

Sensing an intruder, Mr. Manchester kicks the door shut, narrowly missing Brock's nose. He places his hands on my shoulders and holds me out at arm's length. "Now listen, Miss Whittle, if you *ever* pull another stunt like the one you did tonight, you'll be out on your can! Do you understand me?"

Forgetting my lines, I nod silently.

He lets go of me and turns to open the door. "Miss Belle," he says, nodding to Lili Belle, who is now standing in the doorway. "I was just explaining the rules of the Apple Bottom theatre to Miss Whittle. I expect that a seasoned professional like yourself will keep her in line in the future. Goodnight, ladies."

"Wanda!" Lili Belle rushes towards me as Mr. Manchester leaves. "Are you okay, sweetie? You look so pale, as though someone died!"

I look into Lili Belle's kind face and promptly burst into tears.

"Oh, honey! It *was* an accident, wasn't it?" She wraps her arms around me. "I never should have doubted you!"

I bury my face in her neck and continue to sob. "I'm so sorry, Lili Belle. I didn't mean to…"

"Shh," she pats my back gently. "There's no reason to get so upset. I've had my act crabbed before and goodness knows, I've crabbed more than a few acts myself!"

She gives me a squeeze and sits back. "Are you sure it's just the act? There's nothing else bothering you?" Her large dark eyes search me questioningly, "It ain't a man, is it?"

I nod, my sobs interrupted by hiccups. "He … I thought he … wanted *me* but … he doesn't anymore!"

Lili Belle licks her thumb and rubs it gently under my eyes.

"I understand, honey, but try not to cry. There's no man in the world worth ruining your eye make up over."

She stands up and walks to the window. "Look, Wanda," she says as she spreads open the curtains. "The sun will be up soon. There's nothing that ever looks so terrible in the morning."

But I know that Lili Belle is wrong. There are plenty of things that look even worse in the morning.

Midnight Musings

Wanda Wiggles: "Maid" To Please!
Chester Cromwell, Night Beat Reporter

Last night, the patrons at the Apple Bottom theatre received an eye—*and button!*—popping surprise from rising burlesque star Wanda Wiggles. The new pip on the peep-street possesses the fiery red tresses of Clara Bow, the body of Mae West, and the S.A. of Jean Harlow. In other words, she's got *it*; she's got *that*; she's got *those* and *HOW*.

Crabbed of a proper introduction by corny clown Brock Baxter, our curvy cutie swept across the stage in a house-keeping uniform so scant it was *maid* to please! She was joined by voluptuous veteran Lili Belle—the cheers of the audience leaving no doubt that two belles are better than one—and proceeded to do the buxom beauty's bidding.

Wanda's service was nothing short of satisfying, but the demands of our fair maid's own well-built house proved too cumbersome for her corset; the buttress was no longer able to bolster Wanda's curvaceous charms.

Propriety prohibits the pressman from publishing the particularities. However, the censors may permit him to report that the temperature inside the theatre last night could only be recounted as tit-ulatingly *nippy*.

Those who have a predilection for pulchritude need get an eyeful of the Apple Bottom's peepshow prodigy: the wickedly wanton wonder, Wanda Wiggles!

12. CHEAP AND VULGAR

THE POLITICIANS AND THEIR NEWSPAPERS keep declaring the Depression almost over as the breadline outside the Mission grows longer. It is early spring and the air smells like earth. I stand outside the movie theatre, still huddled in my fur coat to spite the sun. The title on the marquee reads *Gold Diggers of 1935*. I finger the three dimes in my pocket, but I don't go inside. The talkies don't excite me as much as they used to.

Two blocks from here, my own name is splashed across the Apple Bottom's marquee:

WANDA WIGGLES:
BLINK AND YOU'LL MISS HER EYE-FULL!

What Mr. Manchester called my "dirty little stunt" turned into an oil well for his theatre. After Chester Cromwell's column hit the newsstands a couple of months ago, ticket sales more than tripled. Joe raised my salary to $45.50 a week and Geraldine custom made a pair of small light pink pasties for me that, while being enough to appease the censors, look like nipples from the cheap seats. The one major drawback is that now I am stuck wearing the maid outfit: the audience loves watching me sweep and scrub, and my breasts popping out of my uniform and into a soapy bucket of water is a new crowd pleaser. *Cheap and vulgar,* I overheard Queenie say to Dottie.

Wanda's act is cheap and vulgar. Now when I'm onstage, I don't fantasize about Mr. Manchester watching me. Not in my maid uniform. Just like the movies, performing at the Apple Bottom no longer gives me a thrill.

"Listen, sister," the pudgy cashier sticks her head out of the movie house ticket booth. "Ya either cough up tha' dough for tha' show or ya scram!" She straightens her little red hat and glares at me. "Ya got that?"

"Sure, sister," I say. "I got that."

I walk away from the movie theatre, in the direction of the Apple Bottom. Ahead of me, a small group of children surround an organ grinder and his monkey. Clad in matching polka-dot vests and straw boaters, the mustachioed man vigorously turns the crank of his barrel organ as his leashed monkey jumps around to the repetitive circus music, waving a small tin cup.

I kneel down and drop my three dimes into the monkey's cup. He stops jumping and looks at me intently with his small ambivalent eyes. Puckering his mouth, he leans over and kisses me on the cheek. The children cheer.

"Listen, mister," I say, shaking my finger at the organ grinder. "You better be nice to this monkey!"

I open the door to the Apple Bottom and walk right into myself, black and white and larger than life: WANDA WIGGLES – MAID FOR MAN! The photo above the tagline shows me kneeling over a bucket of soapy water, clad in my too-tight bosom busting uniform. Smiling, I wink reassuringly at the camera.

Benny walks by, carrying an ash bin.

"Where's Queenie's photo?" I ask him.

He stops and looks at me without interest.

"Who's Queenie?"

"You know Queenie!" I say impatiently. "Her picture used to hang here. Where is it?"

Benny shrugs. "Dunno. All you hoofers look the same to me." He brushes past me, whistling "I'm Forever Blowing Bubbles."

"Lookin' good, baby." Eddie approaches me from behind and slides an arm around my waist. I lean into him; inhaling his familiar scent of fresh soap and old tobacco.

"Are you talking about me or the picture?"

"Both."

"I don't like it," I say, wrinkling my nose at the photograph. "I think I look cheap and vulgar."

"So what?" Eddie lifts my hair and plants a kiss on my neck. "I like 'em cheap and vulgar."

I can feel my body becoming aroused. Benny has left his cart of cleaning utensils and supplies in the lobby. A set of keys are looped around the wagon's handle bar. I smile mischievously at Eddie. "Come on," I grab the keys and hook my finger at him. "Follow me."

"You bad girl," Eddie says as we slip through the side door. "Where ya taking me?"

Wordlessly, I lead him down the hallway of cherry carpet, stopping in front of a charcoal grey door with a brass nameplate.

"But dis is Mr. Manchester's office," Eddie gapes at me incredulously, his hands dropping down to his sides.

I hold a finger to my lips and wink at him as I turn the key. "Shhh," I whisper as we step into the dimly lit room. The air inside smells like ink and Brylcreem. In contrast to his neat, sparse apartment, Mr. Manchester's office is crowded and cluttered, dominated by a large oak desk covered with banking slips, black and white glossies, and newspapers.

"Come on baby, joke's over," Eddie twists a handkerchief in his hands nervously, his eyes on Mr. Manchester's overcoat and hat hanging by the door. "Let's blow."

Ignoring him, I lean over Mr. Manchester's desk and squint at the framed photograph sitting beside his onyx marble telephone. In the photo, Mr. Manchester stands stiffly beside an attractive older woman. Dressed in a smartly tailored suit and with her hair pulled back in a severe bun, the woman's large beautiful eyes peek out from behind sharply raised cheekbones.

Her birdlike hands hold onto the shoulders of a chubby, apple-cheeked young boy, clad in a vest and short pants. No one in the photograph is smiling.

"What a *darling* family!" I exclaim. I pick up the picture and wave it at Eddie. "What do you think of Mr. Manchester's wife? Lili Belle told me that she's the daughter of some big shot real estate mogul. Guess she was a smart investment for Mr. Manchester, huh? Do you think she's pretty?"

"Sure, doll," Eddie takes the photo from me and places it carefully back onto the desk. "She's swell. Can we go now?"

I push the heavy Underwood typewriter aside and hop onto the writing table. "Plenty of room here!" I say. I snap open the clasps of my fur coat. "This is *so* much more comfortable than that fleabag hotel you're so fond of taking me to." I lean back and open my legs. "Won't you join me?"

I bend my legs at the knees, letting my loose skirt fall backwards around my waist. I'm not wearing any knickers. Eddie rubs the back of his neck. His eyes dart uneasily from the space between my legs to the doorway and back again.

"Come on," I purr soothingly, reciting Norma Shearer's infamous line from *A Free Soul*. "Put 'em around me."

"I dunno," Eddie replies in a very un-Clark Gable like fashion. "What if Mr. Manchester walks in?"

"So?" I flip my hair back and smile at him. "I wouldn't mind."

"Well, I would! I can't afford to get canned!" Eddie's voice rises, unattractively so. "I'd hafta go back to driving my brudder's cab for twelve hours a night at half da pay! No dame is worth that."

"Oh, for heaven's sake!" I pull my skirt down and stand up. "Forget it, Eddie!"

"Say," he gently grabs my arm as I try to push past him. "Howz about we go to your dressing room?"

I shake my head. "Lili Belle's in there."

"Well," the smoke has returned to Eddie's voice. "The customers ain't here yet. Whaddya say we sneak in da washroom?"

"*No,*" I say firmly. "I'm not in the mood anymore, Eddie."

"Oh-kay." Eddie's eyes have gone flat. He pulls a cigarette out from behind his ear and sticks it between his teeth. Standing in the doorway, he pauses. "I'm guessin' you don't like me much anymore, doll."

"What a thing to say!" I exclaim, impatient for him to leave. "Of course I still like you, Eddie!"

I wait until I hear the corridor door slam shut. Turning back towards the desk, I pick up the family photo. Mrs. Manchester and her son stare back at me, triumphant in their innocence. I flip the frame over and slide open the latch. Carefully, I remove the photograph.

"Why did you get everything?" I ask Mrs. Manchester. I fold the photo in half. "You don't deserve it," I continue as I rip her and her fat son away from Mr. Manchester. "I deserve it," I say, shoving Henry into the pocket of my fur coat. "Not you." I crumple up Mrs. Manchester and her son and toss them into the wastepaper basket. "*Me.*"

13. JOAN CRAWFORD EYES

"DON'T WORRY, LADIES, WANDA WIGGLES won't steal your husband ... but she might *borrow* him!" I wince, both at Brock's onstage joke and because Geraldine has accidentally pricked me with a garment pin.

"Ouch! Be careful, Gerri!" She looks up at me and shrugs in apology. "Say, what's he greasing his gums over me for?" I ask her. "Isn't Queenie's act next?"

Geraldine shrugs again. She wraps her measuring tape around my burgeoning waist and sighs in disgust. "If you had taken my advice, I wouldn't have to let out your costumes every week," she admonishes through a mouthful of pins. "Steam baths," she shakes her sausage-like finger at me. "Raw carrots and steam baths."

I don't tell her that I still only bathe once a week in the galvanized tub in Mama's kitchen, or that I much prefer boxes of cherry-filled chocolates—like the kind that the stage door Johnnies are so fond of giving me—over raw vegetables.

"The customers don't seem to mind," I say and Geraldine pokes me with one of her pins, this time intentionally.

"Queenie's locked herself in her room!"

Fresh off the stage, Lili Belle bounces into our dressing room, clad in a yellow robe with dyed-to-match rabbit fur sleeves. Her eyes are wide with a half relished panic. "She said she's not going onstage tonight, or ever again! Joe's about to blow his toupée!"

It's because of me, I think. *It's all my fault.* I turn away from Geraldine.

"Oh, honey, that's not a good idea!" Lili Belle says in vain as I push past her toward Queenie's dressing room.

"Queenie?" I knock softly at her door. "It's Wanda. Please let me in." I hear movement inside, the rustling of clothing, but no answer. "Queenie?" I try again and sigh. "Queenie, this is *Winnifred.*"

Queenie opens the door then, looking resplendent in a belted wool suit of forest green. She sits back down at her vanity table and, without a glance in my direction, gestures for me to come inside. "Shut the door, dear," she says, pinning a small velvet cap into place and pulling it down over her right eye. "And for Heaven's sake, take off that ridiculous get up."

"T-t-take off my costume?" I stammer, glancing down at my maid uniform. "But I don't have anything else..."

"I'll give you something else." Bending down, Queenie un-clasps a scarlet red garment trunk. "Let's see," she plunges her tiny, well-manicured hands into the sea of silk and beads; a pile of dresses as vibrant and colourful as a wet rainbow. "Here it is!" Queenie exclaims as she pulls out a shimmering gown of gas blue. "This will look marvellous on you."

She hooks the dress over her right arm and stands up. "Let's get you changed." She wraps her arms around me and unzips the maid costume; the garment obediently falls to my feet. "Don't you like this better?" she whispers. She grabs a handful of my hair and kisses the space between my neck and shoulder. Her bosom, unfairly encased in the wool suit, presses up against my bare breasts. I am too afraid to answer, too afraid that she might disappear again.

Lifting my right breast, Queenie brings her mouth down upon my covered nipple and, looking up at me with her sultry Joan Crawford eyes, jerks her head back in a quick, sudden move-ment. "Oh!" I gasp, out of pleasure or pain I am not sure, as she rips the pastie off with her teeth. She smiles and playfully bites my naked nipple before removing the other pastie. This time my groan is of pure delectation.

Queenie motions for me to step into the blue gown. "There," she says, smoothing the dress over my curves. "How fetching you look!"

"I want to see a mirror," I say, but she shakes her head.

"Beautiful women don't need mirrors; men are mirror enough for you." She turns me around. "You can keep this," she says, zipping up the dress. "It will give you something to remember me by."

"Where are you going?" I ask her.

Queenie places a hand on the curve of my belly. Instinctively, I arch my back, pushing my buttocks against her groin. I feel tingly inside like a wind chime: the same sensation that I had felt with Mr. Manchester. Mr. Manchester—a blur. A million miles away.

"It's not where I'm going," Queenie kisses my neck again. "It's who's going to take me and," she laughs, "who's going to *pay*."

I close my eyes. A stab of hatred for the unknown man—a man no doubt like Guy Bacon. A man who will want Queenie to cry.

"You're still the star, Queenie," I say and I mean it. "Not me."

"You're a very sweet girl," Queenie says. She presses her cheek against mine. "But my daddy worked the vaudeville circuit. 'Always leave 'em wanting more,' he'd tell me. 'Don't drag it out or they'll drag *you* out—by the cane.'"

Our faces are so close now that I can smell her lip rouge. "Queenie," I go to kiss her but she stops me.

"Goodbye, Wanda Whittle," Queenie whispers. She picks up her red trunk. "Don't take any wooden nickels."

I close my eyes. It feels the same as when a phonograph record skips or when the projectionist takes too long to change a reel: the dying *clack, clack, clack* of Queenie's heels on the linoleum floor.

"So that snooty dame left, eh?" Joe's voice slaps me out of my reverie. His nostrils are flared so that even from where I am standing, I can count his every nose hair. "Aaah, who needs her?" His eyes take in the gas blue gown. "Well, whaddaya want? For me to beg ya?" He throws up his hands and groans as I gape at him in confusion. "How come you glitzy dames are always so dizzy? Come on!" He grabs my hand, pulling me toward the door. "You've got less than five, baby."

The chorines, dressed in shimmering onyx black cat suits with a mammoth feather affixed to the back of each girl's bowed head, lock arms as they arrange themselves into the shape of a giant almond. At the sound of Eddie's fat drumroll, the hoofers roll their shoulders backwards and bob their heads: the assembly line of feathers fluttering flirtatiously. I emerge from the centre of the elephantine eye with arms outstretched, spinning atop a small revolving stage like a little ballerina doll in a jewellery box.

Coyly, I peer over my shoulder at the audience. *Is Mr. Manchester in the house tonight? Is he watching me?* I part my lips and slip a gloved finger into my mouth. Slowly, I remove the soft satin grey glove with my teeth, tossing it toward the footlights. The band kicks it into high gear and I wiggle my bottom and shake my hips as the audience roars. I wrap my left arm over my chest and unzip the back of my dress with my right hand. Holding the gown loosely over my breasts, I throw out a wink and a smile to the audience. With the impatient pounding of Eddie's drum, I let the dress fall from my bare breasts as the eye blinks and swallows me whole.

"Not bad, kid," Joe says as he rushes me backstage. "Now get the fuck back into your real costume."

14. BLOOD AND BREAD

"ISN'T IT SO EASY TO BE HAPPY, Wanda?" Evelyn slips off her military-style suit jacket and stretches her plump, freckled arms out towards the cottony sky. "Isn't it easy to be happy when it's Sunday and there's no work to be done and you can sit in a field of dandelions with your sister beside you?"

I yank a dandelion out of the damp grass and smile at her. "Some people call them weeds," I say. I reach out and tap her nose with its fuzzy yellow head.

"They are weeds," Evelyn giggles as she swats my hand away. "Dandelions are friendly little weeds who only want to be loved like flowers."

"You're so different, Evelyn. Have you been hanging around Eddie? Whatever he's got you smoking, I want some please!"

Evelyn closes her eyes and tilts her head back. The sun has turned her skin pink; it clashes with her red hair. "I haven't been doing anything, Wanda. I'm *seeing*. I'm *listening*. Everything that we need is right here. Listen to that robin with his belly full of wriggling wet worms. Do you think Mozart himself could create a more pleasing sound? And look at that big orange Tom creeping towards us, the self-satisfied little carnivore! Do you believe that there is a sculptor or a painter in the whole wide world who could improve upon him?"

The cat flops down beside me in an elegant heap. I run my hand along his thick sturdy body, from his neck to the end of his tail. He hums quietly.

"Like I said, though, it's easy to be happy now," Evelyn continues as the cat and I watch her with lazy interest. "But I feel it indoors, too. I feel it at two a.m. when I'm lying in bed and the roof is leaking and ol' Mrs. Merriweather is coughing up a lung. I feel it when my neck hurts and I've got to get up for work in an hour and the little bride upstairs is slamming doors because her husband came home drunk again. I can feel every nail and termite and I'm happy. Well, maybe 'happy' isn't the right way of saying it. I'm content. Just like Tom here." She makes a kissy sound at the cat. "I guess it's natural though," she says, falling back into the grass. "I guess it's natural for me to feel this way." Her fingers dance absentmindedly along the swell of her belly.

"What do you mean?" I stand up. "Evelyn," I straddle her body with my feet. "Evelyn, are you…?"

She looks up at me. Her eyes have disappeared into the sun. Her plasticine pink smile, with its shiny wet teeth, floats up into the space between us.

"Whose is it?"

Her fingers continue their dance as the smile shrinks and expands before me.

"Whose is it?" I yell. "Tell me!"

The smile crawls back into Evelyn's face and I can see her eyes again. "It's Henry's."

She is now standing in front of me. "Everything's going to be okay, Wanda. Everything *is* okay," she says, with the cool casualness of an ice truck on a summer day; words as clean and simple as a V-16 roadster flying through a horse cart.

I cross my arms under my chest to avoid punching her. "When did you become involved with Mr. Manchester?" I ask through gritted teeth.

"We've been seeing each other ever since I went to talk to him about the hatcheck girl job." Evelyn rolls her eyes toward the sky and the smile returns. "He said he loves my hands. He said that he's tired of showgirls."

"I thought you said he was a capitalist pig."

"I did, but that was before I got to know him."

The clouds above us roll slowly but steadily. My fingernails dig into my palms, in lieu of Evelyn's face. "There are doctors, Evelyn. There are doctors who can fix this. Doctors who can get rid of this."

Evelyn visibly recoils as my words hit the ground with a thud.

I study my sister's face so that I can remember her hurt later. Already it comforts me. I leave her in the field of dandelions: talking to cats and babbling about babies.

Got a few dollars and my sister's pain in my pocket. See a ladder in my stocking so bend down and scratch it, rip the whole thing wide open. Ankle to thigh. Thigh to ankle. Tear it off, let it swim down the catch basin. Swim to the Market. Gotta get back to the World Behind the Market.

"Hiya, baby."

Eyeballs springing forward like turtle heads.

"*Leave me alone!*" I yell.

"Sorry, sister." *Turtle eyes walks on.* "Sorry, sister, sorry."

The world is not a globe. The world is a soggy cardboard box torn open at both sides and I'm gonna fall out of it. But I've got a few dollars and my sister's pain in my pocket and the Market Queen is smiling at me saying, "That's not all you got, honey." Pretty dresses, silk stockings, bills stuffed in a secret hole in my pillow. A fur coat—that's better than a baby. Better than a maid uniform.

I climb the steps to our room. *Every nail and termite.* Mama is still at church dropping her last dollar in the collection plate and bowing her head to our Heavenly Father for blood and bread and faith in good daughters.

I pull my suitcase out from under the bed.

Sixty-five dollars and seventy-five cents stuffed in a hole in my pillow. A fur coat. Queenie's gown. The astrakhan-trimmed cap. The silk stockings. Oh! And the sparkly dress that Lili Belle gave me, the dress that I've never washed.

I add a ruby red lipstick, my toothbrush, a bar of toilet soap, some underpants and two pairs of cami-knickers, more stockings, a garter belt, my girdle, a bottle of lavender water, an ivory comb, and the photo of Mr. Manchester.

I sit on the suitcase, but it won't close. The fur coat doesn't fit. I pull it out and put it on over my plain Sunday shirtwaist dress. Springtime be damned—things shouldn't be coming out of the earth today. Why are things being born now?

There's a bottle of ink, a pen, and some paper on the bedside table. I carry it all into our kitchen, which doubles as Mama's bedroom.

Dear Mama,

  Something very exciting has happened! Mama, you won't believe it. I have met a very nice, very wealthy gentleman and we are going to elope! Please be happy. I will send word and money soon.

  Your dearest girl,
  Wanda

I fold the paper in half and place it carefully in the middle of the kitchen table. Parting the curtain, I take one last look at the Market Queen. Under the brilliant glare of the sun, she doesn't look quite so beautiful anymore.

15. BED BUG BABYLON

"YOU DON'T WANT TO GO IN THERE. It's crawling with cockroaches and whores." The businessman, grey in hue and cigarette thin, leers at me as I open the lobby door to the Grand Palace Hotel. I laugh awkwardly, knowing he's hoping that I'm the latter.

The hotel is neither grand nor a palace. Like so many things, its brilliance tarnishes upon inspection. The stuffed velvet loveseat beside the telephone box looks like it was last cleaned in 1902, while a ceiling mural of a lithe blonde Venus, her serpentine locks shielding her nether regions, is marred by water damage. I drag my suitcase across the gold speckled, scuffed linoleum floor. With a tap of the front desk's silver bell, a pink mountain of a man rises forth from under the cracked sun of the lobby clock, two folded envelopes clutched in his meaty paws like battered white doves.

"What ya want?" His marble blue eyes glare at me under the sweaty folds of his brow.

"I'd like a room please," I clear my throat. "One with a view of the city."

The clerk turns his back to me and shoves the crumpled envelopes into one of the mailboxes behind his desk. "Ya wanna week or ya wanna night? Maybe ya wanna hour?"

"Not just one night," I answer. I hoist my suitcase onto the desk with an angry thump. "And certainly not an hour."

"Ha!" His face, like a pound of raw dough, contorts into

a malicious smirk. "Ya don't know when I'm joking, d'ya?"

"I don't care for your jokes," I reply coolly. "I would just like a room please and since you're so interested, I plan to stay for at least a month."

The clerk slides a card, listing the room sizes and prices, across the desk at me. Rummaging through the stack of mail in front of him, he holds an envelope against the bulb of his desk lamp and squints at it.

"Are these prices in *dollars?*" I ask, my mouth agape. "I thought I told you that I don't care for your jokes."

"They ain't in pennies." He continues to peer at the envelope.

"Geez," I snap open my handbag and surreptitiously pull out enough bills for a one-week stay. "For those rates, will the bed bugs fluff my pillow and tuck me in at night?"

"Two weeks payment in advance!" He slaps his fist onto the desk.

"I only have enough for one week," I say calmly. "But I can get more." I undo the clasps of my fur coat and arch my back.

The man's glassy eyes travel from the bills in my hand to my chest and back again. His toothless red mouth stretches into a lascivious smile. "Girl like you can g'more," he nods. "Lossa more."

I fight the urge to vomit with a smile of my own. "Sure," I say. "Now I'll pay you for the week then?"

All business again, the clerk snatches the bills from my hand hungrily, as though he's suddenly afraid that I will change my mind. "Jim-may!" He snaps his pink sausage fingers at a pimply young man in dungarees, dingy white gloves and a bellhop's cap. "Take this lah-dee's bag to room 502!"

"Oh, no," I say, aware that 'Jim-may' might want a tip. "I can carry it myself."

"It's no trouble, miss." The bellhop picks up my suitcase and smiles shyly at me, his neck blushing as bright red as his pimples. "We'll take the lift."

He turns the key for the elevator and motions me inside.

"You'll like 502, miss. It's a swell room. A nice three-piece bath, radiators—not that you'll be needing those much now—and, oh, gee, it even has a radio!"

"A radio? That does sound swell!" I say, although I am more excited about the prospect of having my own private washroom.

"Here we are!" Jimmy slides the elevator door open. The hallway smells like old cigarettes and regurgitated gin. Small grey clouds rise from the boot-stained carpet as the bellhop leads me to my room.

"Number 502 is a real lady's room," Jimmy says. He smiles over his shoulder at me. "Irving must really like you."

"Irving?" I ask. "Is that the name of the mug at the lobby desk?"

"Yes, only he's not a mug. Irving is a real swell fella. He pays me ten dollars and fifty cents a week."

"You don't say."

"Aw," the bellhop blushes again. "I know it doesn't sound like much, but Irving lets me keep all of my tips. The tips make it worth the while."

"This the room here?" I ask, eager to change the subject. I think of the wad of dough safely tucked away in my handbag. Damned if either one of these birds is getting a penny more from me!

"This is it!" Jimmy opens the door. "Ta-da!"

Room 502 is pinker than Irving: orchid-pink wallpaper, baby-pink milk glass light fixtures, and a queen-sized cotton candy bed with a bright pink cherry blossom painted onto its wooden post.

"It's pretty," I murmur. I touch the ruffled shade of a lamp admiringly and brush the yellow dust from my fingertips. "Say," I open a dresser drawer to reveal a bible and a half empty hip flask. "You ever clean this joint?"

The bellhop laughs in embarrassment and reaches for the flask.

"No, leave it." I smile at him. "It comes with the room, don't it?"

"Sure," Jimmy chuckles again. He bounces nervously on the balls of his feet. "There's a guest phone in the lobby. Irving can take messages for you. Oh, and if you get hungry in the morning, there's a kitchen downstairs. We serve a swell ten cent breakfast: bacon, eggs, and toast." He places my suitcase on the floor by the bed. "Is there anything else you need, miss?"

"No." I throw my fur coat over an overstuffed organdy chair and stretch my arms, yawning dramatically. "I think I'll be getting to bed now. You said there's a bathtub in this room?"

"Oh, yes!" Jimmy's eyes light up. "I'll show you, miss."

He leads me into a small lavender washroom with a matching bathtub, toilet, and sink. The bellhop leans over the tub and begins fiddling with the knobs.

"Left for cold, right for hot. See? It's easy, miss."

"Right for hot," I nod. I unbutton the bodice of my shirt dress. "Yes, I see."

Jimmy's mouth falls open as I slip the dress over my head. I never wear knickers on a Sunday. "Don't worry," I say as he continues to gape at me. "I'll give it to you next time." I slip the room key out of his limp hand. "A tip, I mean."

I chuckle to myself as he stumbles out of the room backwards; his pop-eyed face reminding me of a goldfish we once kept as a class pet in primary school. *The boy got his tip, all right. That show was worth more than a few nickels.*

I drop the key down on the sink. I'm so giddy, I feel like a balloon that's about to burst. My own washroom! My very own bathtub! I get in the tub and turn on the taps: a little cold, a lot hot. Because she's a year and a half older than me, Evelyn always got to wash first. By the time it was my turn, the water in our galvanized washtub would be cold and dirty, with bits and pieces of my sister floating around in it.

I jump out of the tub to grab the hip flask. When I return, the bathwater is high to the brim. I turn off the taps and sink into the tub, the hot water turning my flesh scarlet. I take a slug from the flask: whisky. It burns my mouth.

Think she's got the fire down below, Benny?

I giggle, remembering Joe's crude joke. I look down at myself. *Yep,* I giggle again, *I've got the fire all right.*

I close my eyes. Wouldn't it be nice if Eddie were here? He's not my fella. He doesn't make me feel the way that Mr. Manchester and Queenie do. But he makes me feel nice just the same. If only he had a telephone so I could call him. I gulp down the rest of the whiskey. Maybe the bellhop will come back. Maybe I could spread open the curtains and maybe Mr. Manchester would like to watch. I open my eyes and step out of the tub. Naked and dripping bath water onto the faded pink carpet, I go to the window. The curtains are already open, revealing the lights of the city like paste diamonds on a dime store tiara. The bellhop was right, Irving must like me. From my window, I can clearly see the front entrance to Mr. Manchester's apartment building. Oh, I know Mr. Manchester doesn't really live there. I know it's only where he brings his girlfriends. Like Norma. Like...

I open my fists. Crescent moons mark my palms. Hadn't Daddy always loved Evelyn the best? Even though I was prettier. Even though I loved him more. Still naked and wet, I slip on my fur coat and crawl into bed.

Sleep will soon come, Mama used to say. *Sleep will soon come and tomorrow with it.*

When I wake, my tongue feels like an old sock and itchy pink bumps have broken out along my calves and thighs. Ripping off the bedcovers, I inspect the mattress for tell-tale blood stains. I don't see anything, but I know that there was definitely something sleeping in this bed last night besides me.

Oh well, I touch my own grumbling belly, *I guess we've all got to eat.*

In the red and white checkered open kitchen of the Grand Palace Hotel, the customers are fresher than the grub. Two mugs in crumpled fedoras give me the eye in between slurps of slushy, lukewarm coffee. Holding the morning paper in front of my face like a shield, I scan the "Women Wanted" ads. I can't sew, I don't know how to cook, I flunked typing class, and I hate children. That counts me out for most of 'em. I poke despondently with my fork at the swell ten-cent breakfast that Jimmy raved to me about. No ads for peelers. I guess I'll just have to pound the pavement this afternoon. There are plenty of burlesque joints in the city. I stuff my mouth full of rubbery scrambled egg and swallow without chewing. On the radio, a famous author is being interviewed about the book burnings in Germany. The moderator mentions that Hitler has recently prohibited the publishing of non-Aryan writers. Hitler. I've heard the name before. From Evelyn of course. Over breakfast about a week or so ago.

"Evil is most destructive when it is insidious," she had said, raising her porridge spoon in the air for emphasis. "If you think that what's going on in Germany can't happen here…"

"Shush, Evelyn," Mama looked toward our door as though she was afraid that the neighbours would hear.

"Don't tell me that you *agree* with him, Mama!" Evelyn's face had gone as red as her hair. She stood up, knocking her coffee into her porridge.

"Of course I don't agree with him," Mama waved her down. "But it's not our country and it's not our business."

"'Not our country. Not our business,'" Evelyn sarcastically parroted. "And there you have it—both the excuse for and the cause of all the evil in the world. *Not my people. Not my colour. Not from where I'm from. It doesn't concern me.* Until it does, of course."

"Scary world, ain't it?" The waitress Marion slaps my bill down on the table. "Hey, George!" she shouts at the cook. "Why don't ya change the channel? Put on some music! I'd love to hear some Rudy Vallee." She places a hand on her bosom. "That man's voice, I tell ya. It fills my heart, it does."

"Aw, that sap's voice couldn't fill a tin cup!"

I pay my bill quickly and duck out before Marion slugs George. Never get between a middle-aged woman and Rudy Vallee.

There isn't a door on the lobby's telephone box and when Irving stops to turn his radio down as I ring the phone's bell crank, I understand why there are no telephones in the rooms at the Grand Palace Hotel. I rub at my temples; my belly is full, but my mind is unsettled. It's more than just the crummy food and the bed bugs, this feeling. It must be because of Evelyn and what she's done. It can't have anything to do with what's happening in Germany. Sure, that's scary like Marion said, but it's also so far away.

"Number, please."

I turn my back to Irving in a vain attempt at privacy as I give the Operator the number to the Apple Bottom theatre. After a few clicks and pops, Joe's gruff voice comes on the line.

"Yeah, whaddaya want?"

"Hello, Joe. This is Wanda."

"Yeah, so?"

"So, I've just called to tell you that I won't be in tonight. In fact," I say, taking a deep breath. "I won't be back in ever again. You can tell Mr. Manchester that I'm *through*."

Joe guffaws, emitting a machine gun cackle. "Female trouble, baby?"

"Sure, Joe," I reply calmly. "It's a permanent affliction."

16. LITTLE PIGGIES

Turn around now
Let us see the legs
Girl's a honey
The legs are a little big though.
Turn around now
We've seen your picture in the papers
You know we're not that kind of a joint –
We don't want any flatfoots sniffing around the foot lights.
Turn around now
Lift your skirt
Higher! Higher!
Nice, very nice
We're not hiring today, though
Can't even take care of our own.
Turn around now.

ALL DAY LONG, IT'S BEEN THE SAME ol' song: either I'm not what they're looking for, or they're just not looking. Exhausted, I collapse onto a parkette bench and kick off my high heels. My stockings are full of ladders and there's a hole in my right shoe. I tear off the corner of a discarded newspaper and stuff it into the toe. Leaning forward, I rub at my tired, calloused feet.

"Nice little piggies." A clean shaven man in a double-breasted business suit leers at me.

I shove my swollen dogs back into my shoes as he sits down beside me. "You've got pretty little footsies, baby. Don't hide them." He places a soft, well-manicured hand on my knee and gives it a rough squeeze. "I'd like to take those little piggies to market, buy them silk stockings, and satin slippers. Lots of nice things." He grins at me, flashing his sharp little teeth.

I jump up and he laughs.

"Where you going, little piggy?"

I run back in the direction of the city lights, the man's cruel voice thumping at my back. *"This little piggy went wee-wee-wee all the way home!"*

Daytime was only the opening act; the night is the city's main attraction. Blinking yellow bulbs take the place of the setting sun. *Girls! Girls! Dozens and dozens of girls!*

Everyone is naked under a spotlight.

Across the street, a lineup of men forms in front of a small pink bricked building. The men are too well-dressed, their faces too plump and smug, for it to be a breadline. A barrel-chested doorman in a navy blue, brass buttoned suit grins at me and gestures toward the sign glittering above the gathering men:

FALL IN LOVE WITH YOUR DANCE INSTRUCTRESS!
ALL NIGHT! EVERY NIGHT!

17. THE BOW TIE

WHEN THE LIGHTS ARE DIM and the cigarettes are lit, the dames look like ladies and the mugs look like gentlemen and nobody sees the blood in your shoes at the Bow Tie. The orchestra is swell, but it's hard to make the joint hum with so many flat tires. Even when the band plays a hot number like Cab Calloway's "Jitterbug," the customers just want to sway back and forth, like limp grass in the wind. But I'm not sixteen anymore. I know that the customers don't want me to teach them the Lindy Hop. Sometimes they really do want a waltz. Usually they just want to cop a feel. I don't mind so long as they tip me at least a dollar for the pleasure. Anything less and the next time they see me, they'll get their toes crushed.

Oh, pardon me, daddy! You know how clumsy we taxi dancers can be.

I've gone backwards. From burlesque star dressed in sequins to taxi dancer covered in sweaty palm prints. Forty-five dollars a week downgraded to five cents a dance.

I've worked as a taxi dancer before. But it's different when you're sixteen and you can convince yourself that you're really a dance hall instructress. Back then, it had seemed glamorous. Respectful. Even my parents had thought so.

Someone taps my shoulder. I turn around, arranging my face into a sunny smile. "May I have this dance, miss?"

"Mr. Whipplebum!"

Lili Belle's beau squints at me, a flaccid ticket in his out-stretched hand.

"Now, sugar!" I kick out the words jubilantly. "Don't break my heart by saying you don't remember me!"

He squints again. His piggy eyes travel to my bosom. "You *do* look rather familiar."

"The Stone's Throw," I wink at him. "I'm Wanda, Lili Belle's friend."

Mr. Whipplebum's pie face turns bright red. He looks around, waving the ticket in his hand nervously. "I, uh, I think I better ask one of these other girls to dance."

"Oh, daddy!" I pout. "I guess you think these other gals are so much prettier than me!"

Mr. Whipplebum takes a handkerchief out of his pants pocket. "It isn't that." He wipes his fleshy brow. "But if you're a friend of Lili Belle's, I don't think that I'm your type."

I laugh off my confusion at the meaning of his words. "Why, handsome," I say as I slip the ticket out of his wet hand. "You couldn't be any more my type if you were telegraphed by Western Union."

I feel him watching as I prop my leg up on one of the folding chairs and stick the ticket under my garter belt.

"Well, now," he chuckles. "You sure do have pretty legs." His face has gone from apple-red to worm-pink.

"Thank you, sugar." I pull him onto the floor and into a waltz. The band, obviously feeling cheeky, starts up "Ten Cents a Dance." Mr. Whipplebum places his hand on the small of my back and holds me close as the incompatible combination of cologne and sweat fill my nostrils.

I look up at him, smiling widely so as to breathe through my mouth. "You sure know how to swing a hoof, sugar!"

After the song ends, he pulls out his billfold and loudly counts out my tip. "One, two, three."

Folding the dollar bills into my garter purse, I spot Lacey, a frizzy blonde with an angular figure and an intrusively large nose, strutting toward Mr. Whipplebum. "Hello, big boy," she coos, smiling greedily. She braids her arm through his. "Wanna dance with a *lady*?"

I jump up and grab her by her other elbow. "Listen, sister," I whisper. "Go do your digging in somebody else's gold mine!"

"I don't see your initials stitched on 'im," she hisses back.

I drop down into a folding chair in the bull pen and watch in defeat as Lacey wraps her bony arms around the space where Mr. Whipplebum's neck should be. They sway awkwardly under the paper stars, against the timing of the brass.

Pushing my breasts together, I lean forward in my chair and smile at any mug who so much as looks my way. But it's after midnight now. The room has emptied out and my shoes are filled with blood. Time to cash in my tickets and head on back to Bed Bug Babylon.

"Wanda!" Mr. Whipplebum waddles toward me. "Can I give you a ride home?"

"Leaving so soon, sugar?" I nod at Lacey standing alone by the stage, hands on her raw-boned hips. If looks could kill, I'd be a chalk line on this dance floor. "I thought you were having fun."

"Certainly," Mr. Whipplebum chuckles. He holds my fox coat out for me. "It's all blondes and games until somebody loses their wallet."

"Oh, daddy! You're so witty!" I place my hand on his chest, pressing my palm against the diamond stick-pin in his lapel. "You better watch out," I whisper. "I think I could really go for you."

I'm not surprised when Mr. Whipplebum flags down a taxi. Married men don't drive their own cars to the Bow Tie. Too conspicuous.

In the back of the cab, Mr. Whipplebum pulls me onto his lap and begins nuzzling my neck. The cab driver looks straight ahead, pretending not to notice.

"Oh, sugar, that tickles!" I wiggle out of his embrace and

slide toward the window. The city lights are so bright, I can't see the stars. What am I doing with this stuffed bird? I think of my father coming home the day before Christmas, carrying his eye in his hand, his face obliterated by red, yellow, and blue. I think of Lili Belle's diamond bracelet. Mr. Whipplebum squeezes my thigh as the cabbie's hands clench the steering wheel.

I'm glad to be giving him the merry-go-round!

I lean over and lightly tap the driver's shoulder. "The Grand Palace Hotel, please." I finger the diamond stick-pin in my pocket and wink at him. "It's crawling with cockroaches and whores."

"Mind if I call you 'baby'?" Mr. Whipplebum plops his girth down upon my cotton candy bed and grins up at me, all teeth and flesh.

"'Course not, sugar. So long as *you* don't mind if I slip into something more comfortable."

In the privacy of the washroom, I peel off my sparkly gown. I still haven't had it dry cleaned since that night with Mr. Manchester; there are sweat stains under the arms and the hem is starting to unravel. I toss it into the empty bathtub and stand naked before my mirror. I've lost quite a bit of weight, no doubt due to a diet of ketchup soup (ketchup I'd pinched from the downstairs kitchen mixed with hot tap water) and from dancing six hours a night at the Bow Tie. My hip bones jut out further than my belly, which is now concave, while my breasts are beginning to look like two day old balloons.

I lean over the sink and pinch my cheeks for colour. To-morrow I'll start eating better. I'll wake up early and have Marion's ten-cent breakfast. Maybe I'll buy a dinner of meat and potatoes with the tip that Mr. Whipplebum gave me. I'll be fat again, soon enough.

I step into my new seashell pink nightie. I picked it up at the corner five-and-dime store, but it doesn't look so cheap; the material is soft, almost like silk, and the cut is pretty.

"You coming out, baby? Daddy's getting lonely."

"Yes, daddy." I stick my tongue out at my reflection.

"Holy cats!" Mr. Whipplebum exclaims as I exit the washroom. "I was just admiring the city view, but I think I like this view better." He rubs his hands together, smacking his lips hungrily. "You certainly are an eyeful!"

"Oh, sugar!" I laugh. "It is a nice night though, isn't it?" I say, joining him at the window.

Under a fat, lazy moon, the clouds are growing restless. They're rabbits and then when I blink, they're lions. I press my nose against the glass. A girl is standing outside of Mr. Manchester's building. A red-haired girl in a thin gingham dress. A girl with swollen ankles and a face purple with tears. I try to open the window, but it's stuck.

"Who's Evelyn?"

"What?" I turn away from the window, startled.

"You said 'Evelyn.'" Mr. Whipplebum's pig eyes squint at me.

"Daddy," I say, forcing a giggle. "You must be hearing things." I flop down onto the bed and arch my back. "Have you got a cigarette?" I ask huskily, in an attempt to distract him.

Mr. Whipplebum pulls a silver cigarette case out of his trouser pocket. "I don't really like girls who smoke," he scolds as he hands me a snipe. "I don't think it's very ladylike."

I cup his hands as he lights my cigarette with his gold pocket watch lighter. "Do you know what *I* think, sugar," I say, exhaling. "I think that it is very mean of you to criticize me for smoking cigarettes when you do exactly the same thing."

"I don't smoke them," Mr. Whipplebum squints at me, frowning. "I just like to watch them burn."

"That's not all you like to watch, is it sugar daddy?"

"No."

I pull the straps of my nightie down my shoulders. "What else do you like to watch?"

"I like to watch you." Mr. Whipplebum removes his suit jacket and begins to unclasp his cuff links. "But I want to do more than just watch." He reaches over and takes the cigarette from me, dropping it into a glass of water on the nightstand. Grabbing me by the waist, he tries to kiss me, his bright pink tongue thrashing at my face like the tentacle of an angry octopus. Repulsed, I push him away.

"What's the matter?" Mr. Whipplebum asks, his voice rising with indignation. "You're just like your friend, Lili Belle, aren't you?"

"I don't know what you mean..."

"You're just like her," he grumbles. "I should have gone with that blonde instead. Maybe *she* would have been nice to me."

I roll over onto my stomach and bury my face in my pillow. "Oh, daddy!" I press my mouth against the fabric and cough, knowing that he'll mistake the sounds for sobbing.

"Please—please don't cry," Mr. Whipplebum says, suddenly contrite. "I didn't mean to upset you."

"You don't understand, daddy!" I cry into the pillow. "I *want* to be nice to you, it's just ... oh, it's too awful for me to say!"

"What is it, dear?"

"The doctor says I have a, uh, condition ... *down there.*" I sit up and cover my face with my hands. "H-he said it's curable. He said there's medicine that can make it all better, b-but I can't *afford* it!" I begin cough-sobbing hysterically.

"There, there, baby." Mr. Whipplebum strokes my back. "How much did the doctor say this medicine costs?"

"Two hundred dollars." I peek out at him through my fingers.

"And you really want to be nice to me?"

"Yes, sugar daddy. I really do."

"Okay." He takes out his cheque book. "I'll write you a cheque on one condition. I want you to call me as soon as the doctor says that you're cured."

"I will, daddy!" I exclaim, kissing him on the cheek. "Ain't you the sweetest!"

He pats me on the arm and stands up. "Now where in tarnation did I put my lighter?"

18. BREATHLESS AND RECKLESS

THE AFTERNOON IS HOTTER THAN A SPRING DAY has any right to be. Children play hooky to hopscotch in the streets; men tumble out of saloon doors and women's bare legs dangle from open tenement windows, like the hands of a clock. In the middle of the road, a gang of pigeons, hobo-doves, feast on a filthy, forgotten sandwich. They waddle quickly to the safety of the gutters every time that an automobile turns the corner.

I venture out into the road and pick up the sandwich, holding it gingerly between my thumb and forefinger. "There you go, boys," I say, tossing the food onto the sidewalk. "No need to risk your lives for a little breakfast!"

The pigeons watch, their tiny heads cocked inquisitively, but rather than following me—and the sandwich—back to the curb, they choose to stay in the middle of the road; pecking away at the now bare pavement in earnest ignorance.

Dumb clucks.

The red velvet curtain rises and the thumb-headed middle-aged man seated in front of me surreptitiously folds his coat over his lap. The theatre is empty, save for a handful of teenage shop girls, a fat woman in a flowered house-dress, the bald pervert, and me. It doesn't matter. In a few moments, the newsreel will be over, the crude cartoon characters will finish their dance, the house lights will go down and it'll be *her,* only her. Ravishing, radiant, *Reckless:* Harlow.

I place my hand on the armrest of the empty seat next to me, palm up. If Mr. Manchester was sitting here right now, he would finally understand. Watching me watching Jean. Jean Harlow gliding across the screen, resplendent in short-shorts and ankle socks, her Valentine-red lips expertly mouthing the words to another woman's song.

Mr. Manchester squeezes my hand and nods to the screen. That's *me:* smiling, laughing, dancing, slender arms raised and long legs kicking. Me, Jean. Jean, me. Mr. Manchester is watching and we don't know it. He's watching and we don't...

I stand leaning against his brick building, the sparkly gown nestled in the crook of my arm, chain smoking Mr. Whipple-bum's cigarettes. A little girl in a grimy dress rushes past me, her tiny hands clutching a bouquet of dandelions, a string of the weeds wrapped around her dirty neck. Ugly little dandelions. Ugly little weeds. As bright and ugly as the sun.

"A tad hot for fur, wouldn't you say?" The woman arches her pencil-thin eyebrow at me, before resting her heavy shopping bags down on the curb. She reminds me of Norma, with her shiny up-do and immaculate shoes.

"Just a *tad* hot," I reply. I'm about to undo the clasps of my coat, give her a peek of just how hot, when she motions to a man wearing white gloves and a dark, brass buttoned uniform, his arms laden with hat boxes. I drop my hands to my sides. Maybe he's a cop. Even if he's not a cop, he looks like he'd know where to find one.

I push through the merry-go-round doors. The black-and-white checkered floor makes me feel dizzy, as though I am stepping into a box, a box open at both ends. A box I could easily fall out of.

"May I help you, miss?" The dimpled concierge smiles at me.

"Yes," I answer, adopting a haughty, upper-class intonation to my voice as I slap the dress down onto the counter. "I'd like to leave this for one of your residents, but there's just one problem."

"And what is the problem, miss?" The concierge eyes the rumpled, sweaty gown in confusion.

"I need something to wrap it in. It doesn't have to be anything fancy."

The young man tugs at his shirt collar, looking up at me with the eager solicitude of which I've come to expect from most men.

"Will this do?" he asks. He pulls a brown paper bag out from under the counter.

"Lovely," I nod as he folds the dress and places it carefully into the bag. "Kindly ensure that Mr. Manchester receives it, won't you?"

"Of course, miss." The concierge blushes at my smile. "Who should I tell him it's from?"

I kiss the tips of my fingers and wiggle them at him as I step back into the merry-go-round.

"Jean Harlow."

"Ya can't come in, doll." The scarred, fleshy hand blocks my entrance to the Bow Tie. "Boss says you're through."

I take a step back, puzzled. "Through?"

Louie, the Bow Tie's bouncer, laughs humourlessly; his mouth a dank endless hole of chewed tobacco and wooden teeth. "Canned! Sacked! Fired! Ya got that?" He spits on the ground in front of me, narrowly missing my shoes.

"But why?"

"Why?" Louie smirks at me. "'Cuz we don't want ya spreadin' da clap around, that's why."

"I don't have the clap!" I cry. I look behind me at the gaggle of men waiting in line to get in. "The customers really like me!"

"Yah? Well our *best* customer don't like ya and if our best customer don't like ya, da boss don't like ya and if da boss don't like ya, *I* don't like ya." Louie spits out another wad of tobacco, this time making his mark.

I shake out my foot. "I ... I don't understand..."

"He says you stole from him!"

"Who says that?"

"Mr. Whipplebum!"

"That rat! Why I oughta give him a piece of my..."

"Yah, sure," Louie sneers. "Sounds like ya already gave him a piece!"

"Oh, you nasty man!"

"Say Wanda," he says as I turn to leave. "I sure hope ya like to play ball!"

"What?"

"Da cheque Mr. Whipplebum wrote ya," Louie smiles his wooden-toothed grin. "He told me to tell ya it's made outta rubber."

He opens the door to the Bow Tie. "Come on in, fellas," he says, with a wave to the customers. The men shuffle past, clad in their Friday night best. More than one looks me over with hungry interest.

Unwisely, Louie has turned his back to me. I take a deep breath and kick out my leg, planting a high-heeled shoe squarely between his cheeks. "Ya dirty bitch!"

My stockings slip down around my ankles as I run. Breathless and reckless, I almost trip over a homeless man sleeping on the bottom step of the staircase.

"Go get 'em, Red!" the man cheers. He raises his bottle of rubbing alcohol in the air. "My money's on you!"

19. A BUSINESS PROPOSAL

TIME DOESN'T REALLY MARCH ON. It tends to tip-toe. There's no parade. No stomping of boots to alert you to its passing. One day, you turn around and it is gone. It's been over a month since the Bow Tie sacked me; days and weeks that flew by faster than my pillow-case savings could keep up.

I step out of the pawn shop and onto the dusty street. My bounty is now less one astrakhan-trimmed cap. I slip the bills into my handbag. Twenty dollars. Not even a quarter of what the cap is worth, nor comparable to the work that I put into acquiring it. Twenty dollars to buy me more time in Bedbug Babylon.

I undo the clasps of the fur coat. It's too bright again. It feels as though the sun is sitting on top of me, playing uncle.

"Need a ride, honey?"

I turn at the sound of the familiar voice. Shading my eyes, I squint at the boy, his head sticking out of the driver's side of a taxi cab. "Eddie!"

"Wanda?" Eddie opens the car door and rushes toward me. He removes his newsboy cap and wipes his forehead. "What happened to yer hair?"

"I got it bleached and bobbed." I touch my shorn locks self-consciously. "Don't you like it, Eddie?"

"S'okay but I like yer old hair better." He puts his arms around me. "Ain't ya been eatin'? Yer skin and bones. It's like someone let all the air outta yer front tires!"

"Gee, thanks, Eddie. You sure know how to sweet talk a girl." I turn my chin up, avoiding his attempted kiss.

"Aw, now Wanda, don't be like that. You know yer still a pip. Say, it's been too long! How's the ol' Apple Bottom?"

I pull back from him, puzzled. "You mean you don't know? I left a few months ago."

Eddie lets out a whistle. "Ya don't say! That musta been about tha' same time I got canned!"

"You got fired, Eddie?"

Eddie nods. "Been drivin' my brudder's cab evah since!" He slaps his hand down on the hood of the taxi.

"But why?"

Eddie pulls a cigarette out from behind his ear. "Ya got a match, doll?"

"Sure, Eddie." I hand him Mr. Whipplebum's lighter.

Eddie whistles again. "Solid gold! Where'd ya get that?"

"Why'd you get fired, Eddie?"

"Aw," Eddie takes a drag and looks down at his feet. "They think I stole somethin'."

"*Stole* something?"

"Yeah. Remember that day in Mr. Manchester's office?"

"Yes."

"Well, I guess somethin' went missin'. A picture or somethin'. Mr. Manchester thought Benny did it, 'cuz he's the only one got a key. Well I couldn't let 'em can Benny. He's just an old man."

"So you said it was you."

Eddie nods, his thick orange curls falling into his eyes.

"You should have told them it was me, Eddie." I take his hand and squeeze it. "You know that it was."

"I don't snitch on my friends."

"You sure are regular, Eddie."

He laughs. "A regular sap, ya mean! Say, does this mean I can kiss ya now?"

"I thought you said I look like a flat tire?"

Eddie smiles at me mischievously. "I'll fill ya up, doll."

"Oh, Eddie!" I push him away, laughing. "Don't be crude!"

"At least let me take ya to lunch then." Eddie ruffles my hair. "My treat, Blondie."

He takes me by the arm and leads me across the street. "I know a swell Italian place. Nothin' beats a good plate of spaghetti for fattening a dame up!"

The Italian restaurant is homey and charming, with gingham tablecloths and an open kitchen. "Let's sit by da windah," Eddie says. "I wanna look at ya." He pulls out a chair for me. "Let me take yer coat, doll."

I shake my head no.

"Ain't ya hot in that getup? It's almost summer."

"Really?" I yawn. I open up a menu. "I hadn't noticed." Eddie snatches the menu from my hand.

"Two plates of spaghetti, Tom!" He twists his chair around and shouts toward the kitchen. "And don't be stingy with the meatballs!"

"Oh-kay, Eddie!" The beefy, balding cook winks at me.

"Whatsa matter, baby?" Eddie turns my hand over and runs his index finger along my palm. "Ya seem different and I don't just mean yer hair."

I shrug. "I'm swell, Eddie."

"Ya can't lie to me, doll."

Eddie's right. I can't lie to him. I'm not sure if that's because I really like him or because I don't really care what he thinks of me. Or maybe I really like him because I don't care what he thinks of me.

I sigh. "Things have been lousy, Eddie. I was making nickels as a taxi dancer over at the Bow Tie but then they canned me and I haven't been able to find another gig since. The rent at the hotel where I've been staying is eating away at my savings and the bed bugs are eating away at my skin."

"Why don't ya go back to the Apple Bottom?" Eddie pulls a handkerchief out of his shirt pocket.

"I can't," I say. I blow my nose into the hankie. "Please don't ask me why, Eddie."

He tips his chair back and looks away from me. "I don't hafta ask, doll," he says quietly.

"What about you, Eddie?" I force a smile. "You really do look swell. Do you like driving a cab?"

He shrugs. "It'd be all right, if it wasn't fer the goddam customers."

"What's wrong with the customers?"

"Aw," Eddie takes a drag off his cigarette. "When they feel like bein' chatty, I better chat. When they want silence, I better button up my lip. It gets ta ya, Wanda. Gets so ya don't feel human anymore."

Tom comes by with our plates of spaghetti. "Ya hear about Babe Ruth, Eddie?"

I look out the window as they discuss the baseball player's impending retirement. It's begun to rain. A bevy of bowler-hatted businessmen rush by, opening their black umbrellas in unison, as though they are being choreographed by Busby Berkeley. One of the men holds onto the elbow of a middle-aged woman, a raincoat tied at her thick waist, her left stocking rolling down her fish-white leg as she struggles to keep up in her high-heeled shoes. *Old maid Myrtle.*

"Whatcha lookin' at, baby?"

"Oh, nothing," I say, turning back to Eddie. "I just spotted an old neighbour." I pick up my spoon and twirl the spaghetti around my fork. "I haven't written my mama since I left home."

He looks up at me. "Why not?"

I shrug. "I don't have any money to send her."

"Write her anyway," he says, his mouth full of meat and cheese.

"Eddie," I say suddenly. "Do you pick up a lot of tourists in your cab? A lot of businessmen?"

"Sure do. The tourists are usually da chatty ones."

"Well," I wipe my mouth with a paper napkin and take a deep breath. "I have a proposition for you."

"A what?"

"A business deal." I take a sip of water before continuing. "Eddie, do the customers usually ask you for recommendations on hotels and restaurants, that kind of thing?"

"Of course."

"How about girls? Do they ever ask you where to find a girl?"

Eddie laughs. "Oh yeah, dat's a common one."

"Well, I'm staying at the Grand Palace hotel. Room 502. The next time one of your customers asks for a girl, I want you to send him to me. But only," I lean forward and look Eddie in the eye, my raised spoon punctuating the words, "only if he is wearing a wedding ring or a three-piece tailored suit. Or if he's very rich and looks so old he's about to croak. I'll give you a cut, of course," I add anxiously.

Eddie puts his fork down. "You know what yer askin' me, Wanda?"

"Yes I do, Eddie."

He scratches his jaw. "I dunno. I don't like this."

"Eddie, I need the money. I've made up my mind. If you won't help me, I'll ask another cab driver who will."

He looks at me sadly. "I guess I kin help ya."

"Thank you, Eddie." I squeeze his hand affectionately.

"But I'm gonna stand outside the door the whole time. None of them mugs is gonna hurtcha."

"Okay, Eddie."

He digs into his pocket and throws a dollar bill on the table, along with a twenty-five cent tip. "Let's go."

"Aren't you going to finish your spaghetti?"

"No." He stands up. "I ain't so hungry no more."

20. HEAVY SUGAR

The man with the monocle is gravy.
An easy buck
He doesn't want to kiss or touch:
Just lie back, miss
Hands at your sides, that's it.
Open your legs a little wider
Under the light where it is brighter
So I can see
And I can study
Sniff and inspect
Your pretty little cunny.

"THAT CARTOON DICK THINKS that 'crime doesn't pay', does he? Honey, these days it's about the only thing that *does* pay." I take a bite out of my hotdog and grin at Lili Belle sitting beside me on the park bench. "It ain't such a bad gig either. Last night I fell asleep while the Monocle Man was doing his thing. He didn't bother waking me up, just left a fat tip under my left cheek."

Lili Belle leans forward as I open up my handbag. "That's some heavy sugar!" she whistles, impressed.

"You said it, sister!" I snap my bag shut.

"You must have to deal with some pretty ugly mugs, though."

I shrug. "If they're really ugly, I just think about how kind and selfless I'm being. If they're mean or too rough, though,

I call for Eddie and he gives them a good sock in the beezer."

"Eddie's a good egg," Lili Belle muses. "I sure am glad he told me where you were. I was worried about you."

I toss the remainder of my hotdog bun onto the boardwalk and turn to Lili Belle. "They been talking about me at the Apple Bottom?"

"Sure," she nods, chuckling. "Greasing their gums."

"What have they been saying?"

"Well, for starters, they think you and Eddie ran off and got married."

"That's a hot one!" I laugh. "Is that what Mr. Manchester thinks too?"

"Dunno. Mr. Manchester's the only one who never mentions you."

"Oh." I stretch my lips into a smile as I scramble for something to say. "Well, who's the specialty now?"

"Betty Bop." Lili Belle takes a sip of her soda, wrinkling her nose at the gang of seagulls jostling for a bite of her hotdog. "She's a one-legged tap dancer. A real swell girl, almost as cute as Ruby Keeler."

"Is Evelyn still working in hatcheck?" I ask. Might as well twist my own knife.

Lili Belle nods. "I'm not sure for how long, though. She's not looking too well and boy, is she starting to show! Luckily she's behind the counter so the customers don't really notice, but Joe and Mr. Manchester do and they don't like it." She shakes her head sadly. "Mr. Manchester's always been nice to me, but I've been thinking lately that maybe he ain't so good."

"What do you mean?" I ask. "Did he bounce her?"

"Yes. He told her that the baby ain't his. Both him and Joe are trying to pin it on Eddie. All Joe had to do was whisper in Penny's ear and suddenly the whole joint is buzzing about Eddie knocking up your sister, running out with you, and the both of you leaving Evelyn holding the bag. Who cares about the truth when the lie is so juicy?"

"So Mr. Manchester gave Evelyn the air, huh?"

"Why are you saying it like that and why are you smiling?" Lili Belle narrows her eyes at me. "I know you've always been sweet on Mr. Manchester, honey, but Evelyn's your very own sister."

"I'm *not* sweet on Mr. Manchester!" I snap, feeling as though Lili Belle has walked in on me on the toilet.

She shrugs and pops the last bit of hotdog into her mouth. "Don't go making a big deal over a small heel, sugar."

"Oh, why don't you mind your own business!"

"I'm sorry, sweetie." Lili Belle's saucer brown eyes are instantly contrite. "Gosh, it's been so long since we've seen each other, I don't want to quarrel. I just feel so awful for your sister. She's in a real bad way."

"Here." I open my purse and take out the Monocle Man's tip. "Give this to Evelyn. I'm seeing the Boxer tonight anyway."

"The Boxer?" Lili Belle asks as I press the bills into her hand. "Who's the Boxer?"

The Boxer really is a boxer. He's been in the ring, albeit unsuccessfully, with the heaviest of the heavyweights. He's young and he's handsome. Well, except that his nose is crooked and the top row of his teeth are false. A fella like the Boxer shouldn't have to pay for a girl but in bed, just like in the ring, he has trouble getting up. Even after the count of ten.

Whether he's taking me out for a night on the town, or if we're just staying in, the Boxer likes for me to answer the door dressed to the nines. He likes my Jean Harlow hair and brings me big boxes of cream-filled chocolates, because he likes that I'm fat and he doesn't want for me to ever get thin again. I like the Boxer, because he's better looking than most of the mugs that Eddie picks up for me, and because he's almost as easy to handle as the Monocle Man: all he wants me to do is cock my head to one side and smile and agree with everything he says. When he eventually mounts me, my only job is to make a lot of noise, as though he really is giving me a pickle. One time, I made so much noise that Jimmy kicked open the door, because he thought that I was being murdered. The Boxer really liked that. He left me an extra-large tip that day.

"He's my favourite customer," I explain to Lili Belle. I lock arms with her as we stroll the boardwalk together. Ahead of us, a small group of carnies are setting up a make-shift ragbag fair, no doubt hoping to cook up a little dough before the flatfoots sniff them out. A woman in a wine velvet robe, her neck and wrists laden with bright plastic beads, hangs a sign to the entrance of a sorry-looking tent: YOUR FUTURE FOR A NICKEL.

"Say," I turn to Lili Belle. "The Boxer is taking me to the Orange Blossom tonight and he asked me to bring along a friend for his manager. Don't worry," I say quickly as Lili Belle's eyes widen in alarm. "You won't have to do anything. I'll tell him that you're not part of the racket. But," I add, winking. "I'll get him to pay you just the same."

"Oh-kay, sweetie," Lili Belle says, visibly relaxing. "I guess it will be like how it was with Mr. Whipplebum." She smiles. "A merry-go-round."

"Win a pig!" A moustachioed carny cradling a pink hog with a large silk bow tied around its neck, gestures toward a young boy setting up a dart-ball board. "Three games, ten cents! Winner takes home a pig!"

I wear my fox fur coat over my shoulders, the arms loose like a cape. Queenie's gas blue gown stretches tight across my mid-section; my bare breasts bulging out over the top of its low-cut neckline. Outside of the Orange Blossom, the Boxer tosses his cigarette and rushes to the passenger side of the cab.

"Glad you didn't mind meeting me here, doll," he says as he holds the car door open for me. He gives me the elevator stare and smiles. "You look swell. I like that dress." He slips a hand under my coat, giving my backside a pinch. "Fits ya real nice."

Lili Belle exits behind me, dressed in a black velvet evening gown with fingerless fishnet gloves and a Schiaparelli hat shaped like a shoe. Elegantly, she tosses a fat white fur stole over her right shoulder, attempting a look of cool boredom as the Boxer looks her over. "Who's the tomato?"

"Lili Belle," she answers, extending her hand in greeting. "Fresh, but don't squeeze."

The Boxer grins. "Mr. McDaniel's gonna like you, doll."

The taxi driver loudly clears his throat. "Two bits, mac."

"Oh, right." The Boxer gets out his billfold and peels off a dollar bill.

"Ain't ya Billy da Bronco?" the cabbie jeers. "Say, I lost a sawbuck on ya last week at tha Screwdriver. Dat other mug sure showed ya a good time. Almost knocked yer beezer clean offa yer face!"

"That so?" The Boxer slips the dollar back into his wallet. "Here's a tip, bub: next time bet on the other mug." He tosses a quarter to the cabbie and curls one arm around Lili Belle's waist and the other around my neck. "Thanks for givin' my janes a ride, mac."

With the wave of the barrel-chested doorman's white glove, we float past the line-up of fine-feathered rubes waiting to get into the Orange Blossom. Blinded by the lobby's glittering wall-to-wall mirrors, I jump as a pretty girl in a maid uniform—one almost as tight and short as my Apple Bottom costume—removes my fur coat. She bows to me before moving on to Lili Belle.

"This sure is a classy joint," I say, admiring the large por-celain cats standing guard at the foot of the club's winding black marble staircase.

"Any dame who steps out with me better get used to class," the Boxer thumps his chest and winks at me. "Come on, doll, we're meeting Mr. McDaniel upstairs."

Stepping into the theatre of the Orange Blossom is like finding a doorway to the sun: everything is blindingly gold and sizzling hot. The walls are populated with large-breasted mermaids lacquered in peach copper, and the seats are made of a deliciously inviting velvet in a tangerine colour that matches the stage curtains. Cigarette girls and waitresses in skimpy Cleopatra inspired outfits flirtatiously swing their snake-like hips between little round tables topped with gold table cloths.

A large bejewelled hand rises forth from the blood orange sea. "Billy!" The hand snaps its pink sausage-like fingers.

The Boxer nods. "That's Mr. McDaniel," he stage whispers. "And he's a real big shot." His eyes narrow at Lili Belle. "So play nice."

Lili Belle glares back at him. "I've had bigger, dearie."

Unlike most men, McDaniel doesn't rise from his seat to greet us. Noisily, he chews on a toothpick, his eyes fixed on a cigarette girl two tables ahead.

"Hello, Mr. McDaniel," the Boxer says nervously. "This here is my jane, Wanda. Wanda, say hello to Mr. McDaniel."

"How do you do." I offer my hand to him, but he ignores it.

"And this," the Boxer says as he pushes Lili Belle forward. "This here's a present for *you.*"

McDaniel spits out his toothpick. His cheeks and neck flush scarlet as his eyes travel over Lili Belle's curves, coming to a stop at her Betty Boop-like face. "Christmas came early," he says, grinning with approval.

Lili Belle bares her teeth in a forced smile. "Hows about I call ya Santa, daddy?"

The name seems appropriate: Mr. McDaniel, with his white beard and bloated belly, resembles a Santa Claus, albeit one that fell out of a pawn shop on Skid Row.

"Good thing your fish paid upfront," Lili Belle whispers to me. She nods at the rings on Mr. McDaniel's hands. "Them jewels are paste."

"How can you tell?" I whisper back.

"Honey, it's a gift."

"You want a gift?" McDaniel asks, oblivious. "Sit down here, sweetheart, and tell Santa what ya want." He laughs and gestures to his lap. Lili Belle rolls her eyes at me before perching herself stiffly on his bent knees.

"How many couples are left?" The Boxer asks as he pulls out a chair for me.

"Three," McDaniel answers, his eyes still on Lili Belle. "They're just on a ten minute grub-and-go break." He checks his watch. "Should be back soon."

"Couples?" I ask. I had imagined that the show would be a girlie one—classier than the Apple Bottom of course, perhaps with more leg than breast, but a girlie show all the same. Couples though, now *that* really is class. "Like Fred and Ginger?"

McDaniel snorts. "Where'd ya find this dizzy broad, Billy? Sure, honey," he says, turning to me. "*Just* like Fred and Ginger. Only these folks put the 'rags' in 'glad rags.'"

"It's a dance marathon, Wanda," Lili Belle explains.

"A dance marathon?" I look around at the well-heeled audience in confusion.

"Ya ain't never heard of a dance marathon, blondie?" McDaniel sneers. "Where ya from, anyway?"

"Of course I've heard of dance marathons!" I snap. "I come from the Wor … from behind the Market. Some of my neighbours worked in them. I just didn't think that they'd hold marathons in a fancy joint like this, is all."

It was true: many of my friends had danced in these non-stop dance or walkathons. They considered it a job and why not? Where else would they get three square meals a day with the promise of a truckload full of heavy sugar at the end? If they made it to the end, of course.

"Behind the Market, huh?" McDaniel laughs cruelly. He stomps his feet, bouncing Lili Belle on his lap. "Baby's big night out!"

As though McDaniel's words were a cue, the tangerine velvet curtains open to reveal a shapely redhead in a silver bodysuit and fishnets. The audience hoots and whistles appreciatively as she raises a large sign above her head:

COUPLES REMAINING: 3
HOURS ELAPSED: 742

"Hullo! Hullo! Hullo!" I follow the booming voice to the upper right balcony, where a tiny man in a tuxedo clutches the stand of a wobbly microphone. He reminds me of Brock, with his compact body and ruby-cheeked face. A little toy soldier.

"*And* we're back! If your eyeballs made it all the way to Goldie's sign, then you know folks that we've only got three couples remaining: six people who have been dancing, sweating, *bleeding*, twenty-four hours a day, seven days a week for over a month! All in the name of hope, all with the virtue of faith! Hope that happy days are just around the corner! Faith that hard work *will* pay off. If you give it your all, if you never give up, if you *just keep dancing!*"

The crowd, including Lili Belle and the Boxer clap and cheer with delight. The emcee raises his hand for silence. "Yes, ladies and gentlemen, these are just ordinary folk, these dynamic dames and forgotten men. But *you* haven't forgotten them! And all because of *you* they have kept going. Because of *you* they are going to make it!" The audience roars as the three couples shuffle onstage. "For those of you who are just joining us tonight, allow me to introduce our courageous contestants, starting with *Stanley and Edith!*"

The eldest of the three couples squint under the glare of the spotlight. The man smiles charmingly, in spite of the fact that two-thirds of his teeth are missing. His tweed suit hangs loosely on his small frame and I can see his naked toes peeking out of his broken down shoes. He nudges his wife, a stout tired-looking woman with greasy dishwater hair and fat purple ankles. At his coaxing, she stretches her lips into a wide smile, her teeth shining yellow in the cruel light.

"I hear that congratulations are in order," the emcee bellows. "A little bird told me that just this morning, Stanley and Edith became grandparents to a healthy baby boy!"

The audience claps warmly as Stanley dances a wobbly jig. A few people throw nickels and dimes at the stage, which Edith quickly retrieves, stuffing them into her rolled up stockings.

"And speaking of babies…" The spotlight quickly moves on to a much younger couple, the boy looking around eighteen, the girl no more than sixteen, if a day. "Let's give a big hand for our newlyweds, *Frank and Olive!*"

Frank waves his newsboy cap shyly at the cheering crowd as his wife blushes under a curtain of honey-blonde hair. A portly woman wearing a stuffed bird on her head and a dead fox slung around her neck, jumps up and blows kisses toward the stage. Frank and Olive are clearly an audience favourite and it's easy to see why: Olive is pregnant. As in ready-to-pop pregnant; her swollen belly straining against the thin flowery material of her faded dress. Unlike the other contestants, Olive isn't wearing any shoes: misplaced bones jut out from the sides of her claw-like feet, the toes curled under painfully.

"My money's on them two," McDaniel says.

"You kiddin'?" The Boxer asks, his mouth agape. "Look at that dame's dogs! She can barely stand!"

"Don't matter." McDaniel squeezes Lili Belle's thigh as he reaches across the table for his beer. "I've been goin' to these here marathons since twenty-nine and if I've learned one thing, it's this: tha hungrier they are, tha harder they dance." He raises his drink. "I haven't lost a bet yet."

"Well, my money's on Maude and Charlie." The Boxer nods as the spotlight settles on a sturdy, rather ordinary looking couple in their early thirties. The two wear matching red and white sweaters with the Whipplebum soap logo emblazoned across the front.

"Mr. Whipplebum loves these marathons," Lili Belle whispers to me. "He always sponsors whichever couple looks the healthiest. Gosh, I hope that bloated ol' bugger isn't here tonight."

"Me too," I say, scanning the room nervously. The last thing that my garter purse needs is for Mr. Whipplebum to tell the Boxer that I have the clap.

The orchestra strikes up "Smile, Darn Ya, Smile!" as the contestants shuffle about the stage. "For eleven hundred clams!" the emcee loudly informs us.

"Eleven hundred dollars," I whistle. "What I couldn't do with *that.*"

"It ain't hay," Lili Belle nods in agreement. McDaniel wraps his arms around her waist and she giggles as he whispers something in her ear. Moments later, I notice two sawbucks stuffed down her right stocking. Twenty dollars and she didn't even have to do anything more than giggle. That dame rolls more dough than a baker.

"Whatcha drinkin', doll?" The Boxer snaps me out of my reverie. I begin to order a whiskey and soda before remembering that the drink isn't very ladylike.

"Gin Blossom," I answer, smiling at him sweetly.

The scantily clad waitress who takes our order reminds me of Queenie, with her raven hair and green eyes. I surreptitiously watch the Boxer for interest in her, but he seems oblivious to her charms. The Boxer likes bottle blondes. It's strange how much stock some men put in a dame's hair colour, I think as I watch Queenie's double sashay toward the bar, her body shaped like a violin. I feel tingly, remembering Queenie's hand on my belly, her mouth on my nipples. Maybe Eddie could look her up sometime—the three of us could have a tumble.

"Kiss me, doll," the Boxer whispers, shooting a glance over at McDaniel. "Act like ya like me."

"I don't have to act, big boy." I crawl onto his lap and plant a kiss under his ear. I'm a lot heavier than Lili Belle but the Boxer can handle it.

"Hows about we shake things up a little?" The emcee's smile is wide enough to swallow his microphone whole. Goldie, the dame in the silver lamé, has corralled the dancers off to stage right.

"On your mark!" The audience cheers the command in unison. "Get set!"

Goldie wraps her red lips around a nickel whistle. "*Go!*"

Grinning like thirsty dogs, Maude and Charlie lead the race to the tune of Pop Goes the Weasel. Behind them, Edith props Stanley up by his armpits, lugging him around the stage as he holds a hand to his heart in panic. Coming up last are Frank and Olive, the latter's bare toes dragging across the polished floor like dirty knuckles. As the music speeds up, Olive wraps her arms around Frank's neck, her eyes and mouth open wide in a silent amaranthine scream—a grotesque Halloween mask—while she struggles to stay erect. The audience holds its collective breath as her legs suddenly give out and she topples forward, threatening to bring Frank down with her.

"Knees can't touch the floor!" The emcee shouts. "If her knees touch the floor, she's out!""

Olive crouches centre stage, holding her body up by the palms of her hands; her knees and her belly are inches away from the floor. "*Ee-oowwww!*" she howls.

"Get up, honey," Frank gently coaxes. "You can do it."

"You can do it, Olive!" The fat bird woman jumps up from her seat, a handkerchief pressed to her painted cheek. "Think of the baby!"

"Yes, Olive." Frank bends down beside her. "Think of our baby!"

Olive looks up at Frank and then out at the bird woman. The theatre reverberates with the sound of cracking teeth as she belly flops to the floor.

Two uniformed nurses advance from the wings and rush toward the splayed out girl. Olive turns her head toward the audience, smiling peacefully. She shuts her eyes as the stage curtains close.

"She'll be okay," the Boxer reassures me as the four of us leave the Orange Blossom.

"Sure, honey," Lili Belle agrees. "It's a mighty shame though. All that dancing for nothing."

We stand in a circle outside the nightclub, the men suddenly quiet. McDaniel keeps his gaze set on Lili Belle, who pretends not to notice. When she slips a Lucky out of her clutch purse, both McDaniel and I go to light it. Ignoring the old man's waning flame, Lili Belle leans toward me, cupping my hand with both of hers as she sparks her snipe. Exhaling, she gently takes the lighter from me and turns it over in her palm.

"WWB," she winks at me as she runs a manicured finger over Mr. Whipplebum's engraved initials. "Nice work, sister."

McDaniel whispers something in the Boxer's ear.

"Say, that's a swell idea!" the Boxer exclaims with forced enthusiasm. He turns to me. "Say Wanda, how about we move this party back to your place?"

I smile up at him, blinking my eyes. "Whatever you say, big boy." Lili Belle shoots me a worried look and my grin falters. "Only, I think Lili Belle has to turn in early tonight, don't you dear?"

"That's right!" Lili Belle says, smiling at me in gratitude. She nods at the men. "A dame my age needs all the beauty sleep she can muster!"

"I can help you out there." McDaniel snakes an arm around Lili Belle's waist. "I'll tell ya a bedtime story that'll give you *lots* of sweet dreams." He waves to an oncoming cab. "What way ya goin' honey?"

"Whatever way you're *not* going, sugar!" Lili Belle attempts a run for the cab but McDaniel pulls her back and grabs her roughly by the shoulders.

"Listen you dirty whore!" He screams, spraying tiny droplets of saliva over Lili Belle's finely painted face. "I paid good money for you!"

"Oh yeah? Well *this* bank's folded!" Lili Belle squirms helplessly as she attempts to extract herself from his embrace. "Get your hands offa me!"

I tug at the Boxer's sleeve. "Oh, Billy, do something!"

He shrugs. "Whaddaya want *me* to do, doll?"

As another taxicab pulls up to the curb, Lili Belle lunges for it. McDaniel gets her in a headlock and spins her around. "Ya ain't goin' nowhere, bitch!"

"Oh stop it!" I cry. "Leave her alone!"

McDaniel glances up at us as though he's surprised we're still here. "Shut yer whore up, Billy!"

He turns back to Lili Belle just as she's slipping off her high-heeled shoe. Swinging her arm forward, she smacks McDaniel across the face with it.

"Take that, you mug!" Lili Belle drops her shoe and jumps into the cab as a startled McDaniel rubs his swollen cheek.

"Well how do ya like that?" McDaniel's tone is now light. He spits on the ground as the cab drives off. "I know I told ya that I like 'em feisty, Billy," he says as he bends down to pick up Lili Belle's discarded shoe. "But that's a little too much fire even for *me*!"

"It wasn't anything less than you deserve!" I say, snatching the high heel from his hands. "And you!" I point at the Boxer accusingly. "Why didn't you do anything to help her?"

"Aw, shucks, doll." The Boxer looks down at his feet. "Mr. McDaniel was just foolin' with her. Weren't you?"

"Sure," McDaniel says, his eyes dark. "I was jus' foolin' with her."

"Wanda," the Boxer says sheepishly. "Maybe next time you could bring along a different friend." He shifts his gaze to McDaniel self-consciously. "Someone, uh, a little *friendlier.*"

"Say, yer talkin' like the night is over!" McDaniel wraps an arm around the Boxer's shoulders. "We've still got yer girlie here." He grins at me, flashing sharp teeth the colour of gold. "Hows about a little party of three?"

The Boxer rubs the back of his neck nervously. He understands as well as I do what McDaniel is proposing but I know that I don't have to worry about being the meat in a Boxer-McDaniel sandwich: the last thing Billy wants is for his manager to find out that his hotdog plays dead instead of go fetch.

"Why don't we go down to the Stone's Throw?" The Boxer ventures. "We'll pick up another girl for you there. Why, I know a dame who'll knock your socks off…"

"Aw, Billy." McDaniel thumps the Boxer loudly on the back. "Didn't yer mommy ever teach ya to share yer toys?" He reaches out for me and I stumble backwards, recoiling in disgust.

"Don't touch me!" I hold Lili Belle's shoe out as though it's a handgun. "You–you–you dirty two-bit Santy Claus!"

McDaniel's laughter is like a closed fist. "Yer little filly needs some breakin' in, Billy," he says, his breath reeking of armpit and onions. "Better let me ride 'er first."

The Boxer looks away as McDaniel lurches toward me. Raising my arm, I stab him square in the eye with the heel of Lili Belle's shoe.

"*AHHH-WOOO!*"

McDaniel falls backward into the Boxer's open arms.

"Y-you okay, Mr. McDaniel?" The Boxer stammers.

"Yer bitch!" McDaniel cries, his hand over his eye. "Yer bitch blinded me!" He swings around, pulling the Boxer into a violent bear hug. "She's gonna pay fer this! *Yer* gonna fuckin' pay for this!"

The Boxer holds his arms out in meek protest as McDaniel shoves him against the stained glass door of the Orange Blossom. Quietly, I slip into a checkered taxicab, leaving the two men to fight their battle alone.

"The Grand Palace Hotel, please," I say to the driver. I glance out the car's window as the cab pulls away. Oblivious to my departure, McDaniel and the Boxer clutch at each other's sweaty bodies, wrestling under the flashing hot lights of the city.

It looks as though they are dancing.

21. PETER PICKUP

THE BEST THING ABOUT BEING a "lady of the evening" is that I get to spend my days at the flickers. This afternoon, I watched *Anna Karenina* three times in a row—adrift in Garbo's smoke and cheekbones. Disappearing under the wheels of an oncoming train, Anna Karenina lost all and gave everything. *What do I have to give?* I wonder as I exit the movie theatre. Sugar, of course. Filthy sugar stuffed into little white envelopes to send home to Mama. I slip my hands into the pockets of my fox coat. I'd like a new fur coat with a giant hood, like the one that Garbo wears in her first scene at the train station. Yes, that's exactly what I would like.

I cross the street where another skyscraper is going up, fighting for space among the clouds, bouncing up against the sun. A small grey tabby cat slinks by me, the soft steady *tap-tap-tap* of her little white paws lending a melody to the concrete cacophony of the city. I like the way she walks: like Jean Harlow or like I do when I've got my high heels and girdle on. The cat jumps onto the hood of an ice truck and, after careful calculation of the distance, leaps into the open window of an apartment above a boarded up chili parlor. Evelyn once told me that cats are closer to God than humans could ever hope of being. She said that's why they have all of life's answers. I asked her if that's true, then why don't they share some of their wisdom with us? Evelyn said that they try, but humans are simply not smart enough to understand.

I wish the cat had jumped into *my* open window instead. It'd be nice to have her around. Probably the closest I'll ever get to God.

Passersby in their polo shirts, short-sleeved spectator dresses, and straw hats turn to stare curiously at me in my fox. So what? The cat is still wearing her fur coat, too. It's called glamour, honey. Look it up.

I light a cigarette and lean up against my usual spot, outside the entrance of Mr. Manchester's apartment building. Irving peeks out at me through the dingy yellow drapes of the Grand Palace Hotel, licking his lips. He thinks that I'm working. Well he's right, ain't he? I'm always working.

The merry-go-round doors spit out man after man: middle-aged men in drape suits and wide-brimmed fedoras; young men wearing plus-fours and flat caps. A few of the men pass by me as though I am a potted plant, but most of them turn to gawk at me, either surreptitiously peering at me sideways under their hat brims or leering at me dead-on. The leering ones I don't like; they remind me of the nastier customers that Eddie sometimes brings me, with their twisted smiles and eyes like violence. The kind who don't actually hit me, but whose stare is enough to leave me confined to my bed for most of the next day.

None of the men, though, mean or nice, look at me in the way that Mr. Manchester did on that first day we met.

Shading my eyes, I look up at his apartment window. The curtains are closed. Not that I would really be able to see inside anyway. I picture him opening the brown paper package, slipping out the sparkly dress and lifting the silky cool fabric to his face as he inhales my scent. Even if it made him remember for only a moment, it would all be worth it.

My daydream is interrupted by the clanging bells of the Catholic church a block away. Six o'clock. Time for supper. Time for my real work. I take one last look at Mr. Manchester's window before heading back. I've got a hunk of bread and some leftover tuna in my tiny icebox. I'll need to scarf it all down before Eddie brings home the bacon. I like to drink on the job and the men like it when I do, too, but I have learned that drinking on an empty stomach is just riding for a fall. Best to keep my wits when I'm pulling a trick.

"Hello, Beautiful, are you waiting for someone?"

The young uniformed copper grins down at me. Under the brim of his policeman's visor, all I can see are teeth. My eyes travel toward the gun in his holster and I contemplate making a run before deciding to play it straight.

"Why, yes," I answer. I drop my chin and shyly look up at him through my eyelashes. "My sweetheart said for me to meet him here." I reach into my handbag and take out a hankie to dab at the corners of my eyes. "But I guess he ain't coming."

"Now that *is* a crime." The copper's grin grows wider, his teeth bigger. "Making a pretty girl wait like that."

"Much obliged for the compliment," I nod, stepping out of his shadow. "Now, if you'll excuse me, officer."

"Where was he going to take you?"

"Pardon?"

"Your fellow. He was going to take you out somewhere, wasn't he?"

"Oh, yes. We were going to go to the movies."

"That Garbo picture?"

"Yes," I say, backing away from him. "But I guess I'll be going home now..."

"Oh, no, you're not." The copper grabs me by the forearm and steers me in the direction of the movie theatre. "You didn't get all dolled up for nothing. I'll take you to the picture show myself." I still can't see his eyes, but his wolfish smile looks ready to swallow me whole.

"Oh, I couldn't ask you to do that..."

"Why not? I'm on a break and besides," he says, flashing his sharp wet teeth. "I'm friendly."

Said the spider to the fly, I think. His grip tightens on my arm as we make our way to the theatre. I wonder if he knows what I am, but if he does, he isn't taking me to the slammer—he's taking me to the movies. As though he's reading my mind, the copper removes his cap and winks at me. My first street pick-up, I realize, relaxing. My first street pick-up and he's a flatfoot. What would Evelyn say about *that*?

"What's your name, girlie?" The copper asks me as we settle into the plush red seats at the back of the theatre. I cradle the glass gravy boat in my lap. Wednesday is dish night at the movies. Not that I have any use for a gravy boat, but Mama will like it. I'll mail it to her with my tips.

"Jean," I tell him. "My name is Jean."

"Like Harlow?"

"Yes, just like Harlow."

"You don't look like Jean Harlow," the policeman says. I can see his eyes now and they are blue. Very, very blue. He puts his small-for-a-cop hand on my knee. "You're much prettier than she is."

"Nobody's prettier than Jean Harlow," I say.

"You are." The copper's hand crawls up my skirt. He squeezes my thigh. "I'm Officer Brent, but you can call me Peter."

Peter Pickup, I think, smiling.

I put the gravy boat down on the seat beside me. The theatre has started filling up with people. Those interested in watching the movie take the front and middle seats, while those who are just interested in each other sit in the back. I cross my legs and clamp Peter's hand tightly between my thighs, blocking his path.

"Whatsa matter?"

"Oh, nothing," I answer, sniffling. I snap open my purse and remove my crumpled up handkerchief again. "It's just that my sweetheart…"

"Oh, jeez," Peter groans. "We're *still* playing this game?"

"What game?" I ask, wide-eyed. "I *do* have a sweetheart a-a-and…" I press the hankie to my mouth and let out a sob.

"And *what*?" Peter asks, clearly annoyed.

"Oh, I don't want to bother you with my problems..." I flutter my eyelashes at him, Joan Blondell style.

"You're already botherin' me."

"Well, you see, I'm just a factory girl ...that's right, I had a job packing candy in a bon-bon factory until just last week." I bow my head and cough into my handkerchief.

Peter Pickup sighs. "And let me guess, you lost your job," he says drolly. "And you need some dough."

I nod. "My sweetheart said he'd bring me some money for rent. You see, I'm already two months behind and my landlord's threatening to change the locks!" I cry into my hankie.

Peter's hand tenses between my thighs. A busty, moon-faced brunette fills the screen as the pre-show begins. "I'm really not a bad girl," she says, snapping her gum. Off camera, a male voice asks her if she knew that her former lover, the notorious gangster, Nicky "Knockers" Caprelli, orchestrated the Easter Sunday bloodbath: ten members of a rival gang were lined up against the wall of a speakeasy and shot in the back, execution style. "I don't know nothin'," the moll says, her heavily lidded eyes rolling toward the ceiling. "I never did know nothin'."

Peter Pickup shifts in his seat. Out of the corner of my eye I see him reach into his pants pocket with his free hand and take out his billfold.

"How much is rent?" he whispers.

"Fifty bucks," I whisper back.

"Fifty dollars?" He yanks his hand free from my thighs. "That's some pretty high rent!"

"Worth every penny," I answer as I unclasp the top of my fur coat. I only wear a half slip on Wednesdays. The copper's Adam's apple bobs up and down to the tune of the "Follow the Bouncing Ball" musical short now playing on the screen as he stares at my bare breasts, glowing like white grapefruits under the light of the movie projector.

"I only got a sawbuck," he says, his voice hoarse.

"Then *I* only got to watch the movie." I snap my coat shut.

"No wait, please." Peter opens his billfold. "Oh, hey, whattaya know! I got *two* sawbucks!"

"Whattaya know," I say, dryly.

"Well," he leans in close to me, his thin baby lips brushing my ear. "Will you take twenty?"

"What do you think this is, anyway? A flop house? Will I take twenty!" I scoff indignantly.

"It's all I got," Peter Pickup says, his eyes pleading.

I turn to the screen and feign interest in a cartoon tap dancing cow. When he makes a move to slip the money back into his wallet, I realize that this time he wasn't bluffing.

"Fine," I say. I snatch the bills from his hairless diminutive hand and stuff them into the pocket of my coat. "If that's all you got."

The copper closes his eyes as I reach over and unbutton his fly. Part of me is glad that he only gave me twenty; I don't get down on my knees for less than fifty and besides, I don't want to miss Garbo's entrance at the train station.

Hours later in my hotel room, I remove the copper's pistol from my handbag. I run my hand along its cool shaft before placing it in the third dresser door, beside my whiskey flask, the stolen portrait of Mr. Manchester, and the Bible. I don't like guns but a girl like me needs more than just shoes to get by.

22. LOLLIPOPS AND TUMMY ACHES

I TIE THE GREEN RIBBON AROUND the door knob and into a tight bow as a signal to Eddie that I'm ready for my next customer. With the exception of Peter Pickup on Wednesday, it's been a slow week. Thankfully, the Monocle Man visited earlier this evening. He always tips well. Slipping into a pair of orchid-white silk beach pajamas, I take a swig from my hip flask and count out my earnings, deducting Eddie's cut and putting my tips away in an envelope for Mama. Every Monday, I mail all of my tips from the previous week to her, but I still haven't scrounged up enough courage to include a letter.

Eddie raps on the door, his signature two-four-two knock. I hope that he's reeled in a fat, juicy one. A wealthy whale of a widower or a stock trader shark would be nice.

"Whatcha brung for me, Eddie?"

He stands in the doorway, holding his hat in his hands. "I'm sorry, doll," he says sheepishly. "Da mug wouldn't take no for an answer."

Eddie steps aside as Brock pushes forward.

"Miss Wanda!" Brock's soldier blue eyes gape at me in wonder. "Is it really you? Gee, you look different."

"Y-y-you look different, too, Brock," I stammer. It's true and although I don't say it, he also looks very elegant, having traded in his checkered vaudeville jacket for a charcoal grey double-breasted wool suit.

I look past him to Eddie who shrugs apologetically. "Dis bird heard I knew where to find ya and..."

"I've been looking *everywhere!*" Brock emphatically cries, wrapping his arms around me in a cloud of Boraxo and Brylcreem.

Eddie punches his cap and shifts his feet. "S'okay if I leave you kids?" he asks, clearly uncomfortable. "I'm the town clown tonight; only five minute fares, 'cepting this mug." He nods at Brock.

"Sure, Eddie," I say, wiggling out of Brock's embrace. "Say," I dig into the pocket of my pajamas. "Here's your cut for the Monocle Man."

Brock watches in confusion as I hand the wad of bills over to Eddie, who tips his hat to me in embarrassment.

"What was that about, Miss Wanda?" Brock asks, after Eddie leaves. "Why were you giving him money?"

I flop backwards into the overstuffed organdy chair. "Business deal," I yawn, stretching my arms out to the ceiling.

"What kind of business?"

Brock stares at me intently, the roses fading from his apple cheeks. The sweet voice of Shirley Temple crawls out of the mouth of my neighbour's phonograph, singing a song about chocolate bars and lollipops and tummy aches. The music swells suddenly, like a gust of wind, and then just as quickly disappears. I look back at Brock. The air in the room has gone still. It's like pulling petals from a daisy or stealing a sugar tit from a baby. It's not right, but it's too easy.

"What kind of 'business' do you think, honey?"

Brock slowly shakes his head back and forth, as though trying to push away the meaning of my words.

"This isn't you, Miss Wanda." He falls on his knees before me and takes my hands in his. "I know that this isn't you."

"Really?" I snap, pulling my hands away. "Aren't I the kind of dame who steals husbands? Oh, no," I laugh bitterly. "That's right, I'm the type of girl who *borrows* them."

"Miss Wanda, you know why I made those jokes." Brock hangs his head, his lush eyelashes casting shadows on his pretty pink face. "You hurt me, Miss Wanda. That night at the Stone's Throw was like a knife to my heart."

I slip off the chair, joining him on the dusty rose carpet. "I'm no good, Brock," I whisper sincerely. "I'm sorry."

"That isn't true, Miss Wanda! None of this is your fault." He takes my hands again. "Everything became so clear to me the day that you left the Apple Bottom."

"What became clear?"

"Everything—the Stone's Throw, your flash house act…" Brock squeezes my hands firmly. "He used you, didn't he?"

"Who did?"

"Mr. Manchester."

I nod, turning away from him. "Yes, Brock, he did."

"I knew it!" Brock jumps up. "I told you that he was a masher, Miss Wanda. I tried to warn you." He begins pacing the room, his hands clenched behind his back. "Oh, I've seen it before! A man like him sees a girl like you, as fresh and as untouched as a field of clover after a rainstorm. But men like Mr. Manchester can't appreciate such momentary beauty, can they? Why? Because you can't buy a moment of beauty and men like Mr. Manchester can't appreciate anything that they can't buy! So what does he do?" Brock crouches down with his hands on his thighs and glares at me. "Does he resign himself to just gazing at the field? Allow himself to simply admire it? *No!*" He slaps his palm against his fist. "No, if he can't own such beauty then he must plunder it, *destroy* it! Oh, yes, Miss Wanda," Brock continues, "I don't need you to sing me the song, I already know all the words by heart. You," he points a finger at me. "You, a sweet girl, a *nice* girl, were lured to the Apple Bottom under false pretences. You, an innocent babe who thought that she'd be hoofing in the chorus, like Ruby Keeler in a Busby Berkeley musical. You didn't know you'd have to take your clothes off. You didn't know that stepping onstage at the Apple Bottom was akin to falling down the rabbit hole: a downward spiral of *sin* and *sex*!" He shouts the last words out as though speaking into a bullhorn. "Oh, Miss Wanda," Brock sighs, collapsing on the floor beside me. "How could I have ever blamed *you?*"

His speech has exhausted me. I lean into him, my head dropping to his shoulder, my insides feeling like so much rumpled dirty laundry. "I don't know why you're here, Brock. I don't understand why you like me."

"Like you? Why honey, I'm bugs about ya! Ever since that day you walked in on me in my drawers," Brock smiles and nudges my chin between his thumb and forefinger. "Remember that day, Miss Wanda?"

I nod, smiling. "Yes, Brock. You were so nice to me."

"I knew then how special you were. I knew that a sweet girl like you didn't belong in a joint like the Apple Bottom. Do you remember, Miss Wanda, how you told me all about your dreams of having a husband and lots of babies?"

I don't remember telling him any such thing, but the look on his face is so open and earnest that I second guess myself.

"And do you remember," he continues, "How I told you that I wanted to quit my gig at the Apple Bottom and become a reporter?"

He pulls a piece of newspaper out from his jacket pocket and unfolds it on the carpet in front of us. A large photograph of a bespeckled, unsmiling man accompanies the paper's headline: JOSEPH BREEN KEEPS IT CLEAN!

The proceeding article goes on to praise the Motion Picture Production Code Administrator and his one-year-old amended Code to "govern the making of motion and talking pictures," particularly the Code's promise to ban "Communistic propaganda" from the screen. Wedged in the upper right corner of the column is a tiny black-and-white headshot of a frowning, Trilby-hatted Brock.

"Brock Baxter: Reporter to the *Town Star*!" I read the byline out loud, wrapping my arms around his waist. "You did it, Brock! You've really made it!"

"Part one of my dream accomplished," Brock points his index finger in the air, drawing an imaginary checkmark. "Now I just need to work on part two." He smiles at me shyly.

I look away from him, blushing. "You could get a nice girl now," I muse. "A respectable girl who works at the bank, or maybe a stenographer. Or perhaps a girl who doesn't need to work at all, say a socialite from a wealthy family."

"I had a girl like that. Oh, not a socialite, mind you," Brock laughs at my dumbfounded expression. "Once upon a time, I was engaged to a nice girl who worked in a legal office."

"What happened?"

"I gave her the air," he laughs again, tugging gently at my bleached hair. "I guess I'm just a sucker for a certain platinum blonde."

I laugh along with him. "You're a swell fella, Brock. It's been a long time since someone made me smile like this."

Brock jumps up and grabs me by the hands excitedly. "What are you doing tomorrow, Miss Wanda?"

"Nothing. I don't have anything planned."

"Well, now you do! I'm picking you up at twelve noon for lunch." Brock spins me around the room in a waltz, stopping by the door. "Until tomorrow, my beautiful girl."

I part my lips and tilt my head back, but when he leans in, it's only to plant a dry kiss on my cheek. "Not yet, Miss Wanda," he whispers. "But soon."

We wave goofily to each other while he waits for the lift. After the bellboy slides the elevator doors shut, I untie the green ribbon from my doorknob and let it fall limply to the floor.

"It's rather warm for a fur coat, dear."

"You're right, Brock," I laugh in embarrassment as I toss the fur into the backseat of his modest Pontiac Six. "I guess I keep forgetting that it's summer."

I'm a bit abashed by the plainness of my Sunday shirtwaist but it's the only dress I own that I figured Brock, who himself looks both smart and cool in a crisp linen suit with slightly cuffed trousers, would approve of.

"Where to, Miss Wanda?" Brock tips his straw boater hat and winks at me. "I know a swell French bistro with an outdoor patio, which isn't too far from here."

I shake my head, knowing that I wouldn't fit in at a place like that. "It's such a lovely day, Brock. I'd rather go to the boardwalk."

"That's what I love about you, Miss Wanda," Brock says, beaming. "You have the face of a movie star but the simple heart of a farm girl. There's not a materialistic bone in your beautiful body."

Brock parks his motorcar close to the lake, disrupting a gang of seagulls whose eardrum-busting shrieks make no secret of their annoyance.

"Flying rats," I nod at the birds. "That's what my Daddy used to call them. Rats with wings."

"Flying rats," Brock laughs as he helps me out of the car. "I like that. How did your daddy die, Miss Wanda?"

"How do you know he died?" I ask sharply. "I never told you that."

Brock looks taken aback. "I'm sorry, Miss Wanda. I just figured, because you talked about him in the past tense..."

"Oh. Well, my Daddy died in the war," I say quickly, re-gaining my ground. "That's right. He was a war hero, had lots of medals and things like that." I draw the words out, like a magician pulling brightly-coloured silk scarves from his sleeve. "He captured a German soldier, to um, you know, gather intelligence. His death ended up saving, oh, about five hundred or so men."

"A war hero!" Brock echoes, squeezing my hand. "But you must have been just a tot," he continues, his eyebrows knitted in confusion. "Why you couldn't have been any older than two or three when he died. How exactly did he die though? Did the Germans..."

I take a handkerchief out of my pocket and bring it to my mouth. "I don't want to talk about this," I say, coughing into the hankie.

"Of course not," Brock puts his arm around my shoulders in sympathy and gently guides me toward the boardwalk.

The beach strikes me as rather desolate for such a sunny afternoon. Although, it may be a workday. I really don't know anymore, having lost track of my days a long time ago. A middle-aged woman dressed in a tattered house wrap sits on a large block of ice and sells bottles of soda pop for a nickel. Brock gives her a quarter dollar for two, grandly advising her to keep the change.

Ahead of us, a beach inspector corrals a group of doughy unemployed shop girls into a lineup. Using a wooden ruler, he measures the distance between each girl's bathing suit bottom and right knee cap. Scantily clad offenders, he makes clear, will be promptly booted off the beach.

Brock takes a sip of his cola, his eyes lazily grazing the plump knees and thick thighs of the inspector's herd. "Do you own a swimsuit, Miss Wanda?"

"No."

"Good," Brock nods. "I think the styles today are positively vulgar." He continues to stare at the girls, his jaw tense. "They look like nothing more than an exhibition—an exhibition of flesh!"

"I showed a lot more when I worked at the Apple Bottom," I remind him.

"That was different," he says, frowning at my mention of the burlesque theatre. "You didn't have a choice."

"Say, Mister, wanna take your girl for a ride?"

A boy of about nine, all peach fuzz and jutting bones, gestures toward a battered baby blue rowboat, lying face down by the water's edge. Brock tips his hat at the child and, bending at the waist, meets him at eye level. "How much, little man?"

"Uh..." the boy shifts his feet. "Maybe a quarter?"

The boat isn't his, I'm sure of it and I think Brock knows it, too, but he pays the kid anyway. "I'll have her back in an hour," Brock says to the boy, tossing a wink in my direction.

"Gee, thanks, Mister!" The boy happily runs in the direction of a hot dog stand as Brock turns the vessel over and pushes it toward the lake.

"Come, honey." He steps carefully into the boat and holds out his hand. "I can't think of anything nicer than a boat ride with my favourite girl."

"I don't know how to swim, Brock," I say. The boat rocks unsteadily as I take hold of his outstretched hand. Below us, the water looks like glass, a mirror without a frame. Only, if I fall in, I won't cut myself, I'll just disappear.

"Don't worry, Miss Wanda," Brock smiles confidently as he lifts the boat's oars. "I know how to swim and I'd never let anything happen to you. Ever."

Brock has removed his suit jacket. He isn't wearing a vest—young men seldom do anymore, thanks to Clark Gable—and his unbuttoned sleeves are rolled up around his elbows. He grunts softly as he raises the oars, sighing loudly as they strike the water. In contrast, both the lake and the clouds in the sky are strangely peaceful, as though they are sleeping. I start to relax. I've always liked Brock, but he's never, as Lili Belle would put it, "gotten me hot." Watching him like this, though—under the lazy sky, damp patches forming under his arms—I have the sudden urge to rip his shirt apart with my teeth, press my mouth against his flesh, and mop his sweat up with my tongue.

Brock stops rowing and smiles at me sybaritically, as though he's reading my mind. Kicking my shoes off, I hike up the skirt of my dress and begin to unroll my stockings. Immediately, Brock's smile collapses into a thin, disapproving line. I pull my dress back down, over my knees.

"That's a very pretty dress," Brock says, as he struggles to rearrange his face.

"Thank you." I look down at the careworn frock, with its faded white daisies. "It's just a rag, though. I don't have many day dresses."

"Is that so?"

"Well, working at the Apple Bottom and then the Bow Tie," I shrug. "Most of my gowns are flashy and I guess a little too over the top for everyday wear."

Brock grabs the oars and furiously spins the boat back in the direction of the boardwalk. At first I think he's angry that I've mentioned the Apple Bottom again, but when he looks up at me, he's grinning.

"What are you doing?" I ask, holding on to the sides of the rowboat for balance. "I thought you said we'd stay out here for an hour."

Brock's smile widens. Under the shade of his straw boater, all I can see are teeth. "It's a surprise."

The Blondell perfume girls lift their pastel-powdered faces as Brock passes by, like a row of tulips opening in the sun. Their pebble blue eyes skip over me and although I try to tell myself that it's the hair, deep down I know that it is simply the passage of time; my old work chums have forgotten me.

"Fox fur, like to touch?" An auburn-haired girl in a silver fox fur coat smiles charmingly at Brock. The colours fall from my eyes as she stretches her arm out toward him. I feel as though I am standing on the other side of a screen, watching a movie about dead people. Roughly, I grab Brock by the hand, ripping him out of the scene.

"What's the matter, Miss Wanda?"

"Nothing," I shrug as Brock blinks at me in puzzlement. "It's just strange being back. I used to work here as a model," I explain and Brock's eyes widen with a mixture of admiration and shock.

"On the level? Why, Miss Wanda, that's swell! Where's the hiring office?" he asks, craning his neck. "I bet we could get you your old job back!"

"No," I say firmly. "That's not possible."

"Why not?"

"Brock, why did you bring me here?" I ask, both to change the topic and out of genuine curiosity.

"It's pay day."

"So?"

"So, I'm all paid up for the month; my landlady's satisfied. Now, I've got a few nickels and dimes left over to play with," he winks at me. "So why not buy a pretty dress for my pretty girl?"

"Oh, Brock!" I wrap my arms around his neck. "You're the berries! No fella has ever taken me clothes shopping before."

"Really?" Brock's smile is both pleased and sceptical. "No fellow has ever bought you anything before—dresses, jewellery, a fur coat?"

"Well…" I hesitate. "No, never!" I smile as Brock puffs out his chest, prouder than a rooster.

He signals for a sales girl just as a sporty-looking model clad in checkered culottes and brandishing a tennis racket struts toward us.

"Isn't she darling?" I clutch Brock's forearm and nod at the model's wide legged pants. "Oh, Brock, I'd love a pair of culottes!"

"No, honey. Absolutely not." Brock shakes his head firmly as the model passes. "They aren't proper or ladylike."

"Good afternoon, sir. Welcome to Blondell's."

Ann, looking both proper and ladylike in her store dress-code approved navy blue double-breasted belted suit, focuses her smile onto Brock. "It's getting quite warm outside? We have a spanking new assortment of summery hats and suits?"

"Actually, we're shopping for the lady." Brock pushes me forward. "I was thinking of something high necked with frills."

"Wanda!" Ann's painted pink mouth falls open. "I almost didn't recognize you with that *hair!*"

I run my fingers through my shorn tresses self-consciously. I haven't been to the beauty salon in over a month. With my thick roots growing in, I'm beginning to resemble an albino-ginger skunk.

"It's been a while, Ann. I was just telling my friend Mr. Baxter here how I used to work at Blondell's as a model. Gee, I wish I'd never have quit." I hold her goggle-eyed gaze steadily, silently daring her to contradict me.

"Yes..." Ann looks from me to Brock in puzzlement. "But you did well for yourself," she smiles, attempting to regain her ground. "I read about you in the papers—Wanda Wiggles! Wow!"

"That wasn't me."

"Oh, I just figured with the red hair and the..." She looks down at my bosom, her face turning as pink as her lipstick. "Well, the newspaper stories started coming out just after you were fi—, I mean after you left ... and after you met that gentleman with the funny eyes..."

"It wasn't me." I stuff my hands in the pockets of my dress, my fingernails itching for Ann's face.

"You must have Miss Wanda confused with another beauty." Brock extends his hand to Ann. "Brock Baxter," he says by way of introduction. "Also a former associate of Miss Wanda's." He smiles congenially at Ann. "Now, we are looking for a new day frock for our friend here. Something darling and ducky. Nothing too showy, mind you."

"Of course, sir." The lilt returns to her voice as Ann slips back on her salesgirl mask. "I have the perfect idea of what you are looking for. I'll find you both a fitting room?"

Entering the Blondell fitting room feels like stepping into my first bath in Bed Bug Babylon. I've been in these fitting rooms before, of course, but only as a model. Back then, I was made to walk slowly in tiny circles along the plush marshmallow carpet, being careful to move my ankles and not my hips. I'd had to pull invisible shades down over my eyes and smile vacantly at the customers, never taking in the gold brocade curtains, the royal ornate mirrors, or the sinfully scarlet furnishings.

I sink into the cherry velvet sofa and clasp a hand over my mouth to stop from giggling. Brock removes his boater and sits down beside me.

"Are you ashamed of your time at the Apple Bottom?" He picks up my hand, bringing it to his lips. "I'm so glad if you are."

"I don't know if I'm ashamed, exactly," I say. I stifle a moan as he presses his mouth against my palm. "It's just..."

"It's just that you didn't want your friend to judge you." Brock nods as he finishes my sentence. "I understand, Miss Wanda. The boys down at the office gave me a real ribbing when they found out that I used to work there."

"Brock, you said something earlier." I snuggle into him. "You called me your 'girl.' Am I, Brock? Am I really your girl?"

"Yes, honey," Brock says. He pulls me closer and kisses the top of my head. "At least I want you to be. If only..."

"I'll leave the racket," I say. "I'll tell Eddie I'm through."

"Miss Wanda, that makes me so happy. Why, you're the most marvellous..."

I close my eyes and part my lips as Brock cups my face between his hands.

"A lady's day suit from our new collection?"

Brock quickly drops his hands to his sides as Ann enters the fitting room with a model in tow. The beautiful girl struts before us, toe-heel-toe, in a plum-coloured wool suit, her caramel curls softly bouncing about her delicate shoulders.

Brock jumps up. "I like the length," he says, nodding in approval at the loose skirt that falls eight inches below the knee. "Can you ask her to unbutton the jacket? No, no, that blouse won't do." Brock shakes his head as the model holds open her jacket. "It's too flimsy. I can see her bulbs."

The girl's glossy red smile trembles slightly as Ann instructs her to button back up.

"I'd like something frilly," Brock continues. He pulls me up off of the couch and waves a hand under my chin. "Something high-necked with frills."

"Of course, sir?" Ann nods solemnly. In a few moments she returns with the same model, now clad in a polka dot belted dress with an enormous white bow at the neck.

"This is it!" Brock claps his hands together. "This is exactly the kind of frock that I've always wanted to see Miss Wanda in! Can you ask your girl to sit? I want to make sure that the skirt doesn't ride up. Perfect!" he exclaims as the model perches on a white padded stool. "No knees! Take my girl's measurements and ring it up!"

"Will there be anything else, sir? Hosiery, foundation garments?" Ann raises an eyebrow in the direction of my bosom. "A brassiere?"

Brock nods vigorously as Ann wraps a measuring tape around my chest. "Brassieres are manufactured in a variety of cup sizes now?" She explains to Brock. "Wanda definitely falls into the 'challenge cup' category?" She snaps her measuring tape shut. "I think I have something in the back?"

"I'll wait outside, dear." Brock kisses my cheek as Ann returns with a white bandage-like garment.

I unbutton my dress to the waist unselfconsciously. Ann's a professional and besides, she's seen much more of me before.

"Bend slightly and lean forward," she instructs as she fits me into the brassiere.

"It's too tight," I protest, wincing. I turn away in horror from my mirrored reflection. With my breasts bound in the elastic contraption, I look as though I'm recovering from an automobile accident.

"Listen, Wanda," Ann glares at me sternly as she places her hands on her slender hips. "I'm saying this not only as your former supervisor, but also as a pal. You heard your beau: he doesn't like a dame's bulbs to be showing through her blouse and *you*," she gestures at my breasts. "You've got a couple of blazing oil lamps." She buttons my dress up over the brassiere. "You've got yourself a classy fella now. Don't gum the works."

23. LEAVING THE RACKET

"I CAN'T TONIGHT, EDDIE. I've got the curse." I lean into him so that the rodent-faced mug he's brought for me can't hear. "I need to talk to you."

Eddie nods. "Sorry, mac," he says, turning to the john. "Cookie jar's empty tonight. The lady's indisposed."

The john's elongated snout twitches with annoyance. "Whaddaya mean 'indisposed?'"

"Female trouble," I answer, crossing my arms over my chest. "And unless you want some, I suggest you blow."

The john gapes at me openmouthed, as though surprised that I can speak. He looks at Eddie. "Say, I don't care if she's on her rag." He smiles, exposing a row of yellow and brown teeth. "Her mouth still works, don't it?"

Eddie roughly grabs him by the shoulders. "Get the hell outta here, ya dirty mug!" He shoves the john toward the lift. "Sca-rew!"

Eddie wipes his hands on his trousers as the elevator doors close. "Whaddaya wanna talk to me about, doll?" he asks, stepping into my room.

"I'm leaving the racket, Eddie." I snap open Mr. Whipple-bum's cigarette case and take out two snipes, one for me and one for him. "I've made up my mind," I say, lighting my cig. "So don't try to stop me."

Eddie wipes his forehead with the back of his hand and sticks the snipe between his teeth. "Light me up, will ya doll."

I go to hand him Mr. Whipplebum's lighter, but he reaches out and grabs both sides of my face as though he's about to kiss me, pressing the tip of his fresh snipe against the lit cigarette in my mouth.

"Thanks, baby." Eddie winks at me as he exhales.

"You mad at me, Eddie?" I ask. I stub the cigarette out in the ashtray beside my bed.

"Mad at ya?" Eddie's smile splits his face in two. "Why, I'm over da moon! I always knew ya weren't cut out for dis dirty business."

"But what about the money?" I ask him. "You'll be pulling in a lot less now."

"Dat filthy sugar? Aw, I kin live without it."

He wraps an arm around my waist, pulling me close. "*Dis* filthy sugar on the other hand," he whispers, gently biting my left earlobe. "Dis is some filthy sugar I *kin't* live without." Against my will, my pelvis tilts forward as he unbuttons the shirt of my dress. "I never did like da thought of dem rats with dem grimy paws all over ya. I know ya ain't my girl," he says, slipping a hand over the cup of my new brassiere. "But yer somethin'."

"No Eddie," I squirm. "We can't..."

"Why not?" Eddie stops his fumbling and looks at me, the cigarette dangling from his mouth. "Cuz ya got da curse? Dat don't make no difference to me." He grins. "We'll strip da mattress."

"No," I say. I button up my dress as I back away from him. "I can't be your 'something' or your 'anything' anymore. I'm somebody's girl now."

"Yeah." The cigarette between his lips bobs up and down like a question mark. "Who's girl? Da Bronco's?"

"No. I'm Brock Baxter's girl now."

Eddie laughs so hard that the cigarette falls out of his mouth. He crushes it under his flat, unpolished shoe. "Dat sap? Woo!" He grabs hold of his belly. "Good luck, doll."

"What's so funny about that? He loves me. He wants to marry me." I nod at the boxes piled up on top of my dresser. "He took me shopping today."

"I wouldn't trust any feller who takes a dame shoppin'!" Eddie exclaims, still laughing.

"He bought me a swell dress…"

"Did he buy ya dat brassiere?"

"You hush up!"

"So," Eddie says, wiping his eyes. "Dat's what ya think love is, huh? A ten-dollah dress, a forty-nine cent box o' candy." He picks up the fox fur and tosses it at me. "A fur coat."

"Why are you being so mean? It's not like you ever loved me!" I let the coat fall to the floor between us. "Well, did you, Eddie? Did you ever love me? Even when," I bite my lip. Why am I asking him this? I don't really care. "Even when we were making it together?"

The air hangs heavy, like the grey factory clouds at the edges of the city. We look at each other and I notice for the first time that Eddie has lost his eyes: they've slipped behind two dark half-moons, disappeared under the weight of driving a cab for twelve hours a night and sleeping in the light of the sun.

"Naw," Eddie says slowly, drawing the words out like a knife. "I guess I never loved ya."

There is a defiance to the quiet that follows. It makes me sick. Makes my mouth taste of bile.

"Get out!" I scream so as to be heard above the silence. "Get out of here you … you dirty dime store hoodlum!"

As he turns to leave, I grab the ashtray and throw it at him. It hits him square between the shoulder blades, scattering ashes onto my pink rose carpet like black rain.

A mess.

A beautiful, beautiful mess.

24. HEADLIGHTS

"THREE ON A MATCH." Gallagher, Brock's photographer friend from the *Town Star*, winks at me as he lights my cigarette. His crooked smile is parenthesized by deep scraggly lines that mar his otherwise handsome face. "I hope you're not superstitious, Wanda."

"Three on a match means one will die soon?" Brock snorts disdainfully. "That's just a lot of bunk made up by the owner of a matchstick company to sell more boxes of matches." He takes my hand in his and glares across the restaurant table at Gallagher.

I exhale slowly, enjoying both the photographer's attention and Brock's jealousy. Leaning back in my chair, I cross my legs, surreptitiously giving Gallagher an eyeful. "You going to eat that thigh?" I raise an eyebrow and nod at the chicken and potatoes on his plate.

Gallagher throws his head back in throaty laughter as the waitress comes by to refill our water glasses.

"I don't see what's so funny, Gallagher." Brock frowns. "I'll have you remember that this is a business dinner."

"A business dinner?" I turn to Brock in curiosity.

"Yes, dear." Brock squeezes my hand and waits for the waitress to finish before he continues. "I pitched a story idea to my editor yesterday. He thought it sounded really swell."

"That's wonderful, Brock!" I tip my glass to his. "So we're celebrating, then?"

Brock smiles tightly. "Not yet." He turns his chair around so that he's facing me. "The story is about an innocent young girl—the type of girl who always tries to do right even though she's from the wrong side of the tracks. A girl whose wholesome dreams of being a chorus girl are transformed into a smutty nightmare when she meets the owner of a bawdy nightclub: a malicious masher who sells her down a one-way river of sin and sleaze!"

"And I ... I'm the girl?" I ask, almost choking on my mouthful of chicken.

"That's right!" Brock claps his hands together with glee. "Potter, my editor, he loved it! You see, it fits right in with what I've been writing about the Catholic Legion of Decency and the Motion Picture Production Code. We've cleaned up our screens, now let's clean up our *streets!* Wipe out the girlie bars and their perverted proprietors! It's a movement towards modesty. A revulsion to raunch, a revolution of righteousness!" Brock brings his fist down onto the table, disrupting the water glasses. "And you, Miss Wanda, *you* will be the poster girl of the revolution!"

"Me?"

Brock's words float before me, as delicate and elusive as soap bubbles. I try to hold them still in my mind, to decipher their meaning, but he keeps on blowing more of them.

Dizzily, I gape across the table at Gallagher. He shrugs at me in boredom.

"Yes, Miss Wanda, *you,*" Brock continues. "Potter called your life story 'sordid and inspiring!'"

"M-my life story? Inspiring?" I shake my head. "I don't understand."

"Don't you see, Miss Wanda? You're the heart of the story—it's salvation! Your journey from nice girl to wanton woman and back again is what's inspiring. You, my dear, will provide faith to the parents of fallen daughters and hope to the harlots!" Brock sits back and wipes his now sweaty brow with a handkerchief. "And you wouldn't just be helping others, Miss Wanda. You'd also be helping yourself."

"Helping myself?" I ask, dumbly.

Brock nods and takes my hand into his. "Remember at the department store? When you were embarrassed because your friend recognized you as Wanda Wiggles? Well, what if she knew the whole story—what if she knew that none of this was your fault, that you were just an innocent victim? Would you be embarrassed then?"

"Yes, I think so."

Brock presses his lips together in frustration. "Well, anyway, Potter said the paper will pay you a weekly allowance."

"*Pay me?*" I sit up straight. "How much?"

"Just enough to keep you in rent and food." Brock eyes my dress. "And decent clothes. I'm so glad that you're wearing the polka-dot dress I bought you, Miss Wanda." He turns to Gallagher. "Doesn't she look like an angel?"

Gallagher nods and raises his glass to me. "Like she fell right out of the sky."

"Just one thing," Brock hands me his handkerchief. "Wipe your mouth, Miss Wanda. Only harlots wear red lipstick."

Stunned, as though I'd been slapped, I take the handkerchief from him and drag it across my lips, my face burning.

"Perfect," Brock nods. He straightens the bow on my dress. "Gallagher is going to take your picture for the paper."

"M-my picture?" Panic rises from the pit of my stomach. *Mr. Manchester. Evelyn. Mama.* Mama! A white flash of light smacks my eyes, temporarily blinding me.

"Sorry, honey. That was just a test." Gallagher grins at me from behind his press camera; its flash bulb like the headlights of a speeding car. Instinctively, I arrange my face into what I hope is a provocative smile.

"No!" Brock admonishes. "You need to look pensive. *Remorseful.* Think of something sad." He snaps his fingers. "Think of your father! That's it. Think of your daddy!"

"Baxter," Gallagher's voice darts out from between the flashes of light. "I think she's crying."

"That's perfect!"

Fallen Angel

A Town Star Special Report by Brock Baxter

GIRLS! GIRLS! GIRLS!

If you've ever ventured into the downtown core, or even crept along its periphery, you've seen the signs: blinking, brilliant, brazen promises of GORGEOUS GIRLS! GLAMOROUS GIRLS! GLORIOUS GIRLS!

Blondes, redheads, and brownettes. Long-legged and petite. Skinny, fat, and in-between. An endless array of flavours and types to satisfy the treacherous tide of MEN! MEN! MEN!

But where do these girls come from and how, after being debased and discarded by their supposed benefactors, do their stories end?

Miss Wanda Whittle holds the answer, the answer and the solution, to this most timely of questions.

Sprung from the loins of a scrubwoman and thrust into the slum behind the Market, the little girl was born with only a sliver of a chance; however, we must remember, dear reader, that flowers thrive best in manure and this child was surely the loveliest of roses. When your humble scribe first met Miss Whittle, she was no more than the tender age of nineteen: fulsome of figure and fair of face, this heavenly creature was living proof of our creator's love. But around angels, devils lurk. The particular devil who tempted this angel—who lured her into a life of pecuniary sex and sin—was the proprietor of the Apple Bottom burlesque theatre on Main Avenue. Henceforth, we shall refer to him as Mr. M (you, faithful reader, may be well excused for presuming that the "M" stands for "Masher").

Yes, when your trustful reporter first laid his peepers on Miss Whittle, she was wholesome and unburdened, with the clear eyes and rosy cheeks of youth. You will see from her photo today that her face is now wan, her cheeks sunken, and her eyes filled with such an immeasurable sadness no lash tint can conceal.

In the coming weeks, Miss Whittle will share her sad story with you, dear *Town Star* readers, with the aim of stopping the flow of fallen females and filth that today floods our city streets. It is her humblest of hopes that her story will prevent another angel from falling into the deviant arms of another Mr. M.

For as Miss Whittle herself lays testament to, even a good egg can become hard-boiled.

25. ANGELS WITH DIRTY FEET

I AM VERY LUCKY TO BE BROCK'S GIRL. It's not every man who'd accept and forgive all I've done. If it wasn't for Brock, I probably never would have left the racket. Gosh, I'd probably be like Bette Davis' character at the end of *In Human Bondage*: raccoon eyes, breasts falling out of my torn nightie as I collapse dead to the floor from syphilis. Brock saved me. That swell fella. That sweet, swell fella.

I spread open the dirty drapes and take a slug of whiskey from my hip flask. The clock by the bed reads 5:02 a.m. Already a cluster of hats crowd the streetcars. The memories of my halcyon days of being a department store model nibble at me and for a more-than-fleeting moment, I long to be out there in the soft grey before dawn, walking single file, moving within the shadows of the telephone operators, the brick layers, the shop girls, and the factory workers: strangers unfolding as one, like a string of paper dolls.

The dame next door has her window open. She's playing the Shirley Temple record again—tootsie rolls and bellyaches—giving me a goddamn headache. I scratch at a bug bite on the back of my shin with my big toe. A few months back I tried to approach Irving about the bedbugs.

"What ya talkin' bout?" he had shouted. "Dissah classy joint. Only slums got dem bugs!" Shoving a sausage finger in my face. "*You* brung 'em!"

I never brought it up again. Kerosene, lye soap—after a while,

I just gave up. But I'll be saying goodbye to this joint soon enough. I take another sip from my flask; the whiskey warms my belly like fire. Lightly, I touch my lips. Last night, Brock brought over a copy of the *Town Star* to show me the article that he wrote. He asked me how I liked it and before I could answer, he kissed me. Our first kiss: slow, gentle, and sweet. Afterwards, he hooked his thumb around my ring finger and sang a little song:

I'm gonna take you far away
Buy you a big fat diamond
So you'll never stray
And you're gonna love me, love me, love me
'Till your dyin' day.

I smile, hugging myself to keep my body from flying out the window. Outside, the moon gives one final bow as the sun waits impatiently in the wings. Inside, the dust falls like snow.

"Miss Wanda! Wake up, Miss Wanda!"

The words rattle inside my skull like dice in a palm. I roll over, my naked body breaking out in goosebumps as the sheets fall to the floor beside my bed. A pair of baby-blue marbles roll up and down my body, disappearing between my tits.

"Snake eyes!" I cry, reaching out for the whiskey flask on my bedside table and knocking over the alarm clock in the process. 5:05 p.m. No, that *can't* be right.

"Are you sick, Miss Wanda?" Brock's soldier boy eyes are filled with concern as he drapes a blanket over my shoulders.

"Sick?" I ask, although it comes out as *'thick?'*; my tongue feeling like a fat fuzzy worn out sock. "No, I ain't sick. I just got a headache is all and you ain't helpin', talkin' so loud." I flip over onto my stomach. "How'd you get in here, anyway?"

Brock crouches by the bed. "The bellhop let me in." He places a hand softly on my back. "Are you mad at me, Miss Wanda?"

"Jimmy the bellhop," I mumble into my pillow, its case wet with spit and lipstick. "Last time he's getting a show from me."

"What are you talking about, Miss Wanda?" Brock asks, smoothing the hair away from my face. "Gee, you're as white as a ghost. I think I better go downstairs and call a doctor."

"I don't need a doctor, I need a drink!"

"Right, Miss Wanda."

Brock leaves my side, returning in a few moments with a cup of water. Helping me into a seated position, he brings the cup to my lips and encourages me to drink with such gentleness that I want to cry. "Just a sip, Miss Wanda. There you go."

Shame stirs me into unwelcome sobriety. "I-I'm sorry, Brock. I don't know what came over me."

"Oh, Miss Wanda," Brock says soothingly as I begin to sob. "Your nerves are all shot." He wraps his arms tightly around me. "Let me call a doctor, honey."

"No." I break out of his embrace and wipe my eyes on the back of my hand. "I'll be oh-kay."

"Let me make up your bed, Miss Wanda," Brock says as he picks the sheets up off the floor. "What you need is a proper sleep. I'll call Mr. Potter and tell him that we're not coming."

"Mr. Potter?"

He nods. "My editor. His wife invited us over for dinner tonight, remember?"

"Oh, yes," I say, cupping my head in my hands. "Yes, I remember now. She liked the article…"

"She thinks you're fascinating!" Brock beams. "She's dying to meet you!"

I swing my legs over the side of the bed. "Let's go then."

"No, Miss Wanda. You're not well enough."

"But this is important to you."

Brock bends down and kisses my forehead. "You're more important to me."

I look up at his kind, pretty face. Such a swell, sweet boy. "We're going, Brock." I say firmly.

"You sure, Miss Wanda? You're still so pale…"

"I'm sure, Brock."

"Oh, Miss Wanda!" Brock hugs me again. "You make me so happy!"

I manage a weak smile. "Pass me my robe, please."

"Gladly!" He turns away as I slip into my white satin wrap with the pink rabbit fur sleeves, a birthday present from the Boxer. A whole lifetime ago.

"Miss Wanda," Brock says shyly, his eyes on the nicotine stained carpet. "May I—before we go, that is—may I please wash your feet?"

"You have very pretty feet," Brock says, rolling up his shirt-sleeves as he fills the bathtub with warm, sudsy water. "But they're awfully dirty."

I perch my bottom on the edge of the tub and dip my toes into the water.

"Didn't your mama ever tell you," Brock continues. "*Pure souls must have clean soles if they want to walk through Heaven's Gate?*"

"No, I guess she skipped that lesson."

"I guess she skipped a lot of lessons," Brock mumbles. He lathers up a chubby bar of lavender soap. "You're so beautiful, Miss Wanda," he says, brightening. "Floating above the water in your white satin robe. Why, you really do look like an angel." He picks up my right foot and brings it to his lips. "Lovely little toes," he whispers, giving each one a kiss. "Sweet little toes." Gently, he rubs my foot between his soapy hands. "I'm so glad that you don't wear toenail varnish like some other girls do, Miss Wanda. I hate that."

I want to ask him how he knows what "some other girls" do, but already I'm too aroused. Holding onto the sides for balance, I tilt my pelvis and allow my body to slide midway down the bathtub. Stretching my left leg, I slowly caress Brock's face with my big toe.

"Wanda, my angel," he moans, his eyes cloudy with desire. A deep red flourishes from the nape of his neck all the way to his ears. "Oh, Miss Wanda…"

Suddenly he drops my foot with a thud, a grimace strangling his pretty face. He stands up, angrily tugging at the crotch of his trousers. "I … I better let you alone to get ready."

"What's wrong, Brock?" I ask. "Did I do something to upset you, dear?" I reach out for him but he swats my hand away.

"I just don't want us to be late is all," he snaps, turning his back to me. "I'll meet you downstairs."

I slip down into the filthy water, robe and all, as the door bangs shut behind him. I shouldn't have been so bold. This isn't some masher like Eddie. Brock is a classy fella and he deserves a classy dame. Next time, I won't be so aggressive. I unscrew the cap off my Fitch shampoo bottle and take a swig. I filled the empty container with gin a couple of days ago. Bathtub gin, I call it. A little joke between me, myself, and I. I smile as the dirt swirls around me and the water goes cold. From now on, starting tonight, I'll be a well-behaved, respectable girl. I'll make Brock proud of me. He'll see.

"I ain't got no money but my honey, she's ducky! As long as I'm with her, all my days will be lucky!"

Clad in a smart tuxedo and top hat, Brock serenades me in the Grand Palace lobby, with the dingy blonde Venus and befuddled Irving as captive audience.

"Say," I giggle as I make my way toward him. "Those aren't the lyrics to High Ballin' Hard Times."

"Well, I wrote the song, didn't I?" Brock smiles down at me. "I guess I can change the lyrics. You look lovely, darling," he says, his eyes surveying the ruffled pink dress that he recently bought for me. "I knew that gown would suit you."

I smooth my hands self-consciously over the dress's puffy wide skirt. The ponderous frock is really more suited to a woman half my size; in truth, I look like a bloated pink marshmallow.

"Ya wanna talk ta me 'bout somepin, Wanda?" Irving leers at us from behind the counter, raising his centipede-like eyebrows at Brock. I glance over his shoulder at the Caper Cola wall calendar. A redhead in blue polka-dots reminds me that it's the first of the month. I'll have to ask Brock for the dough but I don't want Irving catching on about our relationship. If he suspects that I have a steady beau—one with both a regular paycheque and a healthy wallet—he might raise my rent.

"I'll get it for you later," I whisper to him as I lead Brock away from his covetous gaze.

"I want to apologize to you, Miss Wanda," Brock says as we step outside. "I didn't mean to blow my top earlier. I just didn't want us to be late. You see, I'm a big shot reporter now," he winks at me. "And you know how us newspaper folks are about deadlines."

"S'okay, Brock."

"Liar! Liar! She ain't wearin' no pants, but if she was, they'd be on fire! Read all about it in the *City Crier*!" The newsboy in plaid plus-fours and a matching flat cap swings a copy of the evening paper in the air.

"Give me one of those, young man," Brock says, tossing a dime to the boy. "Always a good idea to see what the enemy is up to," he smiles conspiratorially at me as he tucks the rival paper under his arm.

"Say, that's me!" I cry, snatching the newspaper from him. Splashed across the front page is a photograph of me in my maid's costume, cupping my breasts and winking at the camera.

VENGEFUL VAMP, screams the headline.

"Those dirty mugs!" Brock exclaims. "They're trying to crab my story!" He cranes his neck to read out loud over my shoulder:

Mr. Manchester, owner of the well-respected Apple Bottom theatre told the *City Crier* in an exclusive interview that Miss Whittle, also known as Wanda Wiggles, is a natural born peeler. In fact, she'll even *play* without *pay*!

"When I first discovered her, she was standing buck naked in the middle of a department store swimsuit display!" Mr. Manchester reveals. He goes on to say that although Miss Wiggles was not a member of the orchestra, she could often be found in the pit tumbling with the tuba player or tickling the skin tickler.

"This dame and her games put the Apple Bottom in danger of being shut down by the flatfoots," Mr. Manchester explains. As a result of her indiscretions, he had no choice but to can her shapely little can. Miss Wiggles thus retaliated by selling her story to the sob sisters at the *Town Star.*

"Why, they're saying that I was fired! That isn't true," I say indignantly. "What do they mean 'tumbling with the tuba player' I never did any such thing! And what's a 'skin tickler?'"

"That's a colourful name for 'drummer,'" Brock sneers, tearing the paper from my hands. "*Sob sisters!*" he spits. "I'll give them something to sob about!"

"Extra! Extra!" the oblivious newsboy sings. "Read all about it! She's a dirty tramp and there ain't no doubt about it!"

Angrily, Brock rips the newspaper sack off the boy's shoulder.

"Hey, Mister!" the startled boy cries. "What are you doing?"

"Putting this rubbish in its rightful place!"

With the wind whipping excitedly at his tuxedo tails, Brock upends the shoulder bag and deposits its contents into the city trash bin. The newsboy begins to howl as Brock strikes a match across the sole of his shoe and, with a dignified flourish, drops the flame into the bin.

"Nobody insults my girl!" Brock says, straightening his bowtie and tipping his hat at the mortified boy.

26. HOW DRY AM I?

"*THE CITY CRIER* DIDN'T CRAB YOUR STORY, my boy. You can bet dollars to buttons that the *Town Star's* readership will increase tenfold by tomorrow afternoon!" His editor thumps Brock's back genially as we settle down around the Potters' walnut dining table.

Mr. and Mrs. Potter are five steps up from the World Behind the Market and six steps down from Mr. Whipplebum. Their dining room, its walls papered in brown and orange stripes, is kept warm by electric radiators; the polar bear rug by the now obsolete fireplace, head still intact, jaws forever frozen in a last ditch effort at self-defence, is unnervingly real. The diamonds dripping from the overhead chandelier, however, are paste; the floral centrepiece bought at a fruit market, and their maid is on loan from an agency.

"I want a new Wanda story in our paper tomorrow morning," Mr. Potter is saying to Brock, his eyes preponderant over his horn-rimmed spectacles. "Think you can have it ready by midnight?"

"Yes, sir," Brock replies, his soldier-doll cheeks still scarlet from the *City Crier* story. "I'm already working on something as we speak. *The City Crier!*" He growls. "I'll settle their hash!"

"Now boys, no shop talk tonight," Mrs. Potter winks at me as the maid fills our wine glasses. The older woman is matronly yet elegant in a forest green tulle evening dress, her silver hair smoothed back in a becoming chignon. "I'd much rather focus on Miss Whittle here," she says, smiling. "This gorgeous, fascinating creature!"

I tip the glass to my lips in an effort to quench my shyness. The wine is sweet and surprisingly non-bitter. "This is delicious," I say. "I've never tasted wine like this before."

"Oh, it isn't wine, dear," Mrs. Potter says kindly. "It's grape juice."

"The drink that's sweet but won't inebriate!" Mr. Potter chuckles, clinking his glass to mine.

"Absolutely," Mrs. Potter nods. "You see, Miss Whittle, we still believe in temperance in this household. I was a member of the local Ladies Temperance Society before Prohibition and I'm not quitting now."

"Well, I think that's perfectly grand!" Brock bobs his head enthusiastically. "Don't you, Miss Wanda?"

"Grand," I agree. Surreptitiously, I search under my poufy dress for my hip flask.

"*Whittle,*" Mrs. Potter muses. "Your mother doesn't happen to be Constance Whittle, by any chance?"

"No, ma'am," I say as the maid scoops stuffed cucumber salad onto my plate. I run my hands over the Mayfair patterned silverware, wondering which fork to use. "My mama's name is Madge."

"Oh, it doesn't matter. I just wondered, that's all. I know a Constance Whittle from the Society."

"My mama was never a member of the Society, but she supported your efforts," I say, deciding on the smaller fork for my salad. "In the beginning, anyhow."

"In the beginning?" Mrs. Potter raises a pencilled eyebrow at me.

"Yes," I say. "My daddy was a teetotaller but some of my uncles and a lot of the other men behind the Market liked to get squiffy at the saloons."

"*Squiffy,* my dear?"

"Ossified," I clarify. "Drinking away their paycheques, coming home drunk, and slugging their wives, that sort of thing."

"How dreadful!" Mrs. Potter exclaims, bringing a hand to her throat in horror. "The women in your neighbourhood must have been overjoyed with Prohibition."

"Well, I was only a little girl at the time but I remember that most of 'em were pretty happy about it."

"They must not be too happy about the Repeal then."

"Oh, no, ma'am, they're *very* happy about the Repeal," I say through a mouthful of cucumber salad. "Gee, this salad is swell."

Mrs. Potter purses her lips. "Why would they be happy about the repeal of a law so helpful to them?"

"Because it wasn't helpful to them. You see, it's like this: before Prohibition their husbands may have fallen down drunk in the gutters, but at least they got up and walked the next morning. After Prohibition, a bunch of them started hobbling around on the Jake Leg."

"The Jake Leg?"

"Yes, they got it from drinking thirty-five cent cans of eighty percent pure alcohol called 'Jake.' The dime-store bootleggers sold it behind the Market. It was the only stuff most fellas could afford. The Jake numbed their feet permanently so they could hardly walk and not just that," I lower my voice to a whisper, "I've heard tell from some of their wives that the Jake crippled more than just their legs—ow!" I cry as Brock delivers a sharp kick to my shin under the table.

"Nonsense," Mrs. Potter says, oblivious to the kick. "Such ghastly cases must be few and far between. Why, the law was designed to *protect* the less advantaged."

"Besides," Mr. Potter injects gruffly. "They deserved no less for breaking the law. If they followed the rules, they'd still have their legs."

"That's absolutely right," Brock says, glaring at me sternly. Knowing how much he loves his gin rickeys, I glare back.

"If the public had fallen in line, we would have been able

to fulfill Prohibition's promise of a return to Eden," Mrs. Potter says. She raises a glass. "And we still can. Nothing is impossible!"

"You said it!" I cry. "Repeal the Repeal! Gee, Mrs. Potter, you've turned my head straight. This calls for a prayer!"

As they bow their heads, I remove the flask from my garter and take a long swig.

Trying to act sober when you're zozzled is like trying to catch hold of a wet pig. Words as tenuous as soap bubbles float in the air above Mrs. Potter's flapping wet mouth; they tip-toe on the ceiling before escaping through a fine crack in the window. I hold onto the table and wonder if it is really the aspic fish that is wobbling or if it is in fact me. The jelly mould gazes at me with wise olive eyes, its rubbery tail curled around an onion chopped up to resemble a rose.

There once was a woman behind the Market who owned a goldfish that could tell fortunes. For three pennies, the woman would scoop the goldfish out of its bowl and toss it gently into your open palm. If the fish moved its head first, it meant you would have luck with money; if it moved its tail, you'd be lucky in love, but if the fish flopped over and played dead, well, that was bad news. At best, it meant you were SOL, at worst it foretold sudden death. *That little goldfish must be worth its weight in copper,* my father had joked when the woman showed up to church one day wearing an ermine stole.

"Some rats wear trousers and walk on two legs."

Brock's words fly into my mind like a brightly-coloured kite. I giggle, picturing a rodent in a fedora, his fat pink tail poking out of pinstriped trousers.

"What's so funny?" Brock looks at me sharply.

"What you just said," I say, giggling. "About rats wearing pants."

"I was referring to Mr. Manchester," Brock says, his cheek

muscles twitching like the fins of the aspic fish. "And there's nothing funny about that masher!"

"Such a wretched man," Mrs. Potter agrees. She reaches for my hand. "I'm so sorry you were exposed to that, dear."

My laughter gives way to a machine-gun burst of hiccups.

"What is it, Miss Wanda?" Suddenly solicitous, Brock rubs my back. "Are you sick?"

"No," I spit the words out between hiccups. "I-it's just … s-s-she said *deer* a-a-and I'm p-p-picturing a *deer* w-w-wearing a bowler hat a-a-and a big trench coat …exposing himself!"

I collapse face first into the coconut chocolate whip.

"She's really very sick," I hear Brock saying. "An attack of nerves. I shouldn't have brought her out tonight."

"The poor darling," Mrs. Potter's tongue makes a fleshy clucking sound. "She should be in bed."

"Oh, please," I sit up in my chair and lick the chocolate from my lips. "Will everyone please keep their voices down? I have a pounding headache."

"Headache?" Mr. Potter's blue eyes shine like car beams behind his spectacles. "We have just the thing for headaches, don't we dear?"

"We certainly do!" Mrs. Potter exclaims, rising from her seat. She opens the looking glass door of her cherry red cabinet and extracts a small wooden box with a finial carved in the shape of an elephant. "Headache powder," she explains as she opens the box to reveal a white, snow-like substance. "You inhale it." She taps her nose lightly.

I reach for the box just as Mr. Potter cuts the fish's head off. He scoops out its eyes with his pinkie finger and pops them in his mouth. Doubling over, I vomit into my lap.

After a car ride fraught with silent tension, Brock carries me up to my room and gently tucks me into bed. His little soldier-doll face is more wooden than ever: his mouth set in a hard pink line, the look in his saucer eyes abstruse.

"I'm sorry, Brock."

"It's oh-kay," he replies, shrugging off my attempt at an embrace. He picks up his top hat, pops it open and places it firmly on his head. "I better get back to the office now if I want to bang out that story before midnight."

"Are you mad at me, Brock?"

He pauses as though giving my question considerable thought. "No," he says finally. "I'm just disappointed."

"I'm sorry," I repeat stupidly.

"I am too, Miss Wanda." Brock sits down on the bed and takes my hand. "To be honest, honey, I *was* mad at you at first, but then when you started talking about what it was like growing up behind the Market and how rotten that was.... Well, I started to get angry with myself. I realized that I had been expecting too much of you. Trying to pass you off as a genteel lady to the Potters was like trying to pass a donkey off as a racehorse—neither fair to donkeys or racehorses. Oh, don't be sore, honey, I didn't mean that as an insult," he says quickly as I sit up. "All I meant was that if tonight was a disaster—and I think that it's a cinch to say that it was—then it was my fault."

"I guess you won't be coming around no more," I mumble, still smarting from being compared to a donkey.

"Oh, Miss Wanda!" Brock cries, the affection returning to his voice. "Of course I'll still be 'coming around' as you put it. Oh, honey," he smiles, chucking me under the chin. "You're not getting rid of me that easy."

"Well you said you were mad at me," I say, play-pouting now that the putty is warm in my hands. "So, I thought maybe you were givin' me the kiss-off."

"People sometimes get angry with those that they love, but it doesn't mean that they stop loving them." Brock kisses me softly on the lips.

"Oh, Brock, you shouldn't do that! You know I was sick and I haven't brushed my teeth yet."

"I know, honey," Brock smiles. "I guess I must be pretty dizzy for you."

"You sure must be to kiss me with sick in my mouth!" I smile back at him.

Brock kisses me again. "I really should go now," he says. "But before I do, I want you to promise to do something for me."

"Anything, Brock."

"The next time that I take you out among respectable people, I want you to sit back quietly and study them. Listen to the way that they talk, examine their mannerisms. And then I want you to mimic them. It will feel strange at first, but keep at it and eventually it will be duck soup."

"And then I won't be a donkey no more?" I ask playfully.

"No, dear," Brock gives my hand a squeeze. "You'll be a lady."

The Svengali and the Gigolo
A Town Star Special Report by Brock Baxter

One need not to have read the 1895 novel by George du Maurier, or to have seen the 1931 John Barrymore film to have encountered the licentious louse that is the Svengali. For this perverted puppeteer lurks not only within the pages of books and on the silver screen, but on the sidewalks of our very city: music halls, streetcars, grammar-schools, and soda fountains are but a few of the seemingly innocuous places where the Svengali hunts his prey. He may only possess two eyes instead of eight, but his blinkers are as shrewd as those of a spider and his clutch every bit as devastating.

It was within the walls of a department store where Masher—er, *Mister*—Manchester first set his predatory peepers on our Miss Wanda Whittle. The naïve lass, as lovely as a rose and twice as delicate, had been employed by the store as a living mannequin. Should there ever be a case for sex-segregated shopping let this be it, for it was in the Ladies Wear department that Mr. Manchester spun his promises of money and fame into a web enchanting enough to entrap the little clothes model, impoverished daughter of a scrub woman.

Just as du Maurier's Trilby could not sing unless under the hypnotic spell of Svengali, Miss Whittle would never have sinned had she not been under the wicked influence of Masher Manchester. After the proprietor of the rotten Apple Bottom burlesque theatre had squeezed the last penny from the franchise of Miss Whittle's flesh and chewed away at her virtuous heart, the bloated rat in trousers tossed her masticated carcass to the maggots to be gobbled up by one parasite in particular: the drummer at the Apple Bottom, known to all who despise him as Gigolo Eddie (and let it be stated that all who know him *do* despise him).

In the days to come, the *Town Star* will bring you the exclusive story of how the now weak and feeble (but still fetching) Miss Whittle became vulnerable to the vulgarities of Gigolo Eddie and how he proceeded to make dollars out of her degradation. For the only thing worse than a Svengali Spider is a lecherous, lazy *leech!*

27. BEAUTY AND THE BROCK

"HURRY, HURRY, HURRY! Step right up and prepare to be transfixed as the tantalizing Mistress Tamara tangos with the terrifying King of the Jungle!" The mustachioed egg-shaped ringmaster waves his stout arms in the air for emphasis. "Believe me, folks, you've never seen a lion taming act like this before and you never will again! Hurry! Hurry! Hurry!"

Brock shakes his head and laughs as we take our seats inside the circus tent. "How did I ever let you convince me to come here, Miss Wanda? Didn't we get our fill of clowns at the Apple Bottom?"

"I like the circus," I say cheerfully. "And besides, sometimes I miss the Apple Bottom. Not Mr. Manchester," I quickly clarify as Brock's cheek muscles twitch with displeasure. "And not any of that stuff you've been writing about in the papers, but *this*," I spread my arms out. "The anticipation of the audience, the excitement of being on stage. I mean, you felt it too, didn't you, Brock?" I ask sheepishly. "When you were up there singing and telling your jokes, didn't you feel that rush, that..." I search for the right word. "That *crackle?*"

"Have some Cracker Jack, Miss Wanda," Brock says dryly as he hands me the box of candy. He watches quietly as a trio of whooping clowns, their faces painted pink and blue, tumble into the arena. The tallest clown proceeds to stand on his head while another tosses the smallest clown, dressed as a cigar-smoking baby, into the air. The audience roars as the little clown lands feet first onto the soles of the upside-down clown's giant polka-dotted shoes. They stay like that for a few moments, wobbling and waving at the crowd.

"No, Miss Wanda," Brock says finally. "I don't miss any of this. Don't you remember? The papers used to call *me* a clown: Brock Baxter, the corny clown of the Apple Bottom. They were right, too. But look at me now, Miss Wanda," he says, brightening. "When I worked at the Apple Bottom, I wore a paper collar and a dickey but now I wear real shirts with cuffs and look at this," He rolls up his jacket sleeves proudly. "Gold cuff links! Someday they'll be diamonds, Miss Wanda. Mr. Potter says I'm really going places. I pitched him a new story today—a fresh angle—and he loved it! He said I'm getting a raise!"

"That's swell, Brock."

"You bet it's swell!" He puts his arm around me. "It's all thanks to you, Miss Wanda. You're my inspiration, my angel!"

"Brock," I say tentatively. "I want to talk to you about your latest newspaper article."

"Aw, you don't have to thank me for that, Miss Wanda. Mr. Manchester, Eddie, those mugs at the *City Crier*—they all had it coming!" He leans his back against the bench, smiling with self-satisfaction. "I was happy to do it!"

"It's just.... Well, I kind of wish you'd lay off Eddie. He's not really such a bad guy, and..."

"Not such a bad guy!" Brock's mouth drops open in disbelief. "That rat! That dime store version of Mr. Manchester! Why, Miss Wanda, *Eddie* was a part of your descent into depravity!"

The clowns disappear as the lion enters the ring, followed by a strutting Mistress Tamara in a silky white bodysuit trimmed with fat fluffy ostrich feathers. The lion, golden and majestic, yawns in boredom as his mistress snaps her whip in the air, directing him to a tacky, paint splattered pedestal hardly worthy of a king.

"But, Brock," I persist, attempting a different tactic. "This story is supposed to be about *me*—my redemption and well, to be honest, I'm not feeling very *redeemed* by it all."

"You're not, huh?" Brock turns to me and smiles. "Eat your Cracker Jack, Miss Wanda."

"Brock…"

"Go on," he winks. "Have a handful. I guarantee it will make you feel better."

Resigned, I stick my hand into the box of candy but instead of popcorn and peanuts, I pull out a delicate pearl ring with a gold cathedral setting.

"Oh, Brock," I whisper. "It's beautiful."

"I'm still going to get you that diamond, Miss Wanda, but in the meantime consider this ring as a promise of my love and devotion. Someday, Miss Wanda, I am going to buy us a house bigger than the Potters'—big enough for a dozen children! Oh, I know how much you want them, my darling. Think of this pearl," Brock continues as he slips the ring onto my finger. "As the world that I will one day give to you."

My fingers are sticky from the candy and my nail varnish is peeling, but the ring makes my hand look elegant. Ladylike.

"Oh, Brock!" I press my lips to his proudly flushed cheek. "I don't deserve you!"

Mistress Tamara flicks her whip and the audience cheers as the king of the jungle spiritlessly jumps through a red and white striped plastic hoop. "Only beauty can do that, folks!" The ringmaster cries. "Only beauty can tame the beast!"

28. BETTER THAN THE MOVIES

"I TOLD THOSE *CITY CRIER* CUBS that if tawdry gossip was what they were fishing for, then they could go ahead and stick their rods in a different pond." Lili Belle drops into my over-stuffed organdy chair and kicks off her high heels. She rubs her stocking clad dogs as I dance about the room in my new lavender crepe evening gown.

"What do you think, Lili Belle?" I ask, attempting a pirouette. "Isn't this a swell dress?"

"Ain't you tired of it, honey?"

"Tired of *this?*" I lift the hem of my frock. "Brock just bought it for me yesterday. I haven't even worn it out yet."

"The newspapers, Wanda," she corrects me. "The manure slinging. Ain't you sick and tired of it?"

"If anyone's slinging manure, it's Mr. Manchester, not Brock," I say firmly. "All Brock is doing is trying to prevent another girl from falling into the same racket that I did. You know how moralistic Brock is, Lili Belle. Why, I've never met a fella with such high ideals."

"High ideals," Lili Belle spits the words out with disgust. "Oh, he's high-hattin' all right. Why, it wasn't so long ago that he was just a lowly nightclub comic, no better than the rest of us mugs."

"Yeah?" I stick my hand out under her nose. "How many lowly comics would give their dames a ring like this? It's real gold," I add as she rolls her saucer brown eyes.

"It's a nice piece of candy," she says caustically.

"Piece of candy!" I raise my eyebrows. "This is a genuine pearl, not a lollipop top."

"Fine. It's swell, Wanda, but is it really worth tossing your own mama under a train for?"

"What are you talking about?"

Lili Belle puts on her coke bottle reading glasses and removes a newspaper clipping from her alligator clutch purse. "'Wanda's mother, Mrs. Madge Whittle,'" she reads aloud in a sharp, mocking tone, "'was too busy cleaning the homes of the wealthy to bother with caring for her own daughter.' Well, what do you think about that?" Lili Belle asks. She rips the clipping in half and removes her reading glasses. "Your beau wrote that. High ideals, huh?"

"He didn't mean it like that."

"Really? How did he mean it exactly?"

"Well," I turn my back to her and survey my reflection in the oval looking glass. "My mama *is* a scrub woman. It's true that she cleans houses."

"Oh, Wanda," Lili Belle sighs. "I guess love really *is* blind. Especially," she adds. "When the blindfold is made of money."

"Money!" I exclaim. "Look, Lili Belle, this is a pearl, not a diamond. Although Brock *did* say that he's going to buy me a diamond one day." I smile and hug myself. "Really, Lili Belle, you're sweet to be so concerned about me, but you needn't worry so much."

"It's your sister I'm really worried about. She's getting bigger and bluer by the day and those nosey newspaper reporters ain't helping any."

"My sister's a tough cookie, Lili Belle."

"She ain't so tough these days. Well, I told Joe that if he didn't tell those chisellin' cubs to go bang their typewriters in some other joint, then he could find himself another hoofer. You shoulda seen the look on his ugly pan!" Lili Belle laughs. "He couldn't get those mugs out fast enough. After you and

Queenie blew, the last thing Joe and Mr. Manchester want is to lose another headliner."

"Those newsfolk don't care about Evelyn; she's just a hat-check girl." I try to keep my tone light but just the mention of my sister brings me down faster than a brick. She seems so far away—Mama, too—both of them belonging to a world that I don't want to be a part of no more.

"Unzip me, will you?" I ask, flipping my hair over to one side.

Lili Belle's fingers fumble with my zipper. "I–I can't, Wanda." She turns away from me, her face burning. "You better do it yourself."

"Why?" I let my dress fall to the floor. "What's wrong, Lili Belle?"

She glances over at me shyly as I stand naked before her. I recognize the longing behind her glance and yet it is markedly different than the lust of Eddie, Mr. Manchester, or even Brock. Hers is a desire without entitlement. I take both of her hands and lead her to the bed.

"Come sit with me, Lili Belle."

She keeps her head bent; her thick-mascaraed eyelashes casting shadows along her cheekbones, like the wings of a broken butterfly. She reminds me of a stray kitten. I can sense that she wants me to pet her, but if I do, she'll run away.

"I should go, Wanda."

"Do you want to go?" I press my open mouth to the spot where her shoulder meets the base of her neck, inhaling her apricot scent. "Is that what you want?"

The neighbour next door cranks up the phonograph. Piano teeth and trombone lungs, marshmallow clouds and upside down skies: suddenly Lili Belle is kissing me or I'm kissing her. Oh! What difference does it make? Her mouth is a choc-olate cherry cream: messy and sweet, scrumptious and sticky. Kissing Lili Belle is devouring an ice cream cone in July; it is a hotdog at the ballpark; it is Jean Harlow slipping into something more comfortable, and it is better than all of those things. Kissing Lili Belle is better than the movies.

Mercilessly, Lili Belle pulls away from me. She unbuttons her cornflower-blue day dress and wiggles out of her slip and tap pants. In the pale pink glow of the milk glass light fixture, she looks like an angel: an angel with red lipstick smeared all over her neck and face. Gently, she pushes me facedown onto the bed. Straddling my hips, she slips her hands under my breasts and softly bites the back of my neck.

"Wanda..." she whispers my name, over and over, in between planting feathery kisses down my spine.

Outside the closed window, a saxophone wails. Lili Belle's kisses travel over the curve of my ass, between my open thighs. The music taps at the window, its knocks growing impatient. I raise my hips as Lili Belle enters me with her tongue. The scream of the saxophone smashes the window wide open, scattering glass like rain. I open my mouth, crying to swallow the music.

"You okay, sweetie?" Lili Belle is beside me now, stroking my hair, bringing my head to her beautiful bare bosom.

"I'm okay," I wrap my arms around her, squeezing tight. I'm crying and now I'm laughing. "I didn't know anything could feel like this."

"I know, sweetie." Lili Belle kisses the top of my head. "Me neither."

"We can do this again, can't we Lili Belle?" I look up at her. "Brock is going to marry me, but we could still do this, once in a while, when he's not home. It's not cheating if it's with another girl." I nuzzle her neck and cup her left breast in my hand. "It's not like this is a big deal."

Lili Belle stiffens under my touch. The music holds its breath until she finally speaks. "Whatever you want, Wanda."

She picks her slip up off of the organdy chair, holding it out as though she can't remember how to put it on. Her face suddenly looks tired. Older. Like a torn ragdoll slowly losing its stuffing.

"You don't have to go right now, do you?"

"I do." She steps into the slip and turns to the mirror. The seams on her stockings are crooked. "I've only got one hour before curtain call."

"Who's your maid, now?" I ask, hoping to make her smile. I jump off the bed and kneel before her, straightening her stockings. "I betcha she doesn't do half as good a job as me."

Lili Belle laughs. "Raul cut that routine after you left. The latest act is an homage to *King Kong*. Penny dresses up as Kong and I scream like Fay Wray while she removes my clothing. Penny *hates* it, though thank goodness Raul doesn't make her sniff her fingers afterwards."

I laugh along with her. "The audience must really go for that."

"They're just bugs about it," Lili Belle says, nodding. She buttons up her dress and slides her clutch purse under her arm.

"Wait, before you go!" Still naked, I cross the room to my dressing table. I pick up the envelope containing the leftovers of this week's *Town Star* allowance. "Can you give this to Evelyn? Tell her it's for Mama."

Lili Belle visibly hesitates as I hand her the envelope. "I don't know, sweetie," she says softly. "I don't think that they want your money."

"Please, Lili Belle. Just sneak it into her purse then. You don't even have to tell her it's from me."

"Okay, Wanda." Lili Belle reluctantly takes the envelope from me and turns toward the door.

"Hey!" I grab her by the arm. "Ain't you gonna at least kiss me goodbye?" I wink at her.

Lili Belle smiles, but only with her lips. "No, Wanda," she says as she steps out into the hall. "That'd make it seem like too much of a big deal."

29. DIAMONDS AND SLUG BURGERS

NOBODY'S CALLED FOR ME IN WEEKS and I'm all out of shampoo gin. I snap my silk stockings into place and wiggle into Queenie's slinky, forbidden-by-Brock frock. I've got seventy-five cents in my change purse, more than enough for a slug burger and a soda. Turning around, I inspect my back seams in the cracked looking-glass. Sure, maybe I'm a little too dolled up for a diner but in my experience nothing beats a little lipstick for banishing the blues. And yeah, some fella might give me the eye, but would that be so horrible? I've only got seventy-five cents, Brock isn't calling, and I'll be needing more dough—after all, a dame can't live on day-old bread alone.

"Any messages for me, Irving?" I ask, slapping my kid gloves down on the front desk.

"Jus' one from me," Irving says. He pulls a cheap fat cigar out of his sopping wet mouth and waves it at me like a finger. "Yer late on da rent."

"Oh, that," I reply dismissively. "I'm workin' on it. Say, how about I give you these earbobs in the meantime." I tuck my hair behind my ears. "Real diamonds."

Irving shrugs. "I ain't got no use for earbobs. Besides, dey look paste to me."

"Paste!" I reply indignantly. "What do you know about paste?"

"Paste or no paste, I don't want no earbobs. Ya either give

me da cash or," Irving smacks his lips together lasciviously and looks down at my chest. "Ya give me somethin' else I want."

"I'll get you the cash!" I pin my hat into place and glare at him. "You dirty old goat!"

Irving shrugs again. "Iffa ya don't have it by midnight, don't come back. I'll change da locks."

I gotta run
(In my stockings)
Where down and uptown meet—
The subway train grumbling
Beneath my feet.

I flip my fox fur coat over my left shoulder and cock out my right hip as I feign interest in a sporting goods store window display. Damn that Brock. Where has he been? How am I supposed to "study the swells" if he never takes me out? The cad. He never even made me hot. Not really. Not in the beginning, anyway. Now he's got me all screwy.

If that mug dares to darken my doorway again, I'll give him a headline all right. And I'll tell him where he can stick it, too.

A nice looking fella in a brown Trilby hat and a camel coat passes by me, stops, and then returns. He stands beside me at the window, his eyes on a pair of canvas spectator shoes.

"Swell evening, isn't it?" I say. I tilt my pelvis so as to display my bust and rump to full advantage. He looks at me with disinterest and nods before turning back to the window. Undaunted, I push on. "Are you waiting for someone special?" I ask. "A handsome fella like you shouldn't be alone on a Friday night."

I reach out to touch his forearm but he jumps backwards as though burned. "Sorry, sister," he says, his eyes like those of a frightened bunny rabbit. He scurries away, furtively looking over his shoulder as though he's afraid that I'll follow him.

"Run on home to your mama, you mug!" I yell after him. "You couldn't afford me anyway."

Aw, nerts. I'll go try my luck at the diner; catch a man's eye and get a burger in my belly. I keep my own eyes on my shoes as I pass the lineup of men outside the Mission. I tried to be a good girl for Brock and I don't want to do a pick-up tonight, but he's left me no choice—it's either that, or I'll be standing in a breadline myself. Tonight will be my last pick-up though. I'll call Brock tomorrow. No reason why a dame can't call a fella—why, it's 1935, after all! My pace quickens with the revelation. Yes, I'll call Brock at the paper and tell him to come up and see me. I smile at Mae West's famous line. He'll come up all right and I'll tell him then and there that he better pay me the dough or ... or what? Or I'll go to the *City Crier!* Not only that, I'll break off our engagement—if it's still even on, that is. I twist the pearl ring off of my finger and drop it in my change purse. Just a piece of candy, like Lili Belle said. A pretty piece of candy. But still, I think with a tug at my heart, I don't want it on my finger when I'm with another fella.

"Lookin' good, Red."

I don't look up. A come-on from a fella in a breadline is almost the same as no come-on at all, at least when your pocketbook is empty.

"Whatsa matter, doll?" the man says, undaunted. "Ya ain't got a hello fer yer ol' pal?"

"Eddie?" I turn to gape at him in surprise. "What are you doing here?"

"Aw, waitin' and prayin' fer a bite of bread and a sip of soup like da rest of dese mugs." Eddie grins at me, his smile bracketed by two deep creases; his face rough with day old stubble. A crumpled albeit fairly clean-looking suit hangs limply on his slouched frame and his shoes look like old batter mitts. He appears almost a decade older than his twenty-three years.

"But Eddie, you're not like these other men here," I protest, my tone both roseate and pleading. "You've *got* a job."

"Not no more I don't. My brudder canned me when he saw

dat newspaper story. Said it'd be bad fer business to keep me on." Eddie shrugs. "Some brudder, eh?"

"Oh, Eddie, I'm so sorry." I snap open my change purse. "Here," I say, handing him the last of my coins. "Take this."

"Naw," Eddie shakes his head from side to side. "I don't take money from dames, not fer nothin' anyhow. Never mind what yer newspaper sap boyfriend says."

"Well," I begin, stepping back as the line-up of men nudges forward. "At least let me buy you supper. I was going to get something to eat anyhow and I've got enough for a couple of sandwiches and sinkers."

"Go on, Mac," the man standing behind Eddie says, grinning at us with his mouthful of grimy grey teeth. "If you don't go with her, I will."

"Aw, beat it, bub," Eddie says, playfully punching his friend on the shoulder. "Come on, doll." He wraps an arm genially around my waist. "I'm gettin' tired of de pigeon toast and da city juice dey serve in dis joint. I sure could go fer a hamburger and a cuppa joe."

We settle into a booth by the window at Dee's Diner and order two slug burgers, two cups of coffee, and a plate of powdery sinkers, all for sixty-five cents.

"Doll, dis is swell," Eddie says, his mouth full of hamburger. "Next time supper's on me, though." I must look dubious because he continues. "No foolin'. I moved five spots up in da unemployment line dis morning. Dis Depression won't last forever." He smiles hopefully. "I'll find somethin' soon."

I remove a handkerchief from my handbag and gently wipe the hamburger juice from his chin. "I told Brock to lay off of you," I say. "I hope those newspaper stories won't make it hard for you to find work."

"Well, dey won't make it easy," Eddie laughs ruefully. "Naw, doll, I ain't too worried 'bout dat. Dose newspapers will end up in da sole of somebody's shoe or toilet papah for canaries. Dey all will forget about me just as soon as dey forgot ol' Arbuckle, and," he snaps his fingers. "Wassa name of dat fifteen-year-old shop girl? Da one wid da burned face dat married dat ol' millionaire?"

"Peaches Browning," I answer.

"Yah, dat's right. Remembah what a fuss dose newsfolk made 'bout dat? Nobody cares now. And hey, I ain't some millionaire or movie star—I ain't even famous. Well," he laughs. "Not *dat* famous. Say, 'Gigolo Eddie', eh? Dat ain't half bad a stage name. Wait'll I get my drums outta da pawn shop—I'll make it big on vaudeville wid a name like dat."

"You sure are regular, Eddie. I thought you'd be sore at me. As a matter of fact, I wouldn't blame you if you slugged me."

"I don't never slug no dames," Eddie says, dunking a sinker into his coffee. "Penny-candy comics turned dime store reporters on da other hand, *dem* I slug."

"I'm with you there, Eddie," I say. "I'm liable to slug Brock myself."

"Yah?" Eddie crams another donut into his mouth. "Trouble in paradise, huh?"

"You said it." I open my change purse and take out the pearl ring. "He said he loved me and gave me this ring as a sort of promise." I shrug. "An engagement ring, I guess. But now he's turned turtle. I haven't heard from him in weeks."

"Don't worry, doll. Baxter'd be bugs to bounce ya. Yer still da best lookin' dish in dis town." He leans over the table and takes one of my curls between his fingers. "Ya let yer hair grow back," he nods approvingly. "And it's red again. I like it dis way."

"Thanks, Eddie." I watch in silence as he unselfconsciously devours the plate of donuts. "Here," I say, sliding the ring across the table. "I want you to have this. Take it to the pawn shop. It's a nice ring and real gold, too. You should be able to get *something* for it, maybe even get your drums back."

"Dat's nice of ya, doll but I don't take gifts from dames."

"No arguing," I say firmly. "You're taking it and that's that.

Besides, Brock's the one who paid for it so consider it as a gift from him."

Eddie picks up the ring and holds it out between his fingers, studying it. "Well, if yer gonna put it like dat, doll. I guess I *kin* get somethin' fer it. Thanks," he smiles. "Yer a swell dame."

And if I don't start hustling, I think, *I'll be a swell dame sleeping on a park bench.*

"I gotta blow," I say, kissing his scruffy cheek. "I'll be seeing you."

There is a chill to autumn's twilight. Perhaps it is the cool weather that makes the men walk quicker or perhaps it is my nervous desperation that makes them look me over with about as much interest as a goldfish would give to an arithmetic book. Whatever the case, when I return to the Grand Palace, I'm no richer than the ten cents in my change purse.

"Yer one minute late!" Irving points his pink sausage finger at the clock above the mailboxes. "I wassa 'bout ta call da locksmith!"

"Well, I guess you'd still better call him, because this," I say, dropping the dime onto the counter. "Is all that I've got. Unless," I snap open the clasps of my coat. "You still want to work something out."

What the hell, I think as Irving's thick purple tongue slides over his upper lip in anticipation. *I've been with uglier mugs than this.*

I let the coat fall to the floor and slip the straps of Queenie's dress down my shoulders, revealing my bare breasts.

"So what do you say, we got a deal?"

Irving's mouth falls open; the cigar that he'd been chomping on bounces off the counter and onto my shoe. "Not here," he says, his voice hoarse. "In da back office."

"Do we have a deal?" I ask again, hands on my hips.

"Yah," Irving says. He is speaking to my breasts. "We gotta deal. Ya won't owe me no rent fer dis month."

"Good." I pick up my coat. "Write me out a receipt that says I'm paid up in full for the rest of the month."

"I'll do it after."

"Do it now," I demand. I begin to pull my straps back up. "Or the deal is off."

"Oh-kay, oh-kay." Irving quickly writes me out a receipt that I stuff down my stocking for safekeeping.

"Just so you know," I say as I follow him to the back room. "You're getting one helluva deal."

The back office is little more than a cluttered closet, furnished solely with a precariously sunken civil war-era couch and reeking of mothballs. "Ain't nice to throw things out," Irving explains, gesturing to the stacks of dusty cardboard suitcases and boxes. "People might come back for 'em."

He takes a handkerchief out of his back pocket and sweeps it over the seat of the couch. Mouse droppings roll into the spaces between the cushions and onto the floor. "Wait," Irving smiles and runs his tongue over his lips as I move toward the sofa. "Take yer dress off first."

I look around in vain for a clean place to drop my coat and dress. "Fine," I sigh, throwing my coat over the sofa's visibly soiled armrest. "But you're paying for my dry-cleaning."

"Mmm," Irving makes a slurping sound and rubs his hands together as I step out of my dress. "Leave yer heels and stockings on," he demands and I certainly don't object.

"Turn around."

Irving squeezes and pinches my buttocks as though he's testing oranges at the grocer. "Nice, very nice. You kin sit down now."

He lifts one of my breasts and bounces it in his hand. "Nice titties, too. Haven't seen titties this big since 1914."

Irving leans toward me and opens his moist murky mouth, full of sloppy wet tongue. I let him kiss me as he tweaks and twists my nipples back and forth, like knobs on a faulty radio.

"Knock yourself out," I giggle in between kisses. "You won't get any reception from me."

"I ain't never been with anything so beautiful," Irving moans, more to himself than to me. He removes his right shoe and sock and I wince as his bare foot steps down onto a ball of mouse poop. Standing up, he unbuttons his trousers, his BVDs falling down around his ankles. I've never noticed this before—I've only ever seen him behind the counter—but Irving only has one leg; the other is a wooden peg.

"Ya lookin' at dis?" He chuckles and raps his knuckles against the peg. "Bet ya only thought skinny fellas had wooden legs, eh?" He laughs.

"How'd it happen?" I ask.

"Aw, jus' an old war injury." Irving's marble blue eyes seem to melt slightly. He turns his face away from me.

"I'm sorry," I say.

"Why ya sorry? Dis ain't nothing." Irving looks at the floor. "Aw, yer a nice girl. I got no right ta do this."

"It's all right."

"No, it ain't. Why don't ya go? Just go."

He picks up my dress and hands it to me.

"Tha deal still stands."

"Really?" I ask, trying not to sound too relieved. "That's swell, Irving." I slip the dress over my head and stand up. "You're not such a bad guy."

"Yah?" Irving waves me off. "Well, don't ya tell anybody dat."

30. THIS IS MY GAME

I SIT IN THE WINDOW, DRINKING MY WHISKEY and having memories about dreams. I left word with Brock at the paper this morning but he still hasn't called on me and I'm still broke. Luckily, I was able to pawn my earbobs. The pawnbroker could see that they were paste but he gave me a few coins for them, anyway—enough for a bottle of booze.

The dark clouds have turned the city blue. The Saturday evening revellers in their rain-soaked tuxedos, velvet orchestra coats, furs, and ostrich feathers pass lightly over the wet concrete, looking as soft and hazy as a Garbo close-up.

A lady, dainty and pretty in a wide-skirted buttercup evening gown, floats out of the merry-go-round doors of Mr. Manchester's apartment building and falls knees first into a rain puddle. A taxi driver jumps from his parked cab to help her up, but she turns away from him, stumbling forward and wrapping her skinny arms around a lamp post. Under the glow of the street light, the woman's familiar lemon-yellow finger waves and doll-like features blossom into sharp focus and I follow the gaze of Norma, Mr. Manchester's mistress, as she raises her tear-swollen face. Mr. Manchester's curtains are open: the blood red sofa, alone in the centre of the snow white room, is as forbidding and menacing as the lips of an evil Queen. The apartment's mirrored walls reflect the sins of the city back upon itself. The light in the window suddenly snaps shut and Norma bows her head as she slouches into the taxicab.

I shed my sweat-stained shell-pink robe and switch the overhead light on. A shadow appears at Mr. Manchester's window.
Arms stretched above my head, I begin to roll my hips slowly,
east and west, north and south, as I wiggle out of my panties.
Mr. Manchester's light flicks back on. I pick up my fox fur
coat and drape it seductively over my naked body. Turning
away from the window, I pull open the middle drawer of my
dresser. There, nestled between the leather bound Bible and
Mr. Manchester's stolen portrait, is the copper's gun. I slide
the revolver into my coat pocket, stuff my dogs into a pair
of rain boots, and head out into the turbid, promising night.

"Miss Whittle, that was quite the show you just gave me!" Mr.
Manchester's voice booms with mirthful malice as he opens
his apartment door. "Won't you come in? I must have a nickel
around here somewhere, but oh, no! That performance was
worth *at least* a dime!"

Keeping my lips pursed in silence, I step into the winter white
room and lock the door behind me. A foolish grin spreads
across Mr. Manchester's face.

"Sit down, my bad girl!" he says, his cheeks flushed with
wine. "We'll make a loving cup!"

I don't move from the door as Mr. Manchester, clad in pea-
cock-blue silk pajamas, toddles to the kitchen.

"I really should thank you, Miss Whittle," he calls out
over his shoulder as he extracts a bottle from the icebox.
"Attendance at the Apple Bottom has gone sky high since
your boyfriend's little newspaper scribblings came out. Now
my wife, on the other hand, wasn't too thrilled with your
stories," he continues, pouring wine into two crystal glasses.
"But luckily for me she's a *very* understanding woman. In
particular, she understands how improper and distasteful a
divorce would look to her high-hat family and friends. How
about a toast?" he asks, returning to the sitting room. He
raises the wine glasses gaily. "To burying the hatchet. After

all, Miss Whittle, as the papers say, you're still rather fetching and I wouldn't mind…"

The snow turns scarlet as the glasses tumble to the carpet.

"Miss Whittle!" Mr. Manchester's mouth drops open like that of a dead sea trout.

"Come a little closer, Henry," I say. I hold the revolver out like a gangster in a Warner Brothers movie. "Be a good boy, now."

"Now really, Miss Whittle," Mr. Manchester attempts to clear his throat. Nervously, he ties and unties the belt of his pajama coat. "I think you should go home now, Miss Whittle."

"And I think you should do as I say, unless you want your brains splattered all over this swell white carpet."

"You don't want to do this, Miss Whittle," he says, visibly composing himself as he steps forward. "What will the papers say? Why, I can just see the *City Crier* headline now: 'Wanda Wiggles hits the bottom of the apple barrel! Glamour girl sinks to dirty new low!'"

"Shut up, Henry," I say. I nod toward the red velvet sofa. "I remember that sofa. We shared a pretty hot time on that sofa, wouldn't you agree?"

"Is that what this is about?" Mr. Manchester impotently attempts a laugh. "You little girls these days take your play much too seriously."

"So you were just playing with me?"

He nods. "Playing *with* you, my dear. We were playing *together.*"

"Like you play with Norma?"

"Of course," he nods again. "But you knew that when you met me."

"And you were just playing with my sister, too?"

At the mention of Evelyn, Mr. Manchester's face turns as red as the wine bleeding into the carpet.

"I never touched your sister!" he cries furiously. "And that bastard in her belly isn't mine! Besides," he says, anxiously combing his fingers through his thick grey hair. "What would

I want with a homely little nobody like her when everyday I'm surrounded by beautiful showgirls?"

"Come a little closer, Henry."

I press the mouth of the revolver against his temple.

"Evelyn is my sister, see? So if she's a nobody, then so am I. And you," I attempt my best Tom Powers sneer, "are going to do everything *this* nobody says."

His mismatched eyes are devoid of their usual chilly confidence. "What do you want, Miss Whittle?" he asks, his Adam's apple bobbing fearfully.

"First," I say, unsnapping my coat open. "I want you to put your arms around my waist. That's right," I nod as he complies. "Pull me closer now."

I can feel him growing tumescent beneath his silk pajama bottoms as he presses against my naked body.

"Mm," I murmur. "That feels nice." I caress the butt of the gun along his cheekbone.

"Kiss me, my fool," I whisper, in vintage Theda Bara vamp mode.

His tongue is disappointedly slithery and supine like the oysters that the Boxer would sometimes order at the nightclubs he took me to. Tired of the limp kisses, I bring his head down to my breasts. Hungrily, he licks and sucks my left nipple while gently pinching the right between his forefinger and thumb.

"Mm, now *that* feels good, Henry."

Fully erect now, Mr. Manchester scoops me up in his arms and throws me down onto the red velvet sofa. He unties the string on his pajama bottoms while simultaneously prying the gun from my fingers. The revolver falls helplessly to the fluffy white rug—I'll let him think he had something to do with that.

Wrapping my arms around his neck, I tilt my hips receptively, but when he enters me, I feel nothing. As he pounds away, oyster tongue pressed firmly to sweaty upper lip, my body grows numb, as though I have been encased in ice. I jump up, pushing him off of me.

"I'm going now, Henry. Thank you though."

Mr. Manchester's mouth hangs open in confusion. "B-but we're not done yet..."

"Perhaps you don't think so, Henry," I say coolly. I retrieve the handgun and slide it back into my coat pocket. "But you see, you're not writing this story." I flip my hair back and smile at him. "I am."

31. BORN BLUE

IT'S TIME TO GET OUT OF BED BUG BABYLON. I have no job. I have no beau. I have no friends—at least none that I deserve. I think of Eddie, his face so sunken in it's no longer anything more than teeth and bone, and of Lili Belle—why do I feel like I have taken something from her? Something that I can't afford to give back.

A blade of sunlight cuts through the heavy curtains and falls upon the blanket of yellow dust, blossoming like an untended garden, on my carpet. Yes, when the only things alive are the rats in the walls and the little vampires under my mattress, it's high time to blow.

Someone knocks on my door, so lightly that I almost can't hear them over the sound of the creatures fornicating in the woodwork. "Just a minute!"

Brock. It must be Brock. *Oh, won't I give him a piece of my mind!* Quickly, I struggle into a tight red pullover and a forest green knitted skirt. *That mug thinks he can give me the air, does he!* "Well, damn him! Damn him to hell!" I curse out loud as my big toe rips a hole in my left stocking. The knocking at the door grows louder. "I'm coming! Keep your pants on!"

That mug thinks he can crawl back here, feed me some pretty music and I'm supposed to fall into his arms like a first grade sap? Well, I'll show him!

Hurriedly, I run a ruby red lipstick across my mouth and pin my hair into a chignon. I may be giving him the brush off but that doesn't mean I can't look good while I'm doing it. "You've got a helluva nerve!" I cry, throwing open the door.

"I'm sorry, honey. Is this a bad time?"

Lili Belle stands in my doorway, her shoulders slumped in a cerise tailored suit with a mink collar and a matching cloche hat. Her eyes are pink and swollen as though she's been crying.

"What's wrong, Lili Belle?" I ask, waving her in.

"If I had known sooner, I would have come sooner," Lili Belle says, dropping onto my bed. She extracts a black silk handkerchief from her jacket pocket and loudly blows her nose. "But I just found out today."

"Found what out today?"

"Your sister" she presses the handkerchief to her eyes as she begins to sob. "She had the baby."

"The baby!" I exclaim. The baby who had been the catalyst for my escape to Bed Bug Babylon. The baby who had come to symbolize a dream I would never realize. The baby whom I had never actually thought of as a real, tangible being. "Boy or girl?" I ask, excitedly.

"Boy," Lili Belle says between sobs. "They named him Albert after your daddy. H-he was born blue!" she wails. "Your mama said it was probably because Evelyn was crying all the time."

"Born blue? You mean he's dead?"

Lili Belle nods, covering her face with her hands.

I rub her back soothingly. "I need to see her," I murmur. "I need to see my sister."

"You need to go tonight," Lili Belle looks up at me. "She's leaving town tomorrow morning."

Composing herself, she opens her jacket and removes a folded up newspaper from the inside pocket.

"Brock's latest witch-hunt," she explains, handing me the paper.

REDHEAD IS RED MENACE, blares the headline, underneath of which is a surreptitious photograph of Evelyn working behind the hatcheck counter at the Apple Bottom. HOMELY HATCHECK

GIRL IS A COMMUNIST! PLOTS TO ORGANIZE HOOFERS!

"The Red Squad visited her this morning," Lili Belle says. "They told Evelyn that she has twenty-four hours to get out of town or they're throwing her in the hoosegow."

"I'd better go to her now." I stand up. "Will you wait here for me, Lili Belle? Please," I say as she begins to protest. "I really need to be with you tonight. It would be," I pause. "It would be a really big deal."

32. SISTERS

WHEN I LEFT THE WORLD BEHIND THE MARKET, things were sprouting from the ground. Now everything is falling from the sky. I tighten my rain hood and push on against the elements as the heavy rain blinds my sight and deafens my ears. Trees are scant behind the Market but the few that exist writhe near naked before the angry winds: trunks bowed in submission, slick bony branches pleading for succor. It's a night for stealthy cats and stray people. Slim felines, finding cover in trashcan alleys, blink out at me, either with curiosity or in solidarity. Behind the abandoned five-and-dime store, the Market Queen still holds court but the sun and the days have pillaged her face—only her eyes remain. Two heavy grey shadows huddle under the Queen, the orange lights of their cigarettes burning like the eyes of Lucifer.

"Where ya off to, honey?"

I duck out of the way as the larger of the two men lunges toward me, his mouth wide open. "Ya bitch!" He tumbles face first into a wet pile of dog shit.

The cacophony of the man's anger and his friend's laughter is louder than thunder. It crawls up my spine and kicks at my heels as I run toward the crooked porch of the rooming house, its storm door flung open in a ready embrace.

"If yer lookin' fer yer mama, she ain't home." Our landlady, Mrs. Merriweather, balances a wash basin on her hip and glares at me behind cloudy spectacles. "She's at church and if ya ask me, that's where *you* should be—you and yer rotten Red sister!" She spits a yellow and green glob of snot and saliva onto the toe of my rubber boot.

"I'm here to see Evelyn," I say, shaking the mucus from my foot. "Is she here?"

"Ya, but not fer long, thank the heavens." Mrs. Merriweather pushes past me toward her kitchen. "Well g'wan and see her. I ain't stoppin' ya."

The bedroom door is open. A small cardboard suitcase sits on what was once my bed, now stripped bare, the lonesome mattress slumped over the bed's splintered wooden frame. Evelyn appears in profile, her arms laden with dresses, her belly hard and round as though still fat with child.

"Evelyn?" I step into the room tentatively.

Her head snaps upward, her mouth a small white "O."

"Wanda." She drops the clothing on the bed. "You're soaked to the bone," she admonishes as I wrap my arms around her. "You'll catch your death."

I hug my sister tightly, as though trying to merge our bodies as one.

"I'm sorry, Evelyn," I say. "I'm so sorry…"

Gently, she pulls away from me. "Lili Belle told you?" She runs a hand along the stubborn curve of her belly as I nod. "I still feel like he's in there, Wanda." She looks up at me, her eyes desiccated from grief. "I can still *feel* him. He was so small, Wanda. So small and so blue…"

"I'm sorry." I hate myself for having nothing else to say.

She turns her back to me and begins packing the dresses into her suitcase. "It's probably good that I'm leaving," she says. "Maybe I'll stop feeling him if I'm somewhere different."

"Where are you going to go?"

Evelyn opens the bottom drawer of her dresser. "There's a bunch of men—former soldiers—heading out on a train to-morrow morning." She pulls out a pile of brassieres, knickers, and handkerchiefs, and tosses them onto the bed. "They gave up their youth for this country. Some of them lost limbs, most of them watched their friends die. Now they're penniless and starving, forgotten by the same government that they gave up everything to fight for. They're going to the Capitol to demand the payment that they were promised and I'm going with them."

"What are you going to do?"

"Offer support," Evelyn shrugs. "Provide comfort."

"But you're not a nurse," I say. I fold her undergarments and place them carefully into her already overstuffed suitcase. "How can you give them comfort?"

"Oh, Wanda," Evelyn gives a short laugh. "You don't need to be a nurse to give a man comfort. *You* of all people should know that."

"Oh."

Embarrassed, I shift my gaze to the tower of books on her night table. "Are you going to take those, too?"

"I guess I'd better." One by one, she drops the books, many bearing the names of Marx and Nietzsche, into an old pillowcase. "If I don't, people might think they belong to Mama and start accusing her of being a Red, too."

"How is Mama?" I ask. "She must really hate me."

"No, Wanda, she doesn't hate you. She's just tired." Evelyn plops down on her bed and lights a cigarette. "She's at church praying for the both of us. I don't mind, you know. I can use all of the prayers that I can get."

"All of this is my fault, Evelyn."

"You can't saw sawdust," Evelyn says, exhaling slowly.

"Do *you* hate me, Evelyn?"

"I tried," she answers. The ash grows on the end of her cigarette but she doesn't flick it off. "I really tried to hate you, Wanda. I worked very, very hard at hating you, probably harder than I've ever worked at anything in my entire life." She shrugs. "But I wasn't any good at it. I couldn't hate you at all, not even a little bit. I guess that's the curse of being your big sister."

"I couldn't hate you, either," I say, taking a seat beside her on the bed. "And I tried, too, but I didn't have a good reason to hate you."

Evelyn takes my hand in hers and gives it a squeeze. "Did you love him, Wanda?"

"Mr. Manchester? N-no," I answer slowly. "I wanted him. I really wanted him, but I don't think that I ever loved him. Did you?"

"Yes, I did." Evelyn drops her head, her frizzy uncombed hair shielding her face. "It was silly, wasn't it? I always kind of joshed you for being so buggy about the flickers, but I guess I bought into them, too. The whole Cinderella story—deep down, I thought maybe that could be me. I guess I learned my lesson though: men like Mr. Manchester may like to go driving through the slums, but they don't park their cars there."

"You're not a slum, Evelyn."

"I know that, Wanda." She squeezes my hand again. "I guess I just forgot for a bit." She ties the pillowcase of books into a knot and places it beside her suitcase. "I guess I shouldn't take any more than this. Mama said she'll give me some bread and stew to eat on my journey." She turns to look at me. "You'll watch out for Mama, won't you?"

"Yes," I nod. "I promise I will. Will you tell her that I came by tonight? Will you tell her that I'm sorry?"

"I'll tell her." Evelyn slides the window open. The rain has stopped and the night is as black and sempiternal as spilt ink.

"You should go, Wanda. Before the rain starts up again."

"Oh-kay." I pause at the doorway. "We'll see each other again, won't we, Evelyn?"

"Are you kidding? We're sisters, Wanda. Of course we'll see each other again. What is it that Lili Belle always says?" Evelyn laughs, her smile almost reaching her eyes. "Why, it's cream in the can, baby!"

33. HOLY CATS

"YOU'VE REACHED THE END OF THE LINE, GIRLIE."

"You got that right, mister."

The conductor glares at me and I scowl right back at him. Outside the train station, the city is lit up like a footlight parade: the windows of the hotels and skyscrapers looking like paste jewels in a peeler's brassiere. The light in my window, however, is warm and comforting—the one real diamond. Lili Belle is waiting for me.

"I saw that your icebox was empty, so I went out and got you some grub." Lili Belle sits cross-legged on the carpet, plates of bread, cheese, sliced meat, and fruit arranged before her like a picnic. Her hair is wet from the rain and she's wearing my orchid-white lounging pajamas.

"I hope you don't mind, honey, but my own clothes were soaked through."

"You look swell in my pajamas, Lili Belle," I say, stretching out beside her. I rest my head on her shoulder and we sit like that as the minutes pass by, not saying a word. She doesn't ask me about Evelyn and when we begin to eat we speak only of subway trains and eighty-one cent pounds of coffee and the weather. *Sometimes,* I think, *small talk can be so tender.*

We wash our dishes in the bathroom sink and I realize, with a sense of contentment, that I've never had so many plates to clean.

"Queenie's back in town," Lili Belle says as we stack the

dishes sideways in my bathtub to dry. "That ol' sugar daddy she ran off with up and croaked. No wives, no kids. Lucky Queenie, though, he left her with some *heavy sugar.*"

"Oh yeah? Then how come she's coming back here?"

"She's going to open a burlesque theatre."

"All by herself?" I ask incredulously.

"No, honey," Lili Belle answers, shaking her head. "You and me are going to help her. Listen, sweetie," she continues as I gape at her in shock. "If a dame can fly across the Atlantic Ocean, three hoofers can certainly run a peeler palace. Say, look at Texas Guinan—she was rolling in dough! At least *we'd* be on the level."

"Holy cats, Lili Belle! You're making it sound so easy."

"Cats!" Lili Belle snaps her fingers. "That's brilliant, Wanda. Queenie was trying to come up with a name for the joint. Something to do with 'cats' would be swell."

"I can't," I say uncertainly. "I don't know how to run a business."

"Nobody knows how to do anything until they do it." Lili Belle sits down on the edge of the bathtub and gives me an inquisitive look. "But maybe you're still waiting around for Brock."

"I am not!"

"I think that's the real reason why you don't want to do it," she says, raising her eyebrow at me. "You're still pining away for that Underwood banger. You're waiting for him to sweep you off to some big ol' house in the country so's you can grow old and have his babies..."

"Button up, Lili Belle!"

"What would he say," Lili Belle smiles, clearly relishing my annoyance. "What would he say if he found out about us?"

Without waiting for an answer, she takes me by the hand and puts me over her knee. "I don't think he'd like it much," she says. She pushes my skirt up around my waist and pulls my panties down. "Do you, sweetie?"

I squirm with delight as she delivers a sharp slap to my bare bottom.

"Do you think he'd like this, honey?" Lili Belle reaches under my sweater and gently tugs on my left nipple. I cry out and she spanks me harder. "Answer me, Wanda!"

"No, Lili Belle," I moan. "He wouldn't like this." I look up at her, parting my lips as she bends to kiss me. "And I don't want babies, anyway!"

34. CHILI AND CADS: THEY BOTH COME BACK

ORPHAN LEAVES DRESS UP THE CITY in shades of yellow, orange, and red. I'm careful not to slip on the wet sidewalk in my strappy high heels, my arms laden with paper bags full of groceries. I can't cook and my hotel room doesn't have an oven anyway, but I like eating at home with Lili Belle. *Lili Belle.* I smile. My friend. My protector. My lover.

"Is this wrong?" I asked her this morning, our bodies tangled in the sweaty bed sheets, my head resting upon her naked belly.

"Does it feel wrong, sweetie?" she answered.

No, it doesn't feel wrong.

A milk truck passes by, the driver yanking his bell at me. November. Today is the first day of November and all at once my grief feels as fresh as yesterday. A man's shadow falls upon me and I stumble backwards as my bags are stolen from my grasp.

"Hello, Miss Wanda," Brock winks at me. "No need for a pretty lady to carry her own bags."

"Brock!" I exclaim. "Wha-where have you been? Give those back to me!"

"Why, Miss Wanda!" Brock ducks as I swing out at him with my fists. "What the devil is the matter with you?"

"What's the matter with *me*?" I cry out incredulously. I attempt to deck him again but he catches my fist in midair. "You ask me to marry you and then you disappear. You print lies about my sister and the Red Squad runs her out of the city. You sell me out to Mr. Potter for a few bucks and a barrelful of ink—*that's* 'what's the matter with me'!" I spit in his face, this time making my mark.

"Oh, darling," Brock sighs. He wipes at his cheek with a polka-dotted handkerchief. "You certainly are a woman. And you get angry just like a woman. And you misunderstand, just like a woman."

He steers me forward, his hand on my right elbow. "I haven't disappeared, Miss Wanda, and I still hope to marry you. I just got very busy with work. And as for your sister, I never called the Red Squad on her, but she *is* a communist—you admitted so yourself."

"I did no such thing!"

"Of course you did." Brock nods with exasperated pity. "You told me over dinner the night we went to the Stone's Throw. You said your own mother knew Evelyn was a Red. You said she liked to read books with strange ideas,"

"I never said that!"

"Perhaps you don't *remember* saying it but you shouldn't be angry with *me*, Miss Wanda, for *your* insufficient memory."

I reach out to slap him but he takes hold of my hand and kisses it.

"I forgive you, Miss Wanda. I forgive your anger and I even forgive your cruel accusations. I still love you. Very much."

"Give me back my bags, Brock," I say, extracting my hand from his grasp. "I'm going home."

He follows me to the lobby door of the Grand Palace. "At least let me talk to you, Miss Wanda."

"We have nothing to talk about."

"Yes, we do." Brock spins me around, his hands on my shoulders. "Look at you, Miss Wanda. Your coat is matted and dirty, your shoes are all scuffed and your hair looks as though it hasn't been done in months. You need some dough, don't you honey?"

"Of course I need some dough!" I reply indignantly. "Who doesn't?"

"Well, that's what I want to talk to you about. I have a swell proposal for you. Let me come up to your room and I'll tell you all about it."

"You gave me a proposal once," I say. "But it turned out not to be so swell."

"Oh, Miss Wanda," Brock sighs. "You really need to let go of this anger of yours. Now let me come up, won't you dear?"

"No."

"Because you're sore at me?"

"Yes." That, I think, and the fact that I have a naked Lili Belle waiting for me in my bed.

"Well then let's talk in here."

*Irving's head snaps up as Brock open*s the lobby door and ushers me toward the ancient sofa beside the telephone box. Clouds of dust emerge from the sofa cushions as Brock takes a seat beside me.

"Fine," I say. "I'll listen to your proposal, but make it snappy." I gesture at my wristwatch. "You've got five minutes."

"Oh-kay." Brock nervously glances at Irving, who has just turned down the volume on his radio. "Is that mug listening to us?"

"'Course he is," I answer nonchalantly. "Say, Irving!" I shout over my shoulder. "Let me know if you need us to speak up. We wouldn't want you to miss anything!"

Irving scowls at me and turns up his radio again. The lobby fills with the sounds of Tin Pan Alley.

I tap my watch face. "You've got four minutes and fifteen seconds now," I say to Brock.

"Oh-kay. I'll cut to the chase," Brock says, taking a deep, dramatic breath. "Does the name Peg Entwistle mean anything to you?"

"No, not really. Well, maybe. Come to think of it, the name sounds kind of familiar. Is she *an actr*ess?"

"She was a stage actress. She moved to Hollywood with dreams of making it in the pictures. She was sweet, naïve, and innocent, the way you…" he pauses, "the way you used to be. The same way the Apple Bottom took your dreams and spewed *them* back out in dirty, masticated chunks, Hollywood crushed hers. One night, she climbed up to the Hollywoodland sign and jumped off the top of the H."

"Did she … did she die?"

"Yes, she died. Hollywood killed her, just like it killed her dreams."

"That's terrible. Why, I wonder how I never heard about this."

"It was a few years ago," Brock says. "But it was very big news at the time. Her tragic death shone a spotlight on the predatory nature of the movie business and how they lure young girls in with promises of silver and glitter, only to pervert those dreams into a reality of sleaze, desperation, and exploitation."

"That's a very sad story, but what does it have to do with me?"

"I want you to threaten to jump off the roof of the Apple Bottom."

"What?"

"Hear me out, Miss Wanda," Brock says, excitement colouring his *face*. "You won't actually jump. I'll talk you down. But your suicide attempt will be big news and a call to arms to the public to rid our streets of peeler palaces and burlesque halls. Mr. Potter thought your story was getting stale but when I pitched him this idea, he went nuts. He said it's one of the best story ideas he's ever heard! He called it historical."

"I won't do it."

"Not even for one thousand dollars?"

"*O-one thousan*d dollars?" I stammer.

Brock nods, a knowing smile on his lips. "That's what Potter says we'll pay you. Have you ever had that much money in your life, Miss Wanda?"

"No," I admit. "I've never had money like that. Gosh, I've never even dreamed of having money like that."

"It's some heavy sugar, Miss Wan*da.*"

"No, Brock," I correct him. "It's some filthy sugar."

35. THE GREAT WANDA WIGGLES

BROCK SAID IT WOULD BE OKAY to dress like a harlot today. I'm wearing a coin-silver grey gown with wide kimono sleeves under my fox fur coat, along with the silk stockings that Eddie gave me for Christmas: bright red seams to match my thickly applied lipstick.

Standing on the rooftop of the Apple Bottom theatre, with the November winds thrashing at my pin curls, I feel ridiculously fearless, as though if I did jump, I really would fly. The small crowd of men below pop their eyes at me and throw back their heads, mouths open like baby birds hungry for worms.

Brock had wanted my suicide attempt to take place during the day but I insisted on sunset. A girl like me can't perform without stage lights and the street lamps, I explained to Brock, would work just as well. Besides, I wouldn't want to compete with the sun.

I throw up my arms and the crowd emits a collective gasp as I teeter precariously on the rooftop's edge. I spot Brock in his brown Trilby hat and beaver coat. He surreptitiously salutes me and nudges Gallagher, who raises his camera in preparation.

"It's a dirty business!" I cry, reciting the lines that Brock had written out for me. "You stole my innocence—do you want my blood, too?"

The front door to the Apple Bottom swings open and Mr. Manchester joins the gaping masses below. He glares up at me, his face a clenched fist.

"It's a dirty city," I say, now improvising as I slip off my fur coat, twirling it in the air like a lasso. "And I'm a dirty girl!" With one final swing, the coat flies out of my hand. It falls on Mr. Manchester's head.

Two female police officers climb a ladder propped against the side of the theatre. Pumping their whistles, they rush to either side of me, employing me in a game of tug-of-war as they violently pull at the sleeves of my flimsy gown.

Brock brings a hand to his mouth in genuine surprise. He had an agreement with the chief of police who, satisfied with Brock's generous bribe, had promised to instruct the flatfoots to turn a blind eye to our stunt. Double-crossed and impotent with shock, Brock sways side to side in the middle of the jostling crowd, like a defective Jack-in-the-Box.

"*Book her, baby!*"

"*Can I come up and see ya, honey?*"

"*Arrest me, baby! Arrest me!*"

The mob whoops with lurid delight as the coppers tear my dress in half.

BA-DA-BA-DA-BOOM! Eddie's drumroll rises forth, behind the horde of horny men.

"*Got some handcuffs, honey?*"

"*Whatta woman! Oh boy, whatta woman!*"

I cross my arms over my bare bosom and shake my G-string clad bottom at the frenzied crowd as Queenie and Lili Belle shimmy out of their faux police uniforms.

BOOM-BA-DA-BOOM!

Queenie and Lili Belle unfurl a giant banner:

THE CAT'S MEOW:
DANCER-OWNED AND RUN BURLESQUE HALL
OPENING SOON!

I spin around, raising my arms to the sky as the girls drop the flag. Cold winds whip my nipples into tight red berries.

The pop of Gallagher's flashbulb joins the cacophony of cheers, whistles, and Eddie's drums. Brock, his baby-doll cheeks scarlet with rage, tries to wrestle the camera from his paper's photographer. He looks up at me, ungodly curses floating out of his angel-boy mouth like grimy soap bubbles.

"What have you got to say for yourself, Wanda?" A reporter from a rival newspaper shouts.

"The Great Gatsby believed in the green light," I answer, with a swing of my hips. "Wanda Wiggles believes in the footlights."

NOTES

CHAPTER 1

Gold Stars: During WWI, families who had lost a son, brother or father in service would hang a gold star in their window to commemorate their loved one.

CHAPTER 2

Dames is a 1934 Warner Brothers musical comedy directed by Busby Berkeley and Ray Enright. Released about a month and a half after the amended Production Code "to govern the making of motion and talking pictures" took effect, *Dames* pokes a great deal of fun at censorship.

Dick Powell: *"I wonder what it's like to be kissed by Dick Powell!"* Martha Merrill swoons in the Warner Brothers featurette, *And She Learned about Dames.* The cutie-pie crooner, Dick Powell, was the heartthrob of the Warner Brothers Busby Berkeley musicals of the 1930s. He was most often paired onscreen with the equally adorable Ruby Keeler and the two shared so much on-screen chemistry that when Powell married actress Joan Blondell in 1936, fans angrily accused Blondell of "stealing" Powell away from Keeler! Never mind that in real life Keeler was married to entertainer, Al Jolson.

Ruby Keeler: As cuddly as a kitten and twice as sweet, Ruby Keeler admittedly wasn't much of a singer, and sure, sometimes she looked at her feet when she tap danced, but who cares? Depression-era audiences certainly did not; they fell head over heels in love with the wide-eyed, leggy sweetheart of the Busby musicals. With her natural charm, winning smile, and knack for playing naïve yet plucky innocents, Keeler boosted the morale of the movie-going public during the darkest days of the Depression.

Toby Wing: Though usually unbilled, Toby Wing stood out from the numerous Busby chorus girls with her bobbed blonde hair and sassy smile. She is most memorable as the "young and healthy snooty cutie" whom Dick Powell serenades in the Warner Brothers 1933 musical, *42nd Street*.

CHAPTER 3

42nd Street: Wanda and Brock's meet-cute is an homage to a scene in the 1933 musical blockbuster, in which Ruby Keeler mistakenly walks in on Dick Powell in his BVDs. *Oh, if only Brock had turned out to be half as swell as Dick Powell!*

Bessie Love: Sexy tomboy, Bessie Love, made seventy-seven silent films from 1916-1928. She successfully transitioned to talkies in 1929 and earned a nomination for Best Actress at the Academy Awards for her turn as Hank, the hard luck older sister in MGM's, *The Broadway Melody*. Watch the film for Love's performance: unlike many of her peers, who had a difficult time adjusting to the new format, Love took to sound like a fish to water. Her snappy wisecracks remain a highlight of the film.

The Broadway Melody: MGM's first "All Talking! All Singing! All Dancing!" 1929 musical was the first sound film to win the Academy Award for Best Picture. It was the top grossing film of 1929 and created a firestorm of show biz-themed musical films. The trend for Hollywood musicals reached its peak in

1930 when over one hundred of such films were released. The public soon grew sick of the formula, until Busby Berkeley revitalized the genre in 1933 with *42nd Street*.

Cab Calloway: Put on one of his records and it's impossible to stay still, but *nobody* can move like Cab Calloway. The jazz singer, songwriter, performer, and bandleader introduced the world to Minnie the Moocher, the Jumpin' Jive, and the Jitterbug. Innovative and always one step ahead of the times, his music helped define the 1930s and 1940s. He collaborated with Fleischer Studios for three "Talkartoon" short animated films starring Calloway and Betty Boop: *Minnie the Moocher, Snow-White* and *The Old Man of the Mountain*. These films set the tone for modern day music videos.

Jean Harlow: Sexpot. Bombshell. Clown. Thespian. The original "platinum blonde," Jean Harlow was many things, but most of all she was a fighter. Perhaps it was her unusual mixture of chutzpah and vulnerability that—even more so than her hourglass figure and platinum blonde hair—made the actress a star and endeared her to Depression-era audiences. She made 'em swoon in *Hell's Angels,* laugh in *Red-Headed Woman*, and cry in *Red Dust*. Harlow proved to the disapproving (mostly male) critics that she was much more than just "a swell look-ing dish." Sadly, the woman who inarguably had the greatest influence on the style and beauty trends of the 1930s would not live to see the decade's end: she died on June 7, 1937, at the age of twenty-six, from acute kidney failure.

CHAPTER 7
Prohibition: From 1920 to 1933, the United States banned the production, importation, transportation, and sale of alcoholic beverages. Daniel Okrent's 2010 book, *Last Call: The Rise and Fall of Prohibition*, is a must-read on this topic: a detailed, engaging, entertaining, and informative read.

CHAPTER 8
"Ooh, you nasty man!": Vaudevillian and Fleischman Hour radio personality Joe Penner's catchphrase caught on in the 1930s and can be heard in many a pre-Code film.

CHAPTER 11
Mae West: Playwright, screenwriter, actress, and singer, Mae became an international sex symbol at the age of forty and her 1933 film, *She Done Him Wrong*, singlehandedly saved Paramount studios from bankruptcy. Mae West believed that language, like sex, should be fun; she is undoubtedly the Queen of the double entendre (i.e., *"Is that a pistol in your pocket, or are you just happy to see me?"*; *"I used to be Snow White, but I drifted."*) and remains one of the most oft-quoted persons of all time.

CHAPTER 12
Clark Gable: When he walked onto the set of the 1931 pre-Code film, *Night Nurse,* co-stars Barbara Stanwyck and Joan Blondell had to hold onto each other to keep from fainting—Gable was *that* sexy. However, an executive at Warner Brothers couldn't see what Joan and Barbara did: Darryl F. Zanuck complained that his ears were "too big," and after several failed screen tests, Gable signed on with MGM. He went on to dominate as a new kind of silver screen hero: one who was able to hold his own against strong, sassy actresses like Jean Harlow and Joan Crawford. The actor, probably best known to modern audiences as Rhett Butler in the 1939 blockbuster film, *Gone with the Wind,* spoke out against racism in the industry long before it was acceptable to do so.

Norma Shearer: Slightly cross-eyed, Norma Shearer was not considered a great beauty, but that didn't stop her from becoming one of the biggest movie stars of the 1930s. Before the enforcement of the Motion Picture Production Code, she portrayed confident and sexually liberated women in hits such as 1930's, *The Divorcee* and 1931's, *A Free Soul.*

CHAPTER 15
Rudy Vallee: The saxophone soloist, bandleader, and crooner became one of the biggest radio stars of the 1930s when his radio series, the Fleischman Hour, debuted the month of the stock market crash. He would go on to dominate the airwaves for a full decade. As Wanda warns, "don't ever try to get between a middle-aged woman and Rudy Vallee": it was reported that a woman shot her husband to death after he demanded she turn off one of the "vagabond lover's" records.

CHAPTER 19
Busby Berkeley: Who needs special effects when you've got Busby? The choreographer who revitalized the movie musical genre never took a dance class or studied formal dance training. Busby possessed something better than training: a dazzling imagination and the innovation to put the camera where a stage audience couldn't go. His military background no doubt helped with his ability to arrange showgirls into geometric patterns and shapes. His work in films such as *42nd Street, Gold Diggers of 1933,* and *Dames* still inspires modern audiences to gasp out loud in amazement. No choreographer before or since has ever been able to do what Busby could do.

CHAPTER 21
Dish Night: In the 1930s, most films were marketed to a female audience: female actors received top billing and scripts were often written by women screenwriters. As a way to entice women to attend the movies during the worst days of the Depression, theatres would have a "dish night" where moviegoers would receive free dishware. Women would come back week after week to complete their dishware sets.

Joan Blondell: Quick-witted and curvaceous, Joan Blondell is the quintessential sassy dame of the pre-Code films. Her first film appearance was in 1930 and she then went on to become one of the hardest working actors of the 1930s, having made almost fifty films by the decade's end. And yes, I named the fictional department store where Wanda works after the great pre-Code cutie.

CHAPTER 22

Shirley Temple: Does she *really* need an introduction? The greatest child star of all time bar none endures as a symbol of the Great Depression, but Shirley Temple is much more than a relic. Her charming and heart tugging performance in 1934's *Bright Eyes* can still crack even the most modern of hardboiled eggs. Her signature song, "The Good Ship Lollipop," is a child's version of "We're in the Money": a blatant fantasy of indulgence.

The Motion Picture Production Code: The amended Production Code "to govern the making of motion and talking pictures" (aka censorship) took effect on July 1st, 1934. The Code was enforced due, in no small part, to heavy-handed boycotting and mass protests led by the Catholic Legion of Decency. The Catholic Legion of Decency felt that Hollywood films had become a hotbed of sex and vice; they feared that common folk would be led down a rabbit hole of salacious sin and depravity by way of Jean Harlow's nipples and James Cagney's knuckles.

CHAPTER 29

Peaches Browning: Frances Belle Heenan was a fifteen-year-old shopgirl when she began dating fifty-one-year-old tycoon, Edward West "Daddy" Browning, in 1926. He nicknamed her "Peaches." The two shared but one thing in common: a hunger for public attention. Their courtship, marriage, and subsequent legal separation trial ignited the public's imagination (and wrath) and gave birth to the tabloid media that we know today. The next time that you read a trashy supermarket tabloid, scroll through a celebrity gossip blog, or watch a reality TV show, give silent thanks to the ones that started it all: Peaches and Daddy. For more on Peaches and Daddy, read Michael Greenburg's excellent (and addictively readable) book, *Peaches and Daddy: A Story of the Roaring '20s, the Birth of Tabloid Media, and the Courtship that Captured the Hearts and Imaginations of the American Public.*

CHAPTER 30

Theda Bara: The silver screen's first sex symbol, Bara made the word "vamp" both a noun and a verb in her 1915 silent film, *A Fool There Was.* She retired before the advent of sound.

Tom Powers: Sociopathic bootlegger, Tom Powers, is the fictional character immortalized by the great James Cagney in the 1931 film, *The Public Enemy* (the granddaddy of all gangster movies).

CHAPTER 32

Evelyn tells Wanda that she is going to join a group of former WWI vets who are protesting for payment from the government. This is inspired by two real life events: The Bonus Army (U.S.) and the On-to-Ottawa Trek (Canada).

The Bonus Army: In 1932, during one of the bleakest years of the Great Depression, an estimated fifteen thousandWorld War I veterans, out of work and hungry, made their way to the nation's capital to demand payment of their bonus for serving in the war. They called themselves the "Bonus Expeditionary Force," and set up camp and ramshackle tents throughout Washington, DC. Their pleas fell on deaf ears, though, when on June 17 the Senate voted against the House-passed bill that would have given WWI vets immediate payment of their bonus. With no money and no place to go, the soldiers remained in their man-made camps. On July 28, 1932 President Hoover ordered the Army to forcibly remove the veterans, along with their wives and children, using a violent force of tanks and cavalry with fixed bayonets and tear gas. Afterwards, the government set the veteran's makeshift homes on fire.

Public sentiment was largely on the side of the WWI soldiers: it didn't matter which political party one followed, no one thought it was okay for the government to be gassing war veterans. In the 1933 musical film, *Gold Diggers of 1933*, Warner Brothers paid tribute to the Bonus Expeditionary Force in the boot thumping closing number, "Remember My Forgotten Man."

On-to-Ottawa: In his excellent book, *The Great Depression*, Pierre Berton called the On-to-Ottawa Trek, which began on June 3, 1935, "one of those historic incidents that illuminate the times and serve as a symbol for future generations." Two thousand unemployed men—strikers from the government run unemployment relief camps—rode the boxcars to Ottawa to confront Prime Minister R.B. Bennett and demand real work and wages (they were being paid twenty cents a day for their work in the relief camps—hardly a fair wage, even by Depression-era standards). The strikers were supported by the public, many of whom greeted them with hot meals and parcels of food and, as Berton recounts in his book, when they arrived in Calgary, a group of fifty women offered to join the men to "provide solace"—the offer was rejected.

CHAPTER 33

Texas Guinan: Clad in only the finest of diamonds and furs, the notorious NYC speakeasy owner was known to greet her customers with a jubilant, "Hello, Sucker!"

CHAPTER 34

Peg Entwistle was a Welsh-born theatre actress who acted in many Broadway plays in the mid-1920s through the early 1930s. In 1932, she had roles in a Los Angeles play and RKO's motion picture, *Thirteen Women*. She committed suicide in September of 1932 by jumping off the "H" of the Hollywoodland sign. *Thirteen Women*, her only film, was released after her death.

GLOSSARY

Filthy Sugar takes place from 1934 to 1935. The characters, particularly Lili Belle and Eddie, use many of the slang words and phrases that were popular during this time period. Perhaps it was the advent of talkies, increased access to radio (and jazz music), the sexual revolution of the 1920s, or a combination of all of these, but in the 1930s, people really had fun with language. The following is a list of definitions for the slang and sayings that pop up in *Filthy Sugar*. Getting into the spirit, I made up a couple of slang words myself (my creations are marked with an asterisk).

And How!:	Very much so; Absolutely!
Beezer:	Nose
Berries (the):	Wonderful (i.e., "Brock bought me a new roadster. It's the berries, and so is he!")
Bird:	A man
Blinkers:	Eyes
Blow:	To leave (i.e., "I'm really tired, so I'm gonna blow. See you tomorrow.")

Broad (noun):	A woman (a rather coarse term, some times used derogatorily)
Brownette:	A woman with light brown hair (origin: Jean Harlow. MGM coined the term in 1935 to describe her new darker hair colour)
Bub:	An impolite way of addressing a man (usually a stranger)
Bulbs:	Nipples
Bunk:	Lies
Button up:	Be quiet; Shut up
BVDs:	A popular brand of men's underwear
Cad:	A cruel and/or dishonest man, particularly in his relations with women
Can (noun):	The buttocks
Can (verb):	To terminate someone's employment (i.e. "You ain't wearing pasties and this ain't no flash house, so we're gonna have to can you!")
Canary:	A female singer
Chorine:	A chorus girl
Cinch (noun):	1. Something that is easy to do; 2. A sure thing

City juice:	Tap water
Clams:	Dollar bills
Crab (verb):	1. To intentionally wreak havoc or ruin something; 2. To imitate something or someone
Cream in the Can:	A sure thing (origin: Bessie Love's catchphrase in the 1929 musical film, *The Broadway Melody*)
Crepehanger:	A cynical person
Cub reporter:	A young inexperienced journalist or reporter
Dame:	A woman
Dish:	A physically attractive woman
Dizzy:	1. Confused; 2. Not very bright
Dogs:	Feet
Doll:	Term of endearment for a woman
Dollars to buttons:	A sure bet
Don't take any wooden nickels:	Don't do anything stupid
Don't gum the works:	Don't ruin things; don't mess everything up

Dough:	Money
Duck Soup:	Something that is very easy to do or learn
Ducky:	Cute, nice, good
*Filthy Sugar:**	Dirty money (i.e., money obtained by dishonest or illegal means)
Flash House:	A burlesque theatre where the dancers don't wear pasties and/or G-strings
Flatfoot:	A police officer
Flat Tire:	A dull, boring person
Flickers:	The movies
Flock of Salami:	Something that is untrue and/or ridiculous (in other words, bullshit)
Flush:	To have a lot of money
Give someone the air:	1. To break up with someone, usually abruptly and without warning; 2. To end a romantic relationship in a passive, uncommunicative fashion (i.e., to stop returning phone calls). Note: This was the 1930s equivalent of "ghosting."
Glad Rags:	Fancy clothes
Good Egg:	A good person

Grand:	Something that is good or great (upper-class version of "swell")
Grub:	Food
Hardboiled:	Used to describe a tough, unsentimental, and cynical person
Harlow Hair:	Hair that is bleached white-blonde like Jean Harlow, the original "platinum blonde" in her pre-Code days (the phrase was coined for her by Howard Hughes)
Heavy Sugar:	A lot of money
Heel:	A jerk; an unlikeable, cruel person
High Hat (noun):	A snob
High Hat (verb):	To "high hat" is to act superior; to be condescending towards others (i.e., "Don't you dare high hat me! I am just as good as you are!")
Holy Cats!:	Wow!
Hoofers:	Dancers
Hoosegow:	Prison
Horse feathers:	Bullshit
How's Tricks?	How are you? What's new?
I'm bugs about you!	I'm crazy about you!

It's like this:	Let me explain...
Jack (noun):	Money
Jane (noun):	A girl or a woman
Joint (noun):	A place; usually nightclub of ill repute
Lash tint:	Mascara
Mac:	Term of address for a man (usually a stranger)
Make it snappy:	Hurry up!
Masher (noun):	A womanizer
Merry-go-round:	To "give someone the merry-go-round" is to string someone along; to keep someone guessing; to make promises that you don't intend to keep
Moll:	A gangster's girlfriend
Mootie:	Marijuana
Mug:	1. Casual form of address for a man, usually derogatory; 2. An untrustworthy man, particularly one involved in criminal activity; 3. The face
Muggle:	A marijuana cigarette
Nerts:	An expression of disappointment and or dismay (basically "oh shit!")

Old Maid:	An outdated term for an unmarried woman "over a certain age"
On the level:	Honest; trustworthy
Ossified:	Drunk
Over the moon:	Overjoyed; very happy
Pan:	The face
Paste diamonds:	Fake diamonds
Peeler:	A stripper or exotic dancer
Peepers:	Eyes
*Pigeon toast:**	Stale bread
Pill:	An unlikeable, disagreeable person
Pip:	1. An attractive woman; 2. Something that is very pleasing
Powder Room:	Polite "feminine" term for washroom
Racket:	An organized, usually illegal, method or scheme to make money
Rat:	An untrustworthy man
Ring-a-ding-ding:	An expression of glee
Romp (noun):	1. A good time; 2. A party

S.A.:	Sex appeal (many newspapers in the 1930s couldn't print the phrase "sex appeal," so S.A. was a polite alternative)
Sacked:	Fired
Sap:	A sucker; a foolish person
Sawbuck:	A ten dollar bill
Sca-rew!:	Get out of here!
Scram:	1. Get out of here! 2. To leave in a hurry
Sinkers:	Doughnuts
Sister:	Casual form of address for a woman, usually a stranger
Skin Tickler:	A drummer
Slammer:	Prison
Slug burger:	Hamburger meat on stale bread
Snipe:	A cigarette
Sob Sisters:	Condescending, insincere journalists, usually ones who cover "human interest" stories
Spare Tire:	The odd one out (i.e., "I went out with Wanda and Lili Belle, but I felt like such a spare tire around those lovebirds.")

Squiffy:	Drunk
Stagedoor Johnnies:	Male fans of burlesque dancers and/or chorus girls
Sugar:	1. Money; 2. A term of endearment; 3. A physical display of affection (i.e., "I know you're broke and you ain't got no sugar, but you're cute anyway so come over here and give me some sugar, sugar.")
Sugar Daddy:	A man (usually older) who is wealthy and looking to spend his dough on a (usually younger) woman
Swell (adjective):	Very good; very pleasing; the 1930s equivalent of "cool"
Swells (noun)	Wealthy people
Talkie:	A moving picture (movie) with sound
That's a hot one!:	That's ridiculous! Bullshit!
That ain't hay:	That's a lot of money
To blow one's top:	To lose one's temper
To bounce someone:	1. To break off a romantic relationship; 2. To fire someone
To buffalo someone:	To bully or intimidate

To bury the hatchet:	To forgive and forget
To be dizzy for someone:	To have a crush on someone
To act fresh:	1. To come on strong sexually; 2. To speak or act in a sassy or rude fashion
To grease one's gums:	To gossip
To settle someone's hash:	1. To get even 2. To silence someone
To slug someone:	To hit someone
To be sore:	To be angry
To turn turtle:	1. To change one's mind abruptly; 2. To suddenly stop showing interest in a lover
To swing a hoof:	To dance
To work someone:	To make sexual advances
Tomato:	A very physically attractive woman
Town Clown:	A term for when a cab driver can only seem to pick up short distance fares
Tumble:	1. Sexual intercourse; 2. To pay sexual attention to someone

Underwood Banger: *	1. A writer; 2. A reporter
Wet blanket:	1. A dull, uninteresting person; 2. A person whose melancholic nature brings down the mood of those around him
You can't saw sawdust:	What's done is done; let it go
You said it:	I agree!; That's right!
You sure are regular:	You are a good person
Zozzled:	Drunk

ACKNOWLEDGEMENTS

First of all, I would like to thank Luciana Ricciutelli, Renée Knapp, and everyone at Inanna Publications. Dreams *do* come true and I should know—I found the publisher of my dreams!

Special thanks to the following writers for your ongoing encouragement and support: Duncan Armstrong, Valentino Assenza, Brenda Clews, Pat Connors, Jeff Cottrill, Lisa de Nikolits, Amanda Earl, Marilyn Goldberg, Cate McKim, Shawn Syms, Patricia Tomlinson, Lizzie Violet, Iris Wilde and Liz Worth.

To Yasmin Aziz, you are truly the greatest friend a girl could ask for and I am blessed to have you in my life. Neil Traynor, thank you for your unconditional love and for believing in me even during the dark times when I didn't believe in myself. Thanks also to Karen Tiveron for your amazing friendship. A special big thank you to my mother and to the rest of my family (my father, my nephew William, Wendy and my dear Lang Lang).

I would also like to thank and acknowledge the following, without whom *Filthy Sugar* would not have been possible: my wonderful landlady for providing me with safe and affordable housing (sadly a growing rarity in Toronto) and the Toronto Public Library, in particular the Brentwood branch's Le@rning Centre, for the research materials and computer access needed to complete the work on my novel.

Photo: Neil Traynor

Heather Babcock has had short fiction published in various literary journals and anthologies including *Descant Magazine, Front & Centre Magazine, The Toronto Quarterly,* and in the collection *GULCHI: An Assemblage of Poetry and Prose* (2009). Her chapbook, *Of Being Underground and Moving Backwards,* was published in 2015 in a sold-out limited edition. She is a co-founder of The Redhead Revue reading series and I Got You Babe: An Evening of Music and Poetry. Heather blogs about silent and classic movies at meetmeatthesoda-fountain.home.blog. *Filthy Sugar* is her debut novel. She lives and works in Toronto.